'Oh, the Countess! That's all you care about!'

'Of course it's all I care about! That's why I married you!' he said.

'And that's why you would bed me! Not because you wished to! Nor because I am pretty or—or—

'Oh, you are selfish beyond belief! I am *nothing*! My life, my past—my identity, even!—is nothing, except as it is useful to you, Claud. And now you will not take me for your wife, despite the fact that I have spent the whole day in a state of high anxiety only waiting for this moment!' Her voice thickened. 'And it will be all to do again when you decide it *must* be done, after all, and you won't care if I *die* of apprehension!'

A burst of sobs ended this speech. Aghast at her words, Claud sat irresolute, unable to think what to do. His conscience pricked at him. He looked at Kitty, all tousled hair and her face crumpled in distress, and instinct took over. The next moment she was in his arms, and his lips were buried in her neck.

Dear Reader

I have often thought with sympathy of that army of sad spinsters in bygone days whose lot in life was to be a governess. Failing a family member willing to take them in, an orphaned female of the landed classes had few options. Without means, marriage was out of the question. And so they entered alien households, to work either as companion or, more usually, as tutor.

In the world of my creation three such young ladies, devoted friends, are just emerging from a charitable seminary in Paddington where they have been prepared for just such a life.

First comes Tender **Prudence**, a soft-hearted creature totally unfitted to be in charge of a pair of enterprising twins. Hopelessly outclassed, Prue struggles for control under the amused eye of their uncle, Julius Rookham, who engaged her services. What she has not bargained for is a wayward tendency of her unruly heart to warm to her employer.

Then there is Practical **Nell**, whose common-sense approach to her unenviable lot is not proof against the trying circumstances of her new position. The strange behaviour of her charge, coupled with mysterious whisperings in the corridors of her employer's Gothic castle, begin to prey upon her mind. Despite his dangerous attraction, Nell is forced to believe that Lord Jarrow is not all that he seems.

Lastly, there is Fanciful **Kitty**, the only one of the trio to escape the future mapped out for her. But her reality is a far cry from the golden ambition of her impossible dreams.

I dedicate these stories to those unsung heroines condemned to a life of drudgery, who deserve all the romance they can get.

Elizabeth

KITTY

Elizabeth Bailey

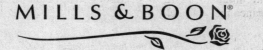

MILLS & BOON®

*MILLS & BOON and MILLS & BOON with the Rose Device
are registered trademarks of the publisher.*

*First published in Great Britain 2003
Harlequin Mills & Boon Limited,
Eton House, 18-24 Paradise Road, Richmond, Surrey TW9 1SR*

© Elizabeth Bailey 2003

ISBN 0 263 83503 0

*Set in Times Roman 10½ on 12 pt.
04-0403-83501*

*Printed and bound in Spain
by Litografía Rosés S.A., Barcelona*

Elizabeth Bailey grew up in Malawi, then worked as an actress in British theatre. Her interest in writing grew, at length overtaking acting. Instead, she taught drama, developing a third career as a playwright and director. She finds this a fulfilling combination, for each activity fuels the others, firing an incurably romantic imagination. Elizabeth lives in Essex.

Recent titles by the same author:

A TRACE OF MEMORY
AN INNOCENT MISS*
THE CAPTAIN'S RETURN*
PRUDENCE†
NELL†

The Steepwood Scandal mini-series
†*Governesses* trilogy

Chapter One

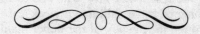

No warning of impending disaster struck the sleepy village of Paddington. A kindly sun obligingly cast its warmth upon the grateful inhabitants, while May bees and butterflies flitted about their business in the hedgerows. The carter's horse plodded slowly around the confines of the Green, and the baker's boy, sauntering from the shop to set out upon the next of his deliveries, let out a jaunty whistle.

He gave a cheery wave as he took in the identity of the young lady perched upon the fence that edged the Green, alongside the road leading to Edgware and thence to the metropolis. The baker's boy was scarce to blame for missing the tell-tale reddened eyes, their brown the more lustrous for having being drowned in tears, for Miss Katherine Merrick undoubtedly added something to the picturesque scene.

A quantity of lush black curls descended halfway down her back, escaping from under a straw hat that framed a countenance undeniably lovely. A straight nose and a pretty mouth, just now turned down in discontent, were worthy of an ensemble more becoming than the dimity gown of faded pink, with its unfashionably low waist and

three-quarter sleeves, and the short hem revealing more
than a glimpse of the white cotton hose that Miss Merrick
thoroughly detested.

Truth to tell, the young lady loathed every item she had
on, from the ancient black shoes to the unmentionable un-
dergarments that confined her curvaceous figure in the
least flattering way. The gown was only marginally less
hateful than the rest. Only how was one to manage upon
a paltry income of three shillings a week?

It was through the agency of the upper maid at the Paddington Charitable Seminary for Indigent Young Ladies—
which had been Miss Merrick's home for more years than
she cared to count—that she had acquired the pink cast-
off gown. Where Parton got it, she could not have said.
Indeed, she took care not to enquire too closely.

'Let's just say as I've a friend of a friend as is friend
to a parlour maid in the house of a great lady hereabouts.
And this one will be three shillings, if it's to your liking,
Miss Kitty.'

It was not much to Kitty's liking, but for want of any
other means of augmenting her wardrobe with anything fit
to wear besides the horrid grey Seminary uniform, she had
handed over the entirety of the week's wages. Now that
she was no longer strictly a pupil, Mrs Duxford had de-
creed that she must receive a little something for her services. And not before time! It was more than a month since
she had been dragooned into the trying task of inculcating
a modicum of grace into the clodhopping feet of the junior
girls. It was like teaching a roomful of elephants!

Kitty dabbed at her eyes again with the sodden pocket-
handkerchief. Perhaps she had best swallow her yearnings
and take up the latest in a series of beastly posts the Duck
wished to thrust upon her. Only what hope had she of
emulating the success of her dearest friends as governess

in a household where the eldest son was but eleven years of age, and there was not a widower in sight?

A fresh deluge of tears cascaded down her cheeks at the melancholy remembrance of Helen Faraday's coming nuptials. The letter handed over to Kitty at breakfast this morning by Mr Duxford, who always dealt with the post, had been couched in rhapsodic terms wholly unlike Nell's usual manner. Kitty held the handkerchief to her eyes as she vainly attempted to stem the flow. She was *happy* for Nell, she told herself miserably. Had she not predicted this outcome the moment she had heard of the widowed Lord Jarrow and his Gothic castle? She had told Nell to fall in love with him, and her friend had done it within a few short weeks. While as for Prue—! Who would have thought that so unpromising a creature would have captured any man's romantic fancy? Mrs Rookham she was now, and disgustingly happy. It was too bad!

But no sooner had this unkind thought passed through her mind than Kitty chided herself for a beast. She could not envy darling Prue. Nor would Kitty have settled for a mere mister! But it was hard indeed to be the only one left, and with no prospects. Of the three, she had been the one to repudiate the future to which she had been raised, and if she ended after all as a governess, it would be the greatest injustice imaginable!

There was but one consolation, her present status permitting her to escape now and then upon the flimsiest of pretexts. This morning she had volunteered to nip out to the village shop in order to procure three pairs of the regulation hose for the latest orphaned arrival, along with a toothbrush and a tin of toothpowder—essential items that had been mysteriously forgotten by the persons who brought the child. Having made the purchases, Kitty had thrust them into her inner pockets and dawdled in the shop as long as she dared without buying anything more. Having used every penny of the last of her pupil's allowance, as well as her new wage, she had no money left to spend.

But the thought of returning to the Seminary, and to the task of listening—her unenviable occupation now of a Friday afternoon—to one of the worst-fingered pupils in the place practising upon the pianoforte, was altogether unbearable. Especially at a time when she was severely moved by Nell's good fortune—and no privacy in which to indulge it. The two other beds in her shared accommodation were now occupied by girls much younger than herself. Seventeen and eighteen—and Kitty was one and twenty in all but a month or two.

One and twenty! It was all of a piece. By rights she should have made her come-out and been long betrothed, if some ill-disposed person had not cut her off from the heritage she was convinced should have been hers. And condemning her thereby to a life of drudgery. She was the unluckiest female in the world!

A sound unusual in this out-of-the-way village penetrated her self-absorption. A vehicle coming down the lane, and drawn by several horses? It could not be the stage, for Mr King's coach boasted but one pair, and it was travelling too fast for a carrier. Distracted from her troubles by an idle curiosity, Kitty looked towards the sound, which was coming from the direction of Westbourn Green.

Around the corner swept a team of matched greys, drawing a smart-looking open carriage. It was driven by a man who looked to be a gentleman, with a liveried fellow up beside him, whom she took to be his groom. Tutored by her avid reading, Kitty recognised a fashionable spencer in the short green jacket, worn over a brown frock coat, the whole topped by a stylish hat. She watched the approach of the carriage with a feeling of envy. How she would love to be driven in so dashing a vehicle! Was it a curricle?

The carriage sailed by, and Kitty could not help but preen herself a little upon seeing its occupant glance in her direction. Especially when she thought she caught an expletive bursting from his lips. She was used to being an object of male attention, even if her admirers were for the most part bucolic yokels like the baker's boy. It did her heart good to know that her features had caught the interest of a personage of this calibre.

And then Kitty realised that the carriage was slowing. In some surprise, she watched it come to a halt, and saw the groom jump down and run to the heads of the leading pair of horses. Had the driver mistaken the way? A riffle disturbed her pulses as an enticing thought struck her. Perhaps he took her for a village maiden, and had leaped to the notion of indulging in a little flirtation.

The horses began to back, guided by the groom, and Kitty experienced a moment of doubt. Hitherto, her flirtations had been confined to the ilk of old Mr Fotherby, who lived in the house at the top of the Green, and knew how to keep the line. Lord, what if this man were to—

There was time for no more, for the carriage was coming level with where she perched, the gentleman's attention fully directed upon Kitty. She took in a vaguely pleasing countenance, just now marred by a heavy frown, and a glimpse of yellow hair under the wide-brimmed beaver, brown in colour. And then the gentleman addressed her, in strongly indignant tones.

'I thought it was you! Dash it, Kate, what the deuce are you about? How did you get here? You haven't run away, have you, silly wench? Didn't I tell you not to fret?'

As Kitty stared at him, utterly bemused, his glance raked

the surrounding area and came back to her face, a pair of blue eyes popping at her.

'What the devil—? Have you come here alone? Where's your maid? Gad, Aunt Silvia will be having a blue fit! I'd best take you home without more ado. Come, get off that fence and hop up!'

Bewilderment gave way to wrath, and Kitty found her tongue. 'I shall do no such thing! Who are you? I do not know you, nor have I heard of your aunt Silvia, and I'll thank you to take yourself off, sir!'

'Oh, will you?' muttered the gentleman grimly. 'Stop playing games, Kate, for the Lord's sake!'

'I am not Kate,' stated Kitty bluntly. 'I do not know who you are, and my name is Kitty.'

'No, it isn't,' argued the young man. 'Kitty indeed! Never heard such flimflam.'

'It's the truth!'

'And I'm a Dutchman.'

Kitty blinked. 'Are you? You sound English to me.'

The young man groaned. 'I'll throttle you in a minute! Now be sensible, there's a good girl. Leave off joking, for I haven't got all day.'

Kitty began to feel desperate. 'Sir, I am not joking. You are quite unknown to me. I am not this Kate, whoever she may be, and—'

'Next you'll be telling me I'm not your cousin Claud!'

'I haven't got a cousin Claud! Indeed, I have no cousin at all.'

Claud—if that was indeed the gentleman's name— gazed at her in a look compound of disbelief and frustration. Kitty pursued what she perceived to be an advantage, and assumed as haughty a mien as she could.

'Be pleased to drive on, sir.'

The gentleman threw his eyes to heaven. 'Will you stop

behaving like a third-rate play-actress? Are you going to get into this curricle, or do I come and get you?'

A rise of apprehension made Kitty grasp tightly to the bar of the fence upon which she was perched. Was the man mad? Her voice quivered a little as she tried again to disabuse him of his strange delusion.

'Sir, I have n-never set eyes on you in my life! You are m-mistaken in me, I do assure you, and I most certainly will not get into your curricle.'

The gentleman cursed fluently, and called to his groom. 'Hold them steady, Docking. I'll have to get down.'

Seeing him move to alight from the curricle, Kitty jumped hastily off the fence and made a dash for safety, running away from the vehicle in the direction of the little bank of shops to one end of the Green. The thunder of feet in pursuit threw her heart into her mouth, and she gasped her fright as a hand seized her from behind.

'No, you don't!'

Kitty shrieked, trying to pull away, as the relentless young gentleman tugged her round to face him. Panic took her.

'Let me go! Let me go!'

But his hold instead strengthened upon her arms, and he berated her with some heat. 'Will you stop making such a cake of yourself? Enacting me a tragedy in the middle of the street, silly chit! Come on!'

'I won't! Let me go!'

'Kate, I won't brook your defiance! Get into the carriage!'

Glancing wildly round for succour, Kitty saw only the empty Green. The hideous truth of a quiet country village hit her. There was no one to come to her aid! Those few inhabitants round about would be stuck in their parlours or out in the gardens that looked away from the Green.

And there was little to hope for from the proprietors of the few shops for which she had been headed, who were in all likelihood snoring at their posts. She was alone with a madman, whose tight hold she could by no means shake off.

Sheer fright drove her then, and she fought like a tigress, shrieking protests and imprecations as her captor struggled to control her.

'You won't make me! Beast! Brute! *How dare you*?'

'If you won't come quietly, I'll pick you up and carry you!'

But Kitty was beyond reason, yowling as much with rage, as panic, as she tried to break free. The man let go of her, and Kitty staggered back, almost losing her balance.

'All right, young Kate, you asked for it!'

How it happened, Kitty could not have said, but the next instant, she found herself flung over the gentleman's shoulder like a sack of potatoes. Half-winded and distressingly uncomfortable, Kitty was borne resistless to the curricle and dumped down without ceremony on to the seat, where she sat mumchance and numb with shock. She gazed in a bemused fashion as her assailant, panting a little, collected up his hat, which had fallen off in the struggle, clapped it back on his head, and leaped nimbly up into his seat, where he settled himself and gathered up the reins.

The horses were given the office to start and the curricle rumbled down the road. The groom jumped up behind as it passed him, and Paddington Green began to recede as it dawned on Kitty that she was being abducted.

Her heart began to hammer. In a shaking voice, she informed her captor of his iniquity. 'You are the h-horridest man I have ever met in my l-life! Set me down at once! Stop the carriage, I tell you!'

'Screech as much as you like. It won't make a ha'p'orth of difference.'

Kitty looked back and saw the familiar Paddington landmarks disappearing rapidly behind them. In a few moments, they would be turning into the Edgware Road. The heavy thump at her chest almost overwhelmed her, and she could barely get the words out.

'This is—is k-kidnapping! You—you may go to p-prison for it!'

But the heartless creature, who, in a few short moments, had turned her world upside down—literally too!—had no other answer for her than a mocking laugh. For a hazardous instant or two, Kitty contemplated jumping from the curricle. But it was travelling faster than she could ever have imagined, and as her glance raked the swiftly passing road beneath the carriage, her imagination presented her with a hideous picture of broken limbs, or worse. Her eyes swept the road ahead, where the rapid approach of the fork told her that hope of a swift return to the safety of the Seminary was receding all too fast. Fright enveloped her, and she descended to pleading.

'Oh, pray, sir, take me back! Indeed, I do not know you, and there will assuredly be the most dreadful uproar when you discover your mistake. Pray, pray stop now, before it is too late!'

A brief glance came her way, and the gentleman addressed her in a conversational way. 'That's very good, Kate. Never knew you were such an actress. You'd best get up some theatricals and give yourself some scope.'

Despair gripped Kitty. Could she make no impression upon him? His conviction of this false identity appeared unshakeable. What could she say to make him recognise that he was making an error, which could not fail to have serious repercussions? She clenched her hands in her lap as the curricle slowed for the turn into Edgware Road.

'You will not believe me, but you will be sorry presently, I promise you.'

His head turned. 'I should dashed well think I will be, if Aunt Silvia chooses to cut up rough! If I don't get you back as fast as bedamned, as sure as check she will have gone to the Countess in hysterics, and then the fat will be in the fire, and no mistake!'

Kitty caught her breath against a rising sob. 'I think you are mad! And if you are not put in prison for this day's work, very likely you will end in Bedlam.'

'Ha! Hark at the pot calling the kettle black! The only thing that would put me in Bedlam is finding that I've got to marry you, after all. Which is what the Countess is bound to say if she gets wind of this escapade.'

So saying, he put the horses into the corner at a speed that raised the hairs on the back of Kitty's neck. The curricle swerved horribly and she clutched hastily at the side, fearful of being overturned. But within seconds, the vehicle had made the turn and was running straight and true down the Edgware Road.

It was a moment or two before Kitty's fright abated enough to think over what he had said. Not that it made sense. Had he mentioned marriage? Certainly, his words bore out that he truly had mistaken her for another. Was she so much like this Kate?

He turned his head again and the blue eyes raked her. 'What in Hades possessed you, Kate? Thought you were a biddable girl. Can't blame you for rebelling, for I want the match as little as you do. Only why go to these lengths? Told you I had the matter in hand, didn't I? Should have known I'm not the fellow to let myself be pushed into it when the female ain't willing. I know my mother's a tartar, but I ain't about to knuckle under over this, and so I tell you!'

Kitty began to be curious, despite her lurking apprehension. 'Is your family then constraining you to marry your cousin?'

She received a disgusted look. 'Don't start all that again! As if you were indeed someone other than Kate.'

The curiosity turned to annoyance. 'But I have told you so! Why you should mistake me for your cousin, I cannot tell, but I am not she.'

'I've had enough of this!' He glanced over his shoulder to address his groom. 'Docking, who is this female?'

Kitty turned in her seat and found the liveried fellow grinning. 'Why, it's Miss Katherine, me lord.'

'And what relation is she to me?'

'Cousin, me lord, being as your ma and her ma be sisters.'

The blue gaze swung back upon Kitty. 'I rest my case.'

But Kitty's attention had caught upon the manner of the groom's address. Almost she held her breath. 'Are you indeed a lord?'

'Don't be a nodcock, Kate. You know I am.'

Kitty experienced a jolting leap in her chest, and turned to stare at the gentlemen's profile. He looked to be pleasant enough—if only she had not discovered him to be anything but!—for his features were clean cut and even, the nose straight and true, the lip rounded. She had taken in little in the brief glimpse she'd had of his hair, except that it was of pale gold. But there was something about the chin. Kitty examined the chin with a certain intentness. It was not a heavy jaw, by any means, only that chin had a stubborn jut. Which explained why his character did not match his appearance! Only he *was* a lord.

'Your name is Claud?' she ventured.

'Devil take it, Kate, will you stop this?'

Then she had recalled it aright. 'And you are unmarried?'

'They could scarce be constraining me to marry you if I wasn't.'

A daring thought occurred to Kitty, and her heart jumbled its beat. 'Is it not the case that if you ruin my reputation by abducting me, you ought in honour to offer me marriage?'

'Lord above!' Claud's horrified gaze swept hers. 'What the deuce will you be at? You ran off only because you don't want to marry me, didn't you?'

The daring notion died at birth. Kitty sighed. 'I keep telling you I am not your cousin. It is true that my name is Katherine, but—'

'Listen!' begged Claud. 'I don't know what your game is, but I'm at the end of my rope! Any more, and I'll tie something round your mouth, so you can't talk!'

Having no reason to disbelieve him—had not the brute thrown her pell-mell over his shoulder in that horrid way?—Kitty refrained from responding in kind and subsided into brooding silence. The pace of the curricle picked up, causing a wind to fly at her for which she was most unsuitably clad. Realisation hit, and the pit of her stomach vanished. She was being driven to London, with nothing but the clothes upon her back! She would likely die of exposure, if she did not expire from sheer terror.

The shock of her enforced capture had in fact receded, although Kitty could not subdue the leaping apprehension. That she had been mistaken for another could not be in doubt, and what would happen when her captor discovered it, she dared not think. Not that she was in any way to blame! If there was any justice, this Claud must acknowledge it. Surely, he would make her reparation? At least he must find a way to send her back to the Seminary.

That he would opt to send her back was all too likely, Kitty reflected a little despondently. He showed no sign of being attracted to her. He clearly did not wish to marry his cousin. And since Kitty evidently resembled her, she could not suppose he would wish to marry her either. A pity, for she desperately wanted to marry a lord! Still, it might not be comfortable to be wed to a stranger, and it was apparent that it would be difficult to bring this Claud up to scratch.

Besides, he was a brute! She recalled the rough treatment she had received at his hands—and the recent threat—with a resurgence of outrage. Oh, but she would serve him out for it! Only wait until he discovered his mistake. For discover it he must, sooner or later. However much she resembled his cousin—

The thought died. Kitty's pulse did a rapid tattoo and shot into a wild thumping that echoed in her ears. Why had she not thought of it at once? If she was this alike to an unknown female, there could be only one explanation. She had stumbled inadvertently upon a member of her lost family.

Buried in his own thoughts, Claud, Viscount Devenick, paid scant heed to his cousin beside him, although she came within the scope of his ruminations. His temper had cooled, but he was at a loss to account for Kate's freakish conduct. Not that he would question her again. If she meant to persist with this ridiculous masquerade, it would only drive him up into the boughs. Thank the Lord she had ceased her nonsensical arguing. Did she think he truly would have gagged her? Should have known him better.

Clearly she did not, as this escapade proved. Silly chit hadn't trusted him!

He reminded himself that she was only eighteen and just out this season. From the vantage point of five and twenty, it was clear how readily this escapade could put the cat among the pigeons. Faced with a niece who ran away rather than marry her cousin, ten to one his mother would force him to the altar on the pretext that Kate had blasted her reputation.

Not that he was such a nodcock as not to realise why Lady Blakemere had taken this notion into her head. If it hadn't been for Grandmama's promised legacy to the girl to give her a decent dowry, the scheme would not have occurred to the Countess. As if he hadn't enough money of his own! And all his mother would keep saying was that the Dowager Duchess's money ought to be kept in the family. A pity he had no brother instead of three sisters. It would have made sense for a younger son to dangle after the loot. But not for Claud to tie himself up in matrimony to Kate, of all girls under the sun!

She was comely enough, but what man wanted to wed his cousin? Besides, she was a thought too much of a milk-and-water miss for his taste. Which made her conduct to-day all the more incomprehensible. He'd never known the chit to be so flighty, nor to face him down as she had. A faint stirring of interest rose up. Perhaps there was more to young Kate than he had thought. He turned to glance at her, and found her studying him, her dark brows lowering. Claud shot instantly to the attack.

'What are you scowling for? You should be grateful to me.'

She continued to stare at him, a pout forming on her lips.

'Lost your tongue?' demanded Claud crossly. 'Answer me, can't you?'

It was too much. Kitty lost her temper.

'*Answer me, can't you!*' she echoed, in almost exact imitation of his tone. 'Why should I answer you, when you can think of nothing better to do than to threaten me? Is it not enough that you have dragged me by force into your carriage?'

'That was your own fault, Kate. Why couldn't you come quietly? Fought like a wildcat!'

'And I would do so again!'

But to his utter bewilderment, the chit abruptly burst into tears. Claud was thrown into instant disorder. He hadn't meant to make her cry.

'Hey, no need to turn into a watering pot!'

'Yes, there is,' sobbed Kitty, hunting frantically for her pocket-handkerchief. 'You don't know what you've done, and I can't tell you. Except that it is terrible!'

Unable to find the handkerchief, Kitty recalled that she'd had it in her hand when this infamous Claud had come upon her. It must have been lost in the struggle. She sniffed, turning on her abductor.

'And you made me lose my handkerchief!'

He transferred the reins to his left hand and dug the right into a pocket of his frock coat. 'Here.'

Kitty snatched the snowy white pocket-handkerchief he presented to her and defiantly blew her nose, wiping away her tears. The desire to weep was receding, but she did not return the handkerchief, instead jerking it between her fingers in a nervous fashion. The wind had begun to make her feel chilled, reminding her of the woeful lack in her costume. She looked round at the author of her plight.

'Do you realise that you have brought me away without a stitch to wear besides this gown?'

The blue gaze travelled briefly down her person and returned to the road. 'Beats me why you'd want the thing! Where did you get it? You look like the farmer's daughter in her Sunday best.'

'How hateful of you to say so! I know it is not fashionable, but—'

'If you take my advice, you'll burn it.'

'Burn it!' shrieked Kitty, outraged. 'It cost me three whole shillings!'

He looked round again, a critical frown between his fair brows. 'You were robbed. Mind you, I can't think why you didn't provide yourself at least with a cloak. Feather-brained, that's what you are, young Kate.'

Kitty glared at him. 'Why should I take a cloak merely for a trip to the shops on the Green on a day like this?'

But Claud was not attending. It had been borne in upon him that his idiotic cousin was shivering. Why she must need escape without proper preparation, he was at a loss to understand. Silly chit hadn't a brain in her head. Thank the Lord he had held steadfast against marrying the wench!

He slowed the carriage, and called over his shoulder to the groom. 'Docking, is there a blanket in this thing?'

'Under the seat, me lord.'

Kitty, who had been lost in the realisation that everything she owned was at the Seminary, came to herself as the carriage was pulled up. Her abductor was rummaging under the seat, and Kitty briefly thought of taking a chance and jumping down. Only he would be bound to come after her, and would have no difficulty in catching her. Besides, how in the world would she manage, left in the middle of the highway, with no notion where she was and no means of getting herself back to Paddington?

Claud straightened, and shaking out the blanket he had found, slung it carelessly around Kitty's shoulders.

'Wrap yourself in this.'

Regretfully abandoning the opportunity for escape, Kitty huddled herself into the new warmth. Gratitude swept through her, and without thinking, she smiled at Claud for the first time in this nightmare journey.

'Thank you.'

For a moment, Claud stared at his cousin's features, oddly troubled by the look that accompanied the smile. It vanished abruptly.

'Oh, Lord! What in the world will the Duck say when she finds me gone?'

'Duck? What duck?' demanded Claud, bewildered. 'What the devil has a duck to say to anything?'

But Kitty, reminded by the idea of Paddington, had realised that in all the horror of her capture, she had forgotten Mrs Duxford. She was supposed in the afternoon to mind the pupils who were practising the pianoforte. When it was found that she had been missing throughout, the Duck was bound to think she was up to mischief. What if it was discovered that she had left the village in company with a strange man? Suppose someone had seen him forcing her into his curricle? She would be utterly ruined.

Almost the thought of Mrs Duxford's inevitable rage made her wish she might never go back. Only the apprehension of what might be awaiting her in the immediate future was worse. If indeed, this abominable Claud's cousin Kate was so very much her image. It *must* be her family! She had longed to find out the truth of her background—believing all these years that it had been kept from her deliberately. But now that the opportunity had arisen, she was more afraid than she had thought possible. They had not wanted her. How would they react if she were thrust upon her?

The curricle had been on the move again for some

while, and Kitty sat silent, from time to time contemplating the profile of the perpetrator of the evils that were gathering about her. What would he say and do when he discovered his mistake? Worse, what would these unknown relatives say?

Time began to have no meaning, and Kitty could not have said how long she had been travelling when she noticed that the passing scenery had begun to change, the rural aspect of the country giving way to an urban feel. The traffic became steadily heavier, with more people shifting on the roadside. They must be approaching the capital.

'Where are we?'

'Coming up to Tyburn Gate.'

'Then we are almost in London!'

Despite the invidious nature of her situation and the horrid uncertainty of her future, Kitty was conscious of a burgeoning excitement. How she had longed to come here! What dreams she'd had of the soirées and balls she would attend; the masquerades and theatres; and the fashionable Bond Street shops!

She gazed about her with new interest, drinking in the sight of persons of all description trotting to and fro. Here a liveried servant, hastening with a message perhaps. There a female in clogs with a yoke about her neck, crying wares which Kitty could not identify. Red-coated soldiers stood about a tavern at the roadside, and several official-looking men were to be seen hurrying into a building, while a fellow in rough garments, with a straw in his mouth, leaned against a wall.

The noise grew to a din. Rumbling wheels, cries from the street, and the yapping of dogs mingled with a clattering and hammering that came at Kitty from all directions. She almost put her hands over her ears. But she was dis-

tracted by a series of emanating aromas that assailed her
nostrils one after the other. Strongest amongst these was
the ordure from the many horses, swept to one side by an
industrious boy. But through that, Kitty identified the smell
of manly sweat here, and there that of fresh baked bread.
Confusion swamped her.

Huddling in her blanket, she felt altogether inadequate,
and ill equipped for this great city. Without realising what
she did, she drew nearer to the man at her side. Despite
his horrid conduct, he was her only hope of succour. She
had no clothes, no money, and no prospect of remedy. And
at any minute, she would be facing the consequences of
her abductor's rash actions.

At last, the curricle entered a less noisome part of the
town, coming into a tree-lined avenue that ran beside a
large park. She pointed.

'What is that, please?'

Claud started out of a reverie. 'Eh?'

'Is it Hyde Park, perhaps?'

Irritation shook him once again. 'Thank the Lord we're
almost there! If I had to take much more, young Kate, I
couldn't answer for the consequences.'

He found himself under scrutiny from his cousin's
brown eyes, a disconcerting expression in them.

'Where are you taking me?'

Claud sighed. 'To the Haymarket, of course. Where else
should I take you but to your own home? Unless my aunt
has already gone to the Countess in Grosvenor Square. In
which case, we'll have to concoct some tale to account for
your absence. Though I'm hanged if I can think what!'

He glanced at her again as he spoke, and the oddest
sensation came to him. For a flicker of time, he wondered
if the chit was indeed someone else. Then he shook off
the moment. It was just what she wanted him to think, he

dared say. And the moment he admitted he had a doubt, Kate would laugh him out of court.

'Still beats me why you did this, young Kate. What did you hope to gain?'

Kitty had no answer. Since he would not accept the truth—and showed an alarming tendency to brutishness in anger!—she judged it prudent to evade the question.

'I know you will come to regret your actions this day, sir,' she said instead. 'Only I hope you will be gentleman enough not to blame me for it in the end.'

'Still at it, eh? Well, I've done. We'll see how you persist when my aunt has an attack of the vapours!'

If anyone deserved to have the vapours, it was herself, Kitty decided. For as they drew nearer and nearer to the destination he had outlined, the thought of what she might discover at the other end all but crushed her.

The house at which the curricle drew up at length was very fine. A tall building of grey stone, with a narrow porticoed entrance, one of a row that had been built in much the same design.

Kitty's heartbeat became flurried again as the groom leaped from his perch and ran first to the great front door, where he tugged on a bell hanging to one side. As he returned to go to the horses' heads, she was impelled to make one last appeal before Claud could alight.

'Sir, pray listen to me!'

His head turned, but his manner was impatient. 'What's to do, Kate? Let's get in and get this over with.'

He was still holding the reins and his whip, and Kitty reached out an unconscious hand to grasp his arm.

'You are making a grave mistake,' she said tensely. 'I very much fear that you may be opening a closet in which I will be found to be the skeleton.'

Claud cast up his eyes. 'Will you have done?'

He turned away without waiting for her answer. Next moment, he had leaped down and was handing both reins and whip to the groom, who left the horses to take them. Vaguely Kitty was aware that the groom was swinging himself up into the driving seat. But her eyes were upon Claud as he came around the back of the carriage to her side. He held up his hands to her.

'Come on, I'll lift you down.'

There was no help for it. Kitty let the blanket fall away and half-rose, moving to find the step. But two strong hands seized her by the waist. There was an instant of helplessness, and she grasped at his convenient shoulders. Then she was set upon her feet, the hands shifting to her arms to steady her. Kitty felt strangely light-headed, and was conscious of warmth where his gloved hands touched her.

She looked up into his face, and found the blue eyes had softened.

'You're a confounded nuisance, young Kate. But I'll stand buff, never fear. I won't let Aunt Silvia bully you!'

This from one who had bullied her unmercifully! Kitty had no words left for protest, for the unpleasant behaviour of her heart was giving her enough to contend with. An imposing individual of great girth and age had opened the door of the Haymarket house. Kitty allowed herself to be shepherded up the short flight of steps and meekly followed the gentleman inside.

The hall into which she stepped was long and somewhat narrow, with a staircase towards the back. There was space only for a table to one side with a gilded mirror above, together with a hat stand and a porter's chair.

Claud stripped off his gloves and handed them, together with his hat, to his aunt's butler. The fellow was fortunately too discreet to say anything, he thought, as he briefly checked his image in the mirror and passed a hand across the cropped blond locks to straighten them. One could not blame the butler for the look he had cast upon Kate, following in his wake. Not that Tufton gave himself away by so much as a flicker. But the fellow could scarcely fail to have been astonished.

'Is my aunt in, Tufton?'

'To you, m'lord, yes.'

'In the yellow saloon, is she?'

The butler bowed. 'As is her custom, m'lord. She is with—'

But Claud was already ascending the staircase, turning to ensure that Kate was following. There was not a dog's chance of keeping this escapade from his aunt, so there was nothing for it but to beard her at once. At least she had not run to his mother. One might entertain some hope of brushing through this with the minimum of fuss. He turned to his cousin as he reached the first floor.

'Looks as if your mama ain't blown the whistle, in which case you may escape with a scold.' Her eyes were as round as saucers. The wench looked scared to death! 'It's all right, silly chit. She can't bite you.'

Kitty swallowed on the choking feeling occasioned by the frantic beating at her bosom. Her hands were trembling, and she was obliged to clasp them together. Her legs felt like jelly, but she trod resolutely behind Claud, her eyes on the back of his fair head, as he strode purposefully for a little way down a corridor and stopped outside one of a series of doors of dark wood. He gave her an encouraging wink.

'Here goes!'

And then the door was open, and there was nothing to do but to square her shoulders and walk into the unknown.

Claud let his cousin precede him, and then strolled into

the well-known yellow saloon. It was aptly named, with
walls covered in a paper of dull mustard, striped in gilt
that was rubbed away in places. The Hepplewhite chairs
of mahogany were cushioned at the seat in faded yellow
brocadé, and cracked gilding enhanced the mantel as well
as the stain-spotted mirror above. That it was a family
room was evidenced by the general air of dilapidation, the
plethora of knick-knacks and ornaments placed upon every
surface, and the wear in the brown patterned rug.

His aunt Silvia, a matron with a tendency to corpulence,
and attired most unsuitably in a gown fashionably waisted
below her ample bosom, was seated in a striped sofa of
yellow and brown set close to the fireside—although there
were no coals burning there today. The small table to one
side held a jumble of the impedimenta required by a knit-
ter. And on the sofa beside her, holding up between her
hands a skein of wool in order to enable his aunt to wind
it into a ball, sat a young female whom Claud knew almost
as well as he knew himself.

In the blankest amazement, he stood staring at his
cousin. The deuce! If Kate was sitting there, then who in
the name of all the gods was the girl by his side? And
why was she the living spit of the Honourable Katherine
Rothley?

Chapter Two

At the back of Claud's mind hovered a realisation that both aunt and cousin, having caught sight of the girl, were staring in a species of shock. But the recognition that he had made a colossal blunder—had not the chit said so over and over?—made him address his immediate feelings to the stranger herself.

'Hang it all, I've made a mistake! Deuced sorry for it—er—' what in the world was he to call her? '—ma'am, only you look so alike! Don't know who you may be, but I've obviously dragged you off to no purpose.'

The girl made no reply. He could not be sure she had heard him. She was in the devil of a tremble, that he could see. Not surprising. He was a thought shaken himself!

A faint moan turned his attention back to the sofa. To his deep dismay, his aunt Silvia had turned ashen. The ball of wool she had been holding had fallen from her grasp and was rolling unchecked across the carpet, unwinding as it went. At any other time, Claud would have leaped to retrieve it, but the sight of his aunt's pallid features, accompanied by a series of palpitating moans that began to issue from her mouth, had thoroughly unnerved him. An attack of the vapours! That was all he needed!

The matron toppled backwards, falling against the upholstered back of the sofa, her eyes rolling alarmingly in their sockets and showing white. Claud darted forward and checked again, irresolute.

But his cousin, whose own rapt attention had been all upon the unknown female, had started at her mother's collapse and jumped up, her skein of wool discarded. She seized her mother by the shoulders.

'Mama! What is the matter? Mama, *pray!*'

Claud took a hand, moving to the sofa. 'No use shaking her like that, silly chit! Here, let me. Haven't you any smelling salts? Give me another cushion!'

In a moment, he had arranged his aunt more comfortably upon the sofa, her head resting upon two cushions. His cousin had darted to an escritoire and was rummaging in a drawer. Claud stood back, looking down at the stricken matron in no small degree of perturbation.

Her breathing was shallow, shown by the rapid rise and fall of her overlarge bosom, and her eyes, sinking into the plump folds of flesh, were closed. But she had not quite fainted away, Claud decided, for a series of protesting groans were escaping from her lips. She had no colour, and it was clear to the meanest intelligence that she had sustained a severe shock.

Claud glanced at the cause of it, and found the girl standing just where he had left her, staring round-eyed at the appalling result of her sudden appearance in the yellow saloon. And all because she looked like his cousin. Not that the girl was in the least to blame. It was his fault, and he must presently face the consequences—which loomed horribly ugly, if Aunt Silvia's reaction was any measure. He brushed this aside for the present. At this juncture, it was of more moment to revive his ailing aunt.

To his relief, Kate came dashing back, armed with a small bottle. 'I have it. Stand aside, Claud!'

Claud stepped hastily out of the way, allowing his cousin to move into the sofa. But it was with mixed feelings that he heard her soothing words.

'Poor Mama. You will be better directly, I promise you.'

He was not at all sure that he wanted to be present when his aunt should feel recovered. It was rapidly being borne in upon him that his arrival with an unknown female who all too closely resembled Kate was a *faux pas* of the first order. He tugged at the short green spencer that had shifted with his exertions, unconsciously smoothing its fit across his chest. What in Hades was there in the stranger to cause this reaction?

Wholly absorbed, and forgetful of the unknown female herself, he watched as his cousin opened the bottle and waved its contents under her mother's nose.

Kitty, standing all the while in a state of petrified shock, could almost envy the large woman lying on the sofa. She could herself have done with a dose of sal volatile. Had she not guessed it? There could be no doubt. She must belong somehow in this family. Else why should the woman become subject to a dramatic collapse? *She must know something.*

Her heart hammered painfully, and her gaze turned upon the girl Kate, for whom her abductor had taken her. The resemblance was uncanny. The female had hair as dark and perhaps as long as Kitty's own, though since it was dressed in a chignon high upon her head, it was difficult to tell. Her figure was masked by a demure gown of white muslin, the fashionable folds of which sent a thrill of envy through Kitty. Was the bosom—which was all the curve visible—as full as her own? Hard to tell. And equally difficult to see at this moment whether Kate had a thought the advantage of her in height. Yet there could be no doubt that in face she looked all too familiar. It was not quite like a mirror, but Kitty could not find it in her to blame Claud for his error.

The reflections left her as she saw that the afflicted matron was recovering. Kitty unconsciously shifted backwards as she saw the woman's eyes flutter open. Finding herself stopped by a chair against the wall, Kitty froze again, wishing she might become invisible.

'There, Mama, that is better, is it not?'

The woman gazed up at her daughter. A frantic look came into her features, and a wavering hand rose up to catch at Kate's fingers.

'Where is she? Did I truly see it? Oh, what a nightmare!'

Kitty shrank away. If only the floor might open and swallow her up! She heard the voice of the girl Kate, but did not take in the words as with a resurgence of dread she saw the woman threshing to get up.

'Pray don't distress yourself, Mama! No, no, don't try to sit up. Stay there, I beg of you!'

The matron's efforts to raise herself ceased, but her eyes, casting about the room, fastened upon Kitty, whose heart jerked as the creature pointed, horror in her face.

'She is there still! Oh, what have I ever done to deserve this?'

'Mama, pray hush!' begged Kate.

Claud, torn between a sense of duty and a strong desire to retire from the coming scene as fast as he could, found his cousin's eyes upon him in a scowl very like that to which he had been subjected by the female he had brought with him.

'Claud, how could you? Look what you've done!'

'How was I to know?' protested Claud aggrievedly. 'I thought it was you!'

His cousin turned to look at her hapless mirror image. 'Well, I can see there is a resemblance. But surely you must have known it wasn't me? Those clothes, for one thing! Where did you find her?'

'In Paddington.'

These simple words acted upon his aunt as if a firework had been set off beneath her. The matron reared up, dislodging her daughter, who fell back in disorder, and gazed upon her nephew with eyes standing wide with dread.

'*Paddington?*'

Claud winced. 'Confound you, Aunt, I wish you would not shriek like that!'

She paid him no heed. 'It is as I suspected. You must take her back! Now. Immediately.' Her arms stretched out towards him, and her voice took on a plea. 'And not a word to your mother, I implore you, Devenick! If Lydia were to hear of it, there is no saying what she would do. Oh, it is too bad! Why, why had you to bring her here?'

She withdrew her hands, wringing them painfully, and casting loathsome glances at the wretched female that was the innocent cause of the brouhaha. Claud's mind was alive with curiosity. Nor was he the only one, for he perceived that Kate, having taken in the gist of her mother's speech, was looking at the girl with a new interest. It became expedient to explain himself.

'The thing is, I was coming back from Westbourn Green—stayed at my friend Jack's place, for we were at cards last night until the small hours—'

'Do get on, Claud!'

Wounded, Claud protested his cousin's impatience. 'I am only explaining how I came to be in Paddington.'

'I can't think why you should suppose I would be in Paddington!'

'That's just it. Couldn't believe my eyes! Only I thought you'd run away.'

'Run away? Why, in heaven's name?'

It occurred to Claud that it was scarcely politic to be giving his reasons in front of Lady Rothley. Not that Aunt Silvia was in any condition to be protesting over that! He gave his cousin an austere look.

'I should have thought that was obvious. But be that as it may, I took the girl for you and thought I'd best bring you back home before anyone got wind of your escapade.'

'But surely this person must have told you that she was not me?'

'She did,' Claud confessed ruefully. 'At some length. Only I would not believe her.' He turned to his aunt. 'You must not blame her, for it was entirely my doing.'

Lady Rothley shuddered. 'Blame her? No, I blame you! I blame Lydia! I blame—'

She broke off, and Claud got the distinct impression that she had recollected herself just in time before giving away whatever secret there was connected with the girl. Vaguely it came to him that the chit had said something about skeletons. Devil take it, there was something in it!

'What's to do, Aunt?' he demanded abruptly. 'What do you know of the girl? *Do* you know her?'

'Of course I don't! I mean—no, I— You must not ask me!'

To Claud's intense relief, Kate took a hand. 'But, Mama, that is unreasonable. After what has passed, I do think you might tell us. Why did you cry out when you heard she came from Paddington? Do you know why she looks like me?'

Lady Rothley waved agitated hands. 'Nothing will induce me to speak of it! You must not ask me! And for

heaven's sake, don't either of you speak of it to anyone.
Least of all to Lydia!'

'But, Mama—'

'Unless you wish to drive me into my grave, Kate, you
won't mention this again.'

There was a silence. Across the room, Kitty eyed the
trio with a burgeoning resentment, which rapidly overlay
the fear and distress occasioned by the woman's horrid
reaction to her coming. She found that she was shaking,
but she resolutely trod a step or two in the direction of the
sofa.

'But I b-believe you owe me an explanation, ma'am.'

Three pairs of eyes shot round, and Kitty blenched. But
she stood her ground, holding her head as high as she
could, and keeping her gaze fixed upon the female. She
saw her abductor move, as if he would come to her, and
quickly held up a hand.

'No, sir, pray don't approach me. It seems that I am
contaminated by my—by my l-likeness to your cousin
there. I did warn you.'

Claud suffered an odd pang of compassion and strode
quickly forward. 'The skeleton in the family closet, you
said. Seems you were right. But you need have no fear. I
won't let you suffer for it! The blame is entirely mine, and
I shall—'

'Devenick, fetch her here!'

He checked, turning his head. 'I'll not let you upset her
any more, Aunt Silvia, and so I warn you! She's suffered
enough humiliation already, I should have thought.'

A riffle of gratitude swept through Kitty. He had shown
himself a brute, but he had a streak of kindness. She looked
quickly at the matron to see how she took this.

The creature was waving plump hands. 'Fetch her! I
want to look at her.'

At which, the girl Kate jumped up and came towards Kitty. 'Yes, pray do come closer.' But instead, Kate came to her. She pulled Kitty about to face Claud and stood close beside her. 'It is extraordinary, is it not? We are much of a height, I think. Only do we really look so very much alike?'

Kitty waited tensely as Claud looked them both over. She was acutely aware of the other girl's hand clutching her at the elbow.

'Peas in a pod,' said Claud. 'If it weren't for the clothes, of course.'

Kitty reddened, and her feelings suffered a reversal. How excessively tactless! As if she was not distressingly aware of the truly enormous gulf between her horrid gown and the elegance of Kate's attire.

But the feeling did not long endure, for a renewed groaning from the sofa drew the attention of both cousins. Kitty was forcibly dragged towards the matron, who had sunk a little where she sat. For all she could sink, with the rolls of extra flesh that made the spotted muslin gown, with its fashionably high waist, appear grossly inadequate for its purpose.

'Mama, who is she?'

Kitty found Claud at her other elbow. 'Good question. Only you'd best refer it to the lady herself!' He gave her a smile that was curiously engaging. 'I know you told me your name, but I wasn't taking notice and I've forgot it.'

The blunt honesty could not but appeal, and Kitty returned his smile. 'It's Kitty.'

'Heavens, you can't be called Katherine!'

This from the girl Kate, who was also possessed of that name. To her chagrin, Kitty heard a note of apology in her own voice. 'But I am called Katherine. My name is Katherine Merrick.'

This information acted powerfully upon the aunt. She closed her eyes in a look of anguish. 'I knew it!'

To Claud's intense annoyance, Lady Rothley addressed him once more in that imploring tone. 'Devenick, you must take the girl away—back to where she came from. And say nothing of this to a soul, I charge you!'

'Yes, you said so before, Aunt Silvia. Only you won't say *why*.'

'I cannot. You must understand that it is a matter of the utmost secrecy. I am sworn to silence!' She turned to her daughter. 'Kate, you must put forth your best efforts to persuade him. I tell you, it will kill me, if Lydia gets to hear of this! To have it all dragged up again—no, a thousand times! I tell you I could not bear it!'

This was more than Kitty could endure. Shaking Kate off, she retreated a few steps, turning in desperation to Claud.

'Pray, sir, will you take me away from here?'

He was frowning. 'Yes, but not until I've got to the bottom of this!'

To his surprise, his cousin balked. 'No, Claud! I cannot ask Mama to betray her promise.' She turned from him to Kitty. 'I am so sorry, Miss—Merrick, wasn't it?—but I think it is best if Claud takes you back.'

'Yes, but wait a bit—'

'Pray, Claud, don't say any more! You can see that poor Mama is upset.'

'That's all very well—'

Kitty cut in swiftly. 'Sir, I have no wish to remain here! It was all a mistake, and there's an end. If you don't wish to embarrass me further, pray take me home.'

It was not an appeal he could refuse. With a sigh, Claud abandoned his attempt to extract the secret. Though he was by no means reconciled. The intelligence that it would upset the Countess had set him on fire to find it out. But his cousin again intervened, moving to the other girl again and taking her hand.

'Poor thing, I am so sorry. We have been dreadfully rude—the shock, you know. I dare say you must be feeling excessively uncomfortable.'

To Claud's intense annoyance, his cousin next turned on him.

'I do think you might have listened when she told you she wasn't me, Claud. Poor Miss Merrick has been disgracefully inconvenienced, and Mama distressed—and it is all your fault!'

'I am well aware of that. Haven't I said so?' He took the girl's arm and pulled her away from Kate. 'Besides, I'm going to make her reparation.'

'How?'

'I don't know yet, but I shall think of something.'

Kitty warmed to him. Indeed, his presence close beside her gave her courage. If his fat aunt Silvia had repudiated her—indeed, her gaze continued to veer towards Kitty at intervals, brimful of revulsion!—at least Claud had the decency to stand by his mistake.

'All I want is to be returned to the Seminary,' she urged, adding bitterly, 'I only wish I had taken one of the posts offered to me weeks ago, and then this would never have happened.'

'Post?' repeated Claud.

'What sort of post?' asked Kate.

Kitty lifted her chin. 'I am meant for a governess. We are all raised for it at the Seminary.'

'Oh, poor thing!' uttered Kate, distressfully. Then her face brightened. 'I know! If you have not yet found a post, perhaps we could help you. Claud, you might recommend her to someone of our acquaintance.'

Claud snorted. 'Don't be so feather-brained, Kate! Present for a governess to some matron I know a girl who looks exactly like you?'

A shriek from the sofa brought his head round, and he winced. His aunt had once again bounced up.

'Upon no account! Dear heaven, only think of the scandal if the girl appeared in town in such a guise! Devenick, I forbid you to help her. Or, stay! You had best see the woman at the Seminary and tell her that the girl must be given a post in a country establishment, among people who will never show their faces in town. Perhaps a well-to-do tradesman, who could never find a place among the *ton*. Yes, that will be the best plan. You will see to it, Devenick. I rely upon you.'

'Lord, ma'am, I can't do that! Who am I to dictate the girl's future? Or you, come to that.'

To his dismay, Lady Rothley surged out of the sofa and came to him, throwing out imploring arms. 'My dear, dear boy, if you knew the agony of mind into which I must fall if this dreadful business should be dragged up all over again, you would not hesitate. Believe me, if anyone has reason to beg your aid in this, it is I. As for authority, your mother took that upon herself long years ago. I tell you, if you do not do as I ask, you risk the worst of Lydia's displeasure!'

Claud evaded her, shifting away to the other end of the mantelpiece, and pulling the girl with him. 'Yes, that's all very well, ma'am, but there's something devilish havey-cavey about all this, and I am not at all sure—'

'For heaven's sake, Devenick, do you wish to drive me demented?'

In a good deal of dudgeon, he watched his aunt totter back to the sofa, Kate fussing about her. He glanced at the girl, whose wrist he had hold of, and realised she was trembling. There was strain in her white face, and the brown eyes looked enormous. A guilty pang smote him, and without thinking, he let go her wrist and put his arm about her, giving her a hug.

'Don't look so worn, young Kate—I mean, Kitty!' he corrected himself, remembering. 'Haven't I said I won't let it harm you?'

Kitty looked up into the even features, and a tired sigh escaped her. 'She is right, sir. If I were seen in town, the resemblance would be remarked. I shall speak to Mrs Duxford myself.' She looked across at the afflicted matron. 'I have no wish to embarrass you, ma'am.'

Kate answered, for the aunt was engaged in moaning softly and rubbing at her temples. 'You are very good, Miss Merrick. I only wish there was something we might do for you.'

Kitty moved out of Claud's protective arm, and took a pace towards the sofa. 'There is one thing. If—if your mother will only tell me that I am indeed a member of this family?'

Claud was beside her. 'That much is abundantly plain!'

'Claud!'

'Well, it's true, Kate. And you needn't look censorious, for I know very well you want to know how it comes about just as much as I.'

Kitty put out a hand. 'Pray don't! I do not care if she does not wish to explain the exact relationship, for I have long suspected there had been a scandal. Only—'

She got no further. A loud groan issued from the aunt's lips, and she waved podgy hands. 'Take her away, Devenick! I cannot bear to look at her!'

Kitty's brief moment of valour was over. The blow struck hard, and she shrank away, feeling all the force of that rejection she had known when persons she only vaguely recollected—strangers to her—had removed her from the place she had called home and dumped her at the Paddington Seminary, leaving her horribly alone.

As if through a cloud, she heard voices, saw Kate's features close to hers, speaking words that had no meaning. She sensed beside her the presence of Claud, and moved as he directed her, going where he led with neither interest nor attention. Only when she was outside the mansion in the fresh air, and being urged into the curricle, did Kitty come back to herself. And to the full realisation of what had happened.

Having packed the girl into his curricle and taken up the reins, Claud did not immediately instruct Docking to stand away from the horses' heads. His mind was sorely exercised by the revelation of the existence of a family skeleton, and he sat irresolute, wondering what were best to do. If his aunt Silvia supposed he would meekly bury the finding under the carpet, she had much to learn of him. Particularly in light of the fear she had exhibited on the notion of Lady Blakemere getting wind of the matter.

A surge of tingling exhilaration rose up inside him at the thought of what this could do to the woman who had long been his Nemesis. She might be his mother, but he had long ago given up addressing her as such. Lydia, Countess of Blakemere, had harried him from his earliest years, and he could not regard her with anything but revulsion. Along with his sisters, he had been terrorised by her frowns and castigated for every fault of character—of which, according to the Countess, he had more than his fair share. He had thanked his stars, and his father's insistence—likely the only time poor Papa had succeeded in standing out against her!—for his schooling at Eton, which had toughened him to withstand the creature just as soon as he was old enough to do so without fear of retribution. Two of his sisters had escaped into matrimony—not that they'd had choice of who they married!—and it was upon the head of poor Babs at seventeen that the wrath of the Countess now fell. There was little young Babs could do against her. But for Claud, always on the lookout for vengeance, an opportunity such as this was manna from heaven. The family skeleton come home to roost!

At this point in his ruminations, it was borne in upon Claud that the skeleton was emitting suspiciously doleful sounds. Turning his head, he found Kitty valiantly attempting to stifle her sobs. Tears nevertheless gathered at her eyes and spilled down her cheeks. Stricken with renewed guilt, Claud cursed.

'Don't cry! Told you I won't let it harm you, didn't I?'

Kitty gulped and sniffed, shaking her head in the hope that he would realise that she could not speak. It evidently did not occur to him that she was less hurt by the possible consequences than her reception in the Haymarket house.

'Where's that handkerchief I gave you? You'd best find it, for I haven't another on me.'

The reminder served to send Kitty's fingers digging into her pockets. One hand came out clutching the handkerchief. In the other was a package tied up in brown paper. Kitty stared at it uncomprehendingly.

'Here, give me that!'

The handkerchief was snatched from her hand, and next instant, her chin was being grasped in a set of gloved fingers and Claud was wiping away her tears. As if she had been a little girl, he held the square of white linen over her nose and requested her to blow. Too startled to protest, Kitty did as she was bid, and then stared into the blue eyes as they inspected her face.

'There, that'll do. You'd best keep this.' Claud released

her chin and stuffed the handkerchief back into her fingers. Then he noticed the package she was holding. 'What's that?'

Kitty looked down at it. 'I cannot remember.' And then she did. 'Oh, it is the hose I purchased for the new girl.' Recalling the toothbrush and the tin of toothpowder, she dived a hand into her other pocket and found the other package. 'Thank goodness! The Duck would scold me dreadfully had I lost it!' It then occurred to her that Mrs Duxford was going to have far too much to scold her over without concerning herself about toothpowder and white hose. A wail escaped her. 'Oh, what am I to tell her? How long have I been absent? The Duck will kill me!'

'What is all this about a dashed duck?' demanded Claud, at last signing to his groom and instructing his horses to start.

Too agitated to be other than forthright, Kitty explained. 'She is the lady who is in charge of the Seminary. Mrs Duxford, only we call her the Duck. Not to her face, for she would be excessively displeased. Not that it matters, for I don't know how I am to explain this. I dare say she will turn me from the door if she hears that I ran off to London with you!'

'Must she hear of it?' asked Claud, turning the horses out of the Haymarket and heading west. 'Can't you make up some tale that will satisfy her?'

'When I have been absent for hours and hours? What should I say? And what if someone had seen you drag me off like that? They would be bound to tell her.'

'Then you will have to tell her the truth.'

'She would never believe it. What is more, I could not blame her. Whoever heard such a rigmarole as you have landed me in?'

Relieved that Kitty no longer showed any disposition to

weep, Claud yet had no solution to offer. 'Well, I admit it's a thought fantastic, but I'm sure you will come up with a likely explanation.'

'It's well for you to say so,' declared Kitty, incensed. 'Do you suggest I tell her that you forcibly abducted me?'

'You know very well it wasn't an abduction,' argued Claud, aggrieved.

'Well, whatever it was, you promised you would compensate me.'

'I intend to.'

'How? The least you can do is help me think up an excuse. You ought to be glad that I am nothing more than a governess, or you would be obliged to make reparation by marrying me.'

'*What?*'

The horses suddenly shot forward, and Kitty was almost thrown from the curricle. She clutched the seat as the groom behind issued a warning.

'Take care, guv'nor, or you'll have us over!'

But Claud was already bringing his cattle under control. Cursing, he turned wrathful eyes upon Kitty. 'What the deuce made you say a thing like that? Made me jump nearly out of my skin!'

A giggle escaped Kitty. 'I didn't mean that you should marry me. But I cannot say I am sorry you got a horrid shock, for it serves you right for what you have put me through today.'

Claud was in no mood for this sort of thing. 'If you think I did what I did for the pleasure of it, you're mistaken. Last thing on my mind was to spend the day ferrying my cousin back and forth to no purpose.'

'But I am not your cousin,' objected Kitty.

'As things stand, it looks deuced likely that you might be!'

This untimely reminder served to throw Kitty back into gloom. 'I wish you will not talk about it. It serves no purpose to recall it to my mind, for it is clear that the scandal is too dreadful to be talked of, and there is nothing to be done about it.'

'Oh, isn't there?' Claud swept round Hyde Park corner and turned north. 'I'm hanged if I let it lie, if it's going to annoy my mother.'

Kitty gazed at him in the liveliest apprehension. 'What do you mean to do?'

'I don't know yet.'

'Why should you wish to annoy your mother?'

'Ha! You don't know her, or you wouldn't ask!'

'Is she horrid?'

'Loathsome!' declared Claud, not mincing his words. 'If you'd to choose between my Lady Blakemere and this Duck you speak of, you'd run to your Duck and hide behind her skirts.'

Kitty eyed the jutting chin in a species of wonder. For all his vehemence, he did not look as if he was in the least afraid of his mother. As for the Duck, Kitty knew her for a just and well-intentioned woman. And she had her moments of kindness. This Lady Blakemere sounded perfectly dreadful. Kitty was glad she would never be called upon to meet her.

It occurred to her that the curricle was travelling so rapidly, despite the press of carriages and people, that in a short space of time she would be leaving the metropolis forever. And with nothing to show for her visit but a headful of unkind memories. It was most unfair! She recalled Claud's promise to compensate her. Did he mean to give her money?

A riffle of excitement bubbled up, followed immediately by a depressing thought. What was the use of his giving her money when she had no means of supplying herself with the things she craved? There was no shop in Paddington where she could purchase the sort of gown she wanted. Nor would the local dressmaker be persuaded to make it up for her—even could she furnish herself with the material.

The daring idea surfaced, and Kitty turned quickly to Claud. 'There is one thing you might do for me.'

His head snapped round, frowning suspicion in his eyes. 'Oh, is there? As long as it has nothing to do with matrimony—'

'Of course it has not.' Kitty drew a deep breath and plunged in. 'Only will you buy me silk stockings and a spangled gown?'

The blue eyes popped. 'Silk stockings and a spangled gown! Have you run mad?' He noted a burgeoning sparkle in the velvety eyes. 'Gad, you mean it! But you are going for a governess. What in Hades are you going to do with a spangled gown?'

'It is just that I have longed to possess such a gown,' said Kitty, breathless with hope. 'Only I had never the means to pay for it.'

'But when are you going to wear it? Besides that it ain't the thing for a governess.'

'I don't care if I never wear it!' Kitty declared. 'If only I might have it, I could be happy for the future.' She brightened. 'I have just had a famous notion! It will give me all the excuse I need for Mrs Duxford. I will tell her that I came to London expressly to purchase it.'

Claud thought this over and found a flaw. 'But you said you couldn't afford it. Don't she know that?'

Kitty summarily dismissed this. 'I shall say that I have been saving my money for the purpose. Oh, and I can say that I have hopes of being invited by one of my two friends, for they are both married—at least, one is already, and the other will be shortly. It is not unlikely that either Prue or Nell will ask me to stay.'

'Not if you've gone as a governess,' objected Claud.

'I wish you will not keep making difficulties!' declared Kitty, annoyed. 'I thought you wanted to make me reparation.'

'So I do, but we're going in the wrong direction.'

'You may turn around then!'

'Yes, but it's already past noon and I've got to drive you all the way to Paddington. Besides, I've an engagement this evening.'

Kitty's bosom swelled. 'How abominably selfish! It is your fault I am in this mess, and you even suggested I may be your cousin after all, and it is not as if I am asking for the moon.'

'No, but—'.

Kitty swept over him. 'If you refuse me, it will be the horridest thing imaginable, for it is *only* a spangled gown and a pair of silk stockings. Unless you have not enough money either to pay for such things?'

Claud slowed the carriage. 'I can stand the nonsense, never fear. It ain't that at all. Only I don't see how I'm to do it without the confounded mantua-maker thinking you're my *chère amie*. A man don't otherwise take a female to buy gowns unless he's betrothed to her, or they are at least related.'

Kitty digested this in silence for a moment. The curricle had drawn in to the side of the road, which at least indicated willingness. If she let this opportunity slip, there might never be another. Desperately she searched her mind, and found a solution. She turned eagerly to Claud.

'I know. You may pretend that I am Kate.'

About to reject this idea on the score that his cousin

would scorn to wear the type of gown Kitty had specified, Claud caught the deeply hopeful look in her face and the words died on his tongue. If he thought poorly of her choice, why should he dash the girl's only hope of pleasure? She had little enough to look forward to. It would make him late for the last ball of the season, but that couldn't be helped.

'You win, Miss Merrick! Let us repair to a mantua-maker.'

Concealed from the eyes of the curious in a private parlour at the White Bear inn, Kitty sat in a happy daze as she partook of the luncheon provided for her by her abductor. It was a trifle stuffy in the little first-floor room, and Claud had been obliged to force the casement window open to let in air. Kitty felt the benefit, for the table at which they were seated was fortunately set parallel to the embrasure, and she was able also to enjoy the comings and goings in the busy thoroughfare of Piccadilly below.

Although she much enjoyed the selection of delicacies placed before her, together with sturdier pasties of which Kitty partook only sparingly, this luxurious entertainment was not responsible for her contentment. Rather it was the thought of the made-up gown that was even now being adjusted to fit her full figure.

The establishment to which Claud had taken her had been disappointingly situated not in Bond Street itself, but in a little lane off the main thoroughfare. Its discreet entrance had been indistinguishable from the other doors except for a small plaque upon the wall. A narrow staircase had led them into a little salon, presided over by a female of French origin, who evidently knew the Viscount of old. She had treated Claud to roguish smiles and, upon hearing that she was to gown his cousin, a suspiciously knowing

look that had made Kitty uncomfortable. She could only
hope the creature's inevitable reflections had been quieted
by Lord Devenick's glib explanation.

'My cousin has taken a fancy to a style of gown that
her mama refuses to let her wear, Madame, and so I have
agreed that she may purchase it so that she may please
herself after we are married.'

If Madame wondered why the lady did not make the
purchase after the wedding, she said nothing of it, but immediately asked after the style proposed.

'I wish for a spangled gown,' had said Kitty breathlessly, fixing hopeful eyes upon the woman. 'Have you got
one?'

'*Bien sûr*. We 'ave zis gown, and many uzzers.'

White muslins, sprigged, spotted and spangled, had
danced before Kitty's eyes as Madame's assistant produced them for her inspection. In her imaginings from the
drawing she had once seen, the treasured vision had been
scattered with gold. But when she was shown a delicate
white gauze, sprinkled over with silver threads and tiny
sparkles of glass beading that caught the light, Kitty fell
instantly in love.

'Oh, this one, this one, if you please!' she had cried,
turning ecstatically to the man who had suddenly become
her benefactor. 'Can it be this one, Claud? Pray say I may
have it!'

'Have it, by all means,' had come the welcome response. 'Only hadn't you best try it on first? No sense in
buying the thing if it don't fit you.'

Hardly able to believe in the good fortune that had come
out of this disastrous journey, Kitty had allowed herself to
be bundled out of the horrid pink gown and into soft folds
of muslin that floated about her. To her intense disappointment, the gown had been a trifle tight across the bosom,

and a little long at the hem. But her mirror image was so delectable that Kitty would willingly have put up with these inconveniences, had it not been for Madame's suggestion that an adjustment could easily be made if *mademoiselle* were prepared to return later for the gown.

'But I cannot! I must go home immediately, and I doubt I shall ever come here again.'

Kitty's distress had been acute, but to her relief, the matter had been resolved by the resourcefulness of Lord Devenick, who had urged the mantua-maker to do the necessary alterations at once, while they repaired to an inn for a meal.

'For I don't mind telling you, Kitty, I'm as hungry as a hunter, and if I'm to drive all the way to Paddington and back, I'd as lief not do it on an empty stomach.'

As long as she might have the precious spangled gown, Kitty had no fault to find with this programme. And indeed, when they had left the little shop and set off in the curricle for the nearby White Bear in Piccadilly, she had discovered that she was also excessively hungry.

For some time, both parties were too preoccupied for conversation, Kitty's attention being divided between the potted beef spread upon hot buttered toast and the mental picture of herself arrayed in the new gown, while Claud concentrated on replenishing his stores of energy. At length he pushed aside his plate, the huge slice of pigeon pie upon it considerably diminished, and sat back, apparently replete.

He did not immediately engage in conversation, but quaffed a tankard of ale, his frowning blue gaze so intent upon Kitty's features that she could not but become aware of it. Disconcerted, she challenged him.

'I wish you will not stare so! Have you not yet accustomed yourself to the likeness?'

Claud shook his head briefly. 'Shouldn't think I ever would. If I were to continue to see you, that is.'

'Well, you won't, so you may cease to look at me in that excessively rude fashion.'

'I'm thinking,' protested Claud, aggrieved.

'About me?'

He took a pull from his tankard. 'Got a notion revolving in my head. No, I won't tell you what it is. Not yet, in any event.'

Curiosity gnawed at Kitty, together with a trifle of anxiety caused by the peculiar intensity of his speech. 'But is it about me?'

'Dash it, who else would it be about?'

Incensed, Kitty exploded. 'Then why will you not say it? I think it is excessively mean-spirited of you to mention it at all if you don't mean to tell me what it is. Has it to do with my likeness to Kate? Do you think you have guessed what your aunt would not reveal about me? Oh, tell me, Claud, pray!'

'Lord, if it was that, of course I should tell you!'

He rose from his seat and began to shift about in the confines of the small parlour, wishing that he had held his tongue. The scheme revolving in his head was fantastic, but it would not do to say a word of it to the girl until he had thoroughly inspected its merits. It was difficult to think with those expressive eyes trained upon him. They were very like Kate's, but with a velvet sheen that was lacking in his cousin's. Even in repose—when Kitty had been sitting in a dreamlike state, unaware of his regard—they had been striking.

However, it was not her pretty features that had brought the notion sneaking into his head, but the effect of them upon his aunt Silvia, and the lively apprehension she had exhibited of Lady Blakemere's reaction should the episode reach her ears.

Claud did not wholly believe that the idea had struck him, but there was no shaking it off. Was it because the girl had herself made mention of it? He had repudiated it then—in no uncertain terms. As well he might. It was madness! Only now that it had planted itself in his head, the temptation was so strong that he doubted he could withstand it. The Countess would be as mad as fire! It was too much to hope that she might go off in an apoplexy, but the blow would assuredly fall hard. Such exhilaration attacked him at the thought that Claud had all to do not to throw caution to the winds on the instant. Kitty's voice checked him.

'You look quite murderous! What are you thinking?'

He uttered a short laugh. 'Thinking of my mother, the Countess.' He was unaware that his lip curled in a manner that was uncharacteristically sardonic. 'That's enough to make anyone look murderous!'

Kitty gave a little shiver, her eyes fixed upon the horrid look in his face. He was the oddest man. All kindness one moment, the next a brutish unpredictable creature. What had his mother done to make him hate her so?

'Is it your mother who wishes you to marry Kate?'

'Aunt Silvia wishes for it too, but yes, the Countess took the notion. Only because Grandmama chooses to settle a dowry upon Kate. She pretends it is for Kate's own sake, but I know better. The Rothleys may lack fortune, but they ain't precisely paupers. Only the Countess had my father make my aunt an allowance, and she thinks to recover something from it.'

'But it was kind of her to do that, was it not?'

Claud's snort was bitter. 'Don't run away with that notion! Kind? Nothing of the sort. The Countess cares only for what Society may say of us. She sets store wholly by appearances, and my aunt was not to be suspected of being purse-pinched, regardless of the fact that everybody knows my uncle Rothley wasted much of his substance.'

This glimpse into the lives of a family of whom she was certainly a part threw Kitty into a combination of excitement and frustration. She longed to know more, yet the horrified reception of her advent convinced her that she had no right to pry. No right, and no reason either. What advantage could it be to her to learn the worst? There had been, in her insistence upon a past couched in mystery, a touch of romance. She had guessed at a hint of unlawful beginnings, convinced that she had been the outcome of an illicit liaison between a peer and an equally high-born married lady. Vague and hazy memories had been at root of her piecing together of this history. But gowned in Kitty's colourful imaginings, it had never been tainted with the disgrace of sordid scandal. At a blow, Claud's aunt Silvia had destroyed the comforting blanket of childish desire, and exposed Kitty for what she truly was—an outcast.

The bleak reality of her situation, which had been held at bay in the joy of her new gown, came in on her. All at once, she wanted to be back in the familiar surroundings of the Seminary, where if she was valued little, she was at least accepted. She pushed back her chair and got up from the table.

'Should we not be starting for Paddington, sir?'

The rapid descent of her mood had not been lost on Claud. The forlorn look in those velvet eyes drew his instant compassion. The words were out before he could stop them.

'We are not going to Paddington. I've thought better of that notion and have settled upon a new plan. We are going to Gretna Green.'

Chapter Three

Kitty gaped at him. Convinced she could not have heard aright, she uttered a fluttery laugh. 'You cannot mean you wish to elope with me!'

Did Claud's features look paler? Had she shocked him? She recalled his horrified reaction when she had merely mentioned his being forced to marry her to make reparation. But if he had indeed said they were going to Gretna Green, he must mean an elopement. He was frowning heavily, his blue gaze clouding.

'I don't wish to! At least—'

He broke off, cursing himself for an impetuous fool. He should have held his tongue! Only he hadn't, and here was the girl, staring at him with those distressful brown eyes that were beginning to show hurt again. He moved to the table, grasping the back of a chair with both hands as if he might draw strength from it.

'What I mean is, I didn't intend to say it yet. Been thinking it over, you see, while we were eating.'

'You have been thinking of taking me to Gretna?'

The disbelief in her voice was patent. He shifted his shoulders, acutely uncomfortable. 'Not exactly. Thinking of marriage. Only said Gretna because I supposed you to be under age.' It occurred to him to question this. 'How old are you? Much of Kate's age, I'd have thought. She's nineteen.'

Kitty lifted her chin. 'Well, I have the advantage of her, for I am one and twenty.'

'Are you, by Gad?' uttered Claud eagerly. 'Then we needn't go north, after all!'

She was obliged to dash this hope immediately. 'I should have said *almost* one and twenty. My birthday is in July.'

Claud's face fell. 'That's a pity. It will have to be Gretna then. Can't marry you otherwise without the consent of your guardians.'

'I have no g-guardians,' objected Kitty unsteadily. 'And Mrs Duxford would have a f-fit!'

Her pulse was behaving in a distressingly irregular fashion, and her brain was reeling at the realisation that Claud had indeed put forward the idea of marrying her. The protest bubbled up without volition.

'And when I said it in your curricle, *you* nearly had a fit!'

'I know, but—'

'You said distinctly that I must not think of such a thing!'

'Yes, because I hadn't thought it over. Changed my mind since then.'

Kitty eyed him in mounting perplexity, sinking back down into her chair. He did not look as if he had taken leave of his senses, but then she scarce knew him. Except to be aware that he was both rash and impulsive. And both to her cost. Oh, he was mad! It was an impossible notion, she had at least brains enough to see that. She drew a resolute breath, gripping her fingers together in her lap.

'You cannot have considered, sir. There can be no question of our being married. Only think what your aunt Silvia would say!' In automatic mimicry of his obese aunt, she uttered, *'Don't do it, Devenick, I implore you!'*

A shout of laughter was surprised out of Claud. 'That's very good, Kitty! Sounds exactly like her.'

But Kitty, whose talent in aping the voices of others was almost second nature, was hardly aware of doing it. She brushed it impatiently aside.

'Never mind that! Only think of your mother's reaction if we were to be wed, for your aunt distinctly told you I don't know how many times that—'

'Yes, and that's just what decided me to marry you!' declared Claud, pulling out a chair and reseating himself. He leaned across the table. 'I don't doubt the Countess will kick up the devil of a dust, for she's bound to. But there ain't anything she can do once the deed's done.'

Appalled, Kitty blinked dazedly. 'You cannot mean it, Claud! You know that I am the family skeleton. How can you possibly marry me? What about the scandal?'

Claud thumped the table. 'That's just it. We don't know that there will be any scandal. If there was one, it must have happened eons ago. I dare say only the family would remember it, and—'

'You are forgetting that I look just like Kate,' interrupted Kitty. 'Even if nobody remembers it now, they will do so the moment they see me.'

'Don't see that at all. In my experience, the *ton's* memory ain't long. They'll be too busy blessing themselves at the likeness to be concerned how it comes about.'

'That is exactly what will concern them, and the gossip will be hateful!'

'It won't. We'll think up a tale that will satisfy people, and there's an end to it.'

Kitty erupted. 'If that is not just typical of you! It is

exactly what you said to me when I asked you what I should say to the Duck.'

'Yes, and wasn't I right?' he argued. 'You thought of that spangled gown!'

'That is nothing to the purpose. This is entirely different. *What* tale will we think up? What tale could there possibly be to account for my likeness to Kate, except that I am somebody's natural daughter?'

Claud sat back, the frown returning to his brow. 'Someone's by-blow? Hang it, I suppose you must be! I wonder who it might be?'

Kitty gazed at him dumbly. Was that all he cared for? Had he no pride? It was all of a piece with his selfishness. Could he not see how she must suffer if people were to whisper about her dubious antecedents? She began at last to wonder why he had determined upon such a course. He was not in love with her. How could he be? Nor she with him, if it came to that. He was personable enough, the more so without his hat when the fair locks did much to improve him. But in character—well, suffice it that his attraction diminished rapidly the more she knew of it!

Only to have such an opportunity dangled in front of her nose—and by a self-confessed lord!—was altogether too tempting. Had it not been for that dreadful reception at the Haymarket house, Kitty could well have been persuaded into taking him at his word. But if Claud had no pride, she had little else!

'It is useless to think of who might have fathered me,' she said, not without a touch of resentment, 'for I doubt we shall ever know. And I have no intention of going to Gretna Green. All I wish for is that you will deliver me safely to the Seminary.'

Claud eyed her with misgiving. She was looking a trifle stormy. Perhaps it was the manner of his offer—if one could call it such—that had offended her. She was a sensitive little thing, that much he had deduced from their short acquaintance. Should he give up the scheme? No, he was hanged if he would! He hurried into speech.

'You can't pretend you'd rather go for a governess than marry me, Kitty. Not that I'm a coxcomb, but it ain't reasonable. And if I take you back to the Seminary, what else is there for you?'

'And if I were to marry you, I might as well have been a governess, for I don't doubt that your family will repudiate me, if Society did not.'

'Aha! But they can't repudiate you, can they? Mean to say, there you are, as like to Kate as makes no odds. No one can say you ain't related, be it to the Rothleys, the Cheddons or the Hevershams. *And* you're known to Aunt Silvia as well as the Countess, and I'll lay any odds they know exactly how you are related to us. What's more, it can't be an accident that you were christened Katherine, for it's a name common in our family. M'sister Kath is one, as well as Kate. Called after my grandmother Litton. Dare say if there'd been a Heversham girl, she'd be Katherine too.'

His words were torture to Kitty. She longed to ask about the names he was throwing out. Yet, the knowledge of having already been repudiated—and as a helpless child to boot—could not but whip up her resentment. And Claud expected her to expose herself to the censure of all these people!

'I wish you will not talk of it! I told you before, I don't care to hear about your family.'

'*Your* family, you mean,' corrected Claud.

'They are not my family! If they are, they do not deserve to be, and I will not thrust myself upon them for any consideration in the world, so you may forget this silly idea of marrying me. I will not do it! And why you should have thought of it at all has me in a puzzle.'

But Claud did not intend to expound his reasons. Not the deep truth of them, at any rate. It was not for Kitty to recognise the violent pull of the vision in his head of his mother—utterly confounded! He had it all fixed in his mind.

'Why, ma'am, what is the matter?' he would say. 'You wished me to make a union with my cousin Kate. To all appearances, I've obeyed you. This girl is undoubtedly my cousin, too, and as you can see, she is Katherine Rothley in all but name.'

Glee enveloped him as he imagined the features of the Countess, contorted with rage and chagrin—as they would be, by Jupiter! It would be worth any inconvenience, any unfortunate consequence, only to pay her back for the ills he had endured at her hands.

But it began to look as if Kitty was beyond persuasion. He searched his mind for arguments to sway her. He must do so, for now that the scheme had come to him, he was loath to give it up. She had averted her gaze, and was sipping at the remains of the lemonade she had drunk with her luncheon. There was no denying she was likely to be a handful, though she was a comely piece. Not that he had doubts of being able to handle her. He might be obliged to take drastic measures now and then, but it would not be beyond his power to gain the mastery over her, rebellious though she undoubtedly was.

'I suppose you realise,' he said conversationally, 'that there's little you can do about it, if I do choose to take you to Gretna Green.'

Her head jerked round, the brown eyes round with shock. 'You would not dare to force me!'

'Why not? Abducted you easily enough once, as you

insisted on calling it. I can readily do so again. Only I should much prefer not to have to go to so much trouble.'

Kitty stared at him, her pulses in disarray. Why had she allowed herself to forget what a brute he was? That stubborn chin was jutting dangerously, and the blue eyes held an inflexible glint. She quailed inwardly, and could not keep the dismay from her voice.

'But why should you wish to? I don't understand!'

Claud uttered a short laugh. 'Isn't it obvious? If I'm married to you, the Countess and my aunt will have to give up the notion of my marrying Kate. And I'll tell them the family owes you something and I'm repaying it. No denying you'd be a deal more comfortable married to me than slaving as a governess.'

Kitty was far from denying it. But she had been brought up to recognise right from wrong, and this was indubitably wrong. She hardly knew that she spoke aloud.

'Nell would counsel me to refuse, I know she would. Indeed, even Prue would say I must not do it.'

A vague recollection of having heard these names before came to Claud. 'Don't know who they may be, but why should they object to me?'

'Not to you! Nell and Prue were my dearest friends at the Seminary, only they both went out as governesses and Prue has married Mr Rookham and Nell is betrothed to Lord Jarrow.'

'Why did they go as governesses then, if they planned to be married?'

Kitty tutted. 'You don't understand, sir. Mr Rookham hired Prue to look after his two little nieces, and Nell went as governess to Lord Jarrow's daughter.'

'Good Gad! D'you mean to say they both married their employers?'

'Well, Nell is not married yet, but was it not the most romantic thing imaginable?'

'I don't know about that, but I can't see why either should put a bar in the way of your marriage, if that's the way of it.'

Kitty sighed. 'Had you been another man, perhaps they would not. But I know they would say I must not marry you in the circumstances. Though I must confess it is what I have always wanted.'

Claud blinked. 'You always wanted to marry me? But you didn't know me!'

'I wanted to marry a lord,' explained Kitty, adding wistfully, 'Indeed, I have believed all my life that it was my true destiny. I could not believe that I was meant for a governess.'

'Well, you couldn't choose better than me,' put in Claud briskly, 'for I am a viscount, you must know, and heir to the Earldom of Blakemere.'

Kitty's heart skipped a beat. 'An earl? Oh, no!'

'What's wrong with an earl?' demanded Claud, nettled.

'Nothing indeed. Except that it is too much of a temptation!'

She smiled abruptly, and Claud was conscious of a faint warmth at his chest. She was a taking little thing, there was no doubt of that.

'It would be like Cinderella,' Kitty told him. 'You could change my life at a stroke. You have no notion how much I have yearned to go to parties and balls, and to wear such gowns as I have seen in the *Ladies Magazine*.'

Claud knew a cue when he heard one, and lost no time in pursuing his advantage. 'So you may. In fact, you can do just as you like, provided you don't expect me to change my way of life. As for gowns, I'll buy you a dozen, if you wish.'

'A dozen!' Kitty's pulses were rioting. She could not help a breathless question. 'Are you rich?'

'Don't know what you'd call rich. Mean to say, in your situation, I should suppose anything above a thousand a year would be a fortune.'

'A thousand a year? I would give my right arm for a thousand a year!'

Claud grinned. 'No need for such a sacrifice. You may have twice that and more just for your pin money. I'll stand the nonsense for any other gewgaws you choose to buy. Spend as much as you like.'

'Oh, don't,' begged Kitty, a catch in her voice. 'You must not tempt me so! Why, you must be as rich as Croesus!'

'Since I don't have a clue who he may be, I can't comment. But I've a fair fortune to hand, and that's without the Earldom. I've a place here in London of my own as well as the family house—which will be mine too at some distant date—and m'father gave me one of the smaller estates to live in when I came of age, so you won't live with the family, never fear.'

'How many estates are there?' asked Kitty, awed.

'Can't remember offhand. Four or five, I think. Unless you count the hunting box as well. It's why they're content for me to marry Kate, for I don't need more. The Countess knew what she was doing when she married m'father, that's certain.'

It was more than Kitty could withstand. Dazzled by the vision of herself as mistress of all this wealth, she was no longer capable of clinging to the hideous reality. After all, she had a right to accept, had she not? She belonged in the family that contained Claud. How and why seemed less important now. Why should she not benefit? It was not as if she had looked for it. If her dream had come true, it

must be what Fortune intended. The sneaking little voice
of conscience that whispered of a horrible mistake was
crushed. Opportunity was knocking on the door, and it
might never come again. Fatal words fell from her lips.

'It is of no use! I cannot possibly resist you!'

To her disappointment, Claud showed no sign either of
pleasure or relief. 'That's settled, then.' He dug a hand
into his fob pocket and pulled out a watch, flipping open
the lid. 'Deuce take it, it's past three! We'd best make a
start as soon as may be. Only if I'm to go all the way to
Gretna, I'll need more luggage than I've got with me, for
I only had enough for one night. We'll be five or six days
on the road there and back at the least. Ain't even got my
driving-coat, and I'm bound to need that. Never know
what the weather's going to do. Can't start on a long journey without a bath and a change of clothes, what's more.
I'd best repair to my lodging and pick you up again later.
I'll have to forgo the party tonight, but it can't be helped.'

Kitty listened to him in growing dudgeon. Had he no
thought for anyone but himself? Did it not occur to him
that she might have needs too? She lost no time in placing
these before him.

'Have you forgot that I have nothing but the clothes I
stand up in?'

'What are you talking about?' demanded Claud.
'Haven't I bought you that spangled gown?'

'If you suppose I can travel all the way to Scotland in
a spangled gown, you must have windmills in your head!
And what is more, you never got me the silk stockings
you promised!'

'We'll pick them up from that Frenchwoman.' But he
scratched thoughtfully at his chin. 'Pity we didn't think of
getting your clothes before we left Paddington.'

'How should we have done so when you were abducting

me?' uttered Kitty with scorn. 'Besides, none of my clothes are suitable for a viscountess. Indeed, there is little at the Seminary that I care to keep, except perhaps one or two personal items like the letters from my friends.'

'We can fetch those after we're married,' said Claud, dismissing this. 'Nothing for it but to get one or two more gowns from that mantua-maker.'

In the event, this programme proved inadequate. Repairing to the little salon off Bond Street, Kitty found herself in possession of two additional gowns, both muslin, one plain and one spotted in black, and a thick cloak to wear upon the journey. But Madame was able to supply neither silk stockings nor those essential items of underclothing of which a young lady going upon a journey stood in crying need. When Kitty, prompted by Madame, also mentioned hats and shoes, it was borne in upon Claud that his blithe intention to enter upon matrimony was going to prove a good deal more complicated than he had anticipated.

Already shaken by hints from the mantua-maker that she had divined his purpose, he came within an ace of abandoning it altogether. The remembrance of the inevitable confrontation with the Countess strengthened him, however, and he had the happy notion of paying one of Madame's sewing-women to take Kitty beyond Bond Street and into a less fashionable arena further north where a plethora of shops of every description might furnish all she required. Meanwhile he could attend to his own needs.

Armed with a roll of bank notes—which was more money than she had ever dreamed of—Kitty spent an exhilarating, if bewildering, couple of hours shifting from one thoroughfare into another. The woman who accompanied her, delighted to be released from incarceration below stairs at the salon, entered into her requirements with

great enthusiasm, bustling her from shop to shop and bar-
gaining in a merry way with the tradesmen. Kitty could
only be glad of her escort, for she had no idea where she
was, nor how to choose of the myriad wares offered for
sale. The streets were so busy that passers-by could not
but jostle her, and her confusion grew as she was led past
all manner of window displays and enticing signs. Fish-
mongers rubbed shoulders with snuff makers, and busts
with glass eyes stared out at her to show off the wigs of
the perruquier. The milliner she visited was placed beside
an apothecary's with curious bottles of remedies; the shoe-
maker was found beside a jeweller's, and the discreet requirements of her toilette were next door to a shop selling
exquisite lamps of glass and alabaster.

By the time Kitty returned to the salon, exhausted, both
she and her companion were burdened with so many packages that she was unable to remember what was in them.
She plonked down upon a chair proffered by Madame to
wait for Claud's return, daunted by the rapidly gathering
apprehension that he would scold her for having spent so
much money. But time passed, and his lordship put in no
appearance.

Madame, whose expression became more pitying as the
afternoon wore on, suffered her assistant to shift the packages out of sight behind a curtain while another customer
was served, and at length had a dish of tea brought for
Kitty's refreshment. She sipped it gratefully, desperately
trying to hide her growing dismay under a cheerful front.
What would she do if Claud had chosen to abandon her?
No matter how many times she told herself stoutly that
this was unlikely, the horrid thought would keep obtruding.

But just as Madame was making noises about closing
the shop, and Kitty had begun desperately to think of how
she could get herself back to Paddington—never mind ex-

plaining the money she had left and the acquisition of so much finery!—a commotion below signalled the arrival of her betrothed.

Only it was not Claud, but his groom Docking, sent in his stead to collect Kitty and drive her to his lordship's lodging in Charles Street. This proved to be a roomy apartment occupying the better part of one floor of a large mansion. Kitty was unloaded into it, together with all her packages, and into the hands of a disapproving individual who introduced himself as Mixon.

'I am his lordship's valet, miss.'

Mixon showed Kitty into a masculine bedchamber, with a dwarf bookcase and a whatnot, besides the bed and the press. It served, so the valet informed her, for accommodation for any of his lordship's friends who might happen to stay the night. There was, to her chagrin, no sign of Claud himself.

'Where is Lord Devenick?'

The valet bowed. 'His lordship has gone out for the evening. He requested me to make you comfortable. A meal has been ordered and will be served presently.'

Kitty gazed at the man, stupefied. 'Gone out for the evening? But we are supposed to be—'

She broke off, suddenly and acutely aware of the invidious nature of her position. She could scarcely discuss her elopement with his lordship's valet!

Mixon coughed. 'His lordship informed me that you are taking a journey, miss, but he thought it rather too late to set out. It is his wish that you rest yourself, ready for an early start in the morning. As for these, miss—' indicating the packages littering the bed '—would you wish me to lend you one of his lordship's portmanteaux?'

But Kitty was in no mood to think about packing. In vain did she strive to repress an enveloping sense of outrage and indignation. She was to rest, while his horrid lordship disported himself at some jollification! Had he not complained of having to miss a party? Not content with leaving her for hours to wait for him at the mantua-maker's, he not only neglected to fetch her himself, but left her—a stranger to the town and his betrothed to boot!—without explanation or reassurance, to the ministrations of his valet and her own devices. He was the most selfish creature she had ever met in her life! And nothing would induce her to marry him.

Attired in silk breeches of his favourite green and a coat of similar hue over a fancy flowered waistcoat, Claud had just come off the floor after a dutiful country dance with his sister Lady Barbara Cheddon, just out this season, when he was accosted in the outer gallery by his cousin Kate.

'Claud, I must talk to you alone!'

Lady Barbara pricked up her ears. A pretty, fair-haired creature, whose even features closely resembled those of her brother, she was correctly and demurely gowned, like her cousin, in the ubiquitous white thought suitable for debutantes, but augmented with a half-robe of lilac net. Noting how his cousin was similarly elegant in a vest of crimson velvet, Claud was assailed by a vision of that overblown spangled gown Kitty had insisted on buying. He made a mental vow to oversee her wardrobe for the future. His attention was drawn swiftly back to his sister.

'Secrets? Fie, Kate! But if it is about your betrothal, you need not mind me, for I know all about it.'

'That'll do, Babs!' scolded Claud, casting a quick glance about to make sure that his mother was nowhere within earshot. The gallery contained several odd groups seeking relief from the heat, who stood about chatting and fanning

themselves, but there was no sign of the Countess of Blakemere. Relieved, Claud returned his attention to his sister.
'It ain't that at all. Besides, we are not going to be betrothed.'

Claud came under the beam of his sister's questioning
blue gaze. 'But Mama says you are, and if she wants you
to marry, I don't see how you couldn't.'

'You'll soon see how,' he declared, with more force
than he intended, impelled by the image that had been
revolving in his mind all evening.

'Even your mama cannot force us,' Kate put in, her
voice low.

Babs looked from one to the other, and Claud detected
scepticism in her eye. 'How will you withstand her? Mary
and Kath couldn't. And I should suppose I shall find myself obliged to marry whomever she chooses for me too.'

'Never you mind how,' said Claud dismissively.

'But I do mind,' objected his sister, 'for if you have a
means of holding out against Mama, I want to know of it.
I feel sure she is thinking of Lady Chale's youngest for
me, and I can't bear him.'

The Countess of Chale had the distinction of holding
the last ball of the season, and the entire first floor of the
mansion had been given over to the accommodation of her
many guests. A vast saloon, done out in blue with white
trimmings in the Adams style, had been formed into a
ballroom, the furniture having been set apart in another
room for the accommodation of those who were not dancing. The drawing room was as full as it could hold of
chattering fashionables who had wandered in from the adjacent dining room next door, where the supper tables were
laid out with a succulent feast of patties, sliced meats and
a variety of sweets. And two further smaller rooms were

given over to the dedicated card players, who could be seen from a distance, grouped around green baize tables.

Contrary to his expectation, Claud was not enjoying himself. Far too many members of his family were in attendance for his liking. There was all too much danger of making a slip and mentioning Kitty, and he was only too well aware that it was upon the subject of his disastrous mistake that Kate was clamouring to talk to him in private. Since he was determined to keep his intentions to himself, he had rather not engage in conversation about the chit. With a vague thought of holding his cousin at bay, he responded more sympathetically to his sister.

'Don't suppose the Countess is thinking of turning you off just yet, Babs. Only seventeen. Besides, she'll be looking for a fellow a thought more eligible than a younger son.' His tone took on sarcasm. 'Never forget, m'dear, you're not only the daughter of an earl, but the granddaughter of a duke.'

'As if any of us cared for that,' put in Kate scornfully.

'No, Claud is right. It is exactly what Mama cares for. Only she says there are no eligible heirs just at present, and she is looking instead at a younger son with good prospects.'

'You don't say so!' exclaimed Claud. 'If that don't beat all! Never knew she was so mercenary, as well as all else. It's only Kate's expectations from Grandmama that made her take the notion of our marrying into her head in the first place.'

'Yes, and Lady Chale's youngest son is to inherit his godmother's money, which is said to be a fortune. Only besides having a face like a frog, he is the most tedious young man of my acquaintance!'

'If you don't choose to marry him, Babs, you need only hold fast to your refusal,' said Kate, adding hastily, 'But will you please excuse us? I have something urgent to discuss with Claud.'

'It's well for you to say that,' retorted Babs, ignoring the request, 'for Aunt Silvia would never go to the lengths Mama would, and I dare say Cousin Ralph could persuade her to let it alone if you asked him. Whereas Claud—'

'Has more gumption than you give him credit for!' he interrupted, incensed. 'Only it ain't a particle of use thinking the Countess would take notice of anything I said, for she won't.'

His sister clasped both hands fondly about his arm. 'That's what I meant to say, Claud. I know you can't be blamed if she won't listen to you. Why, she calls you a nincompoop and says you haven't a brain in your head.'

Claud removed her hands from his arm. 'Obliged to her! And I'll thank her to keep her insulting opinions to herself, the insufferable witch!'

'Hush!' warned Kate, leaning close. 'She is coming out of the ballroom.'

Lady Barbara promptly left them, slipping through two groups of guests to enter the drawing room by a door around the corner of the gallery and diving out of sight among a coterie of chattering maidens.

'She has seen us!' uttered Kate, *sotto voce*. 'She is coming this way.'

Wishing he might follow his sister's example, Claud turned to confront his formidable mother, unable to suppress the inevitable rise of mixed emotions that invariably attacked him in her presence. Defiant he might be, but no weight of years had served to subdue the tight knot of apprehension that settled in his stomach, overlaid with— in his own view—a justifiable sense of outrage. Such derogatory remarks as that relayed by his sister had been commonplace throughout his life, hedged about as he had been by rules and shibboleths that would have driven a saint into rebellion. Transgressions against which had been summarily, and painfully, dealt with.

On this occasion the Countess, as he immediately divined, was disposed to be lenient. She was attired in the grand manner, in an open robe of white muslin spotted in her favourite blue, with a draped sash trained to the floor at the back, epaulettes to her sleeves and a turban head-dress from which rose three tall plumes. But there was approbation in the strongly aristocratic countenance, with the high wide brow, the straight nose—the only feature bequeathed to Claud who otherwise favoured his sire's pleasant looks—and the thin-lipped mouth, which in Claud's memory was usually pinched in disapproval. Lady Blakemere actually smiled as she reached him.

'Well, children?' The perfectly modulated voice was the epitome of good breeding. 'I am glad to see you enjoying one another's company. I hope you have saved a dance for your cousin, my dear Katherine?'

This last did not fail to fan Claud's irritation. Alone of their elders, the Countess refused to use the pet names that served to distinguish her niece and her own eldest daughter. Lady Blakemere instead addressed her child as *Lady Katherine* in public, just as she spoke of her sister as Lady Silvia, raising her over the despised Rothley, mercifully deceased, who had been 'a mere baron'.

Claud watched Kate curtsy as she answered, 'I believe we are engaged for a country dance later in the evening.'

A pained expression flitted over the Countess's face. 'Would that you were more fully engaged.' Her lips curved, but the smile did not reach her eyes. 'Well, I shall say nothing on that score here, although I had not expected to come to the season's close without matters being settled between you.'

'As usual you are right, ma'am,' said Claud, an edge to his voice. 'Neither the place nor the time for such a discussion.' Prompted by a wicked devil within, in the suavest tone he could manage, he added, 'Though I hope soon to be able to allay your ladyship's concerns in that direction.'

Surprise lifted his mother's brows, and a guilty leap of satisfaction entered his chest as the grey eyes—slate grey they were, and as cold as a winter sea—appeared momentarily disconcerted. The look was quickly veiled, and next moment Lady Blakemere was regarding him with all her accustomed contempt, ice in her voice.

'I am not deceived, Devenick.'

'Can't think what you mean, ma'am.'

'You have no intention of yielding, I see that.'

'In the matter of marriage? I might be tamed yet.'

'You *will* be, Devenick, make no mistake about it. I have more armour to hand than you can conceive.'

Claud controlled his temper with difficulty. 'You forget, ma'am. I am more than familiar with your armoury. But you know little of mine.'

With which, ignoring his cousin's claims to his escort, he bowed and walked quickly away. He passed around the corner of the gallery and entered the drawing room, seething so hard that he scarce knew where he went. Jupiter, how he hated her! To the devil with the woman! With a surge of elation, he remembered his scheme. What a coup was going to be his! How he would triumph when he wiped the self-satisfaction from her face. And there would be nothing she could do. *Nothing*. She would be obliged to swallow it, though it be wormwood and gall to her.

Catching up a glass from the tray of a passing waiter, Claud threw the wine down his throat. What sleight of fortune had it been that had caused the girl to be sitting on that fence this morning just when his curricle had

passed? As if she had been sent by Providence, giving into
his hand the surest weapon with which to best his bitterest
enemy. He could not have planned it better had he cudg-
elled his brains for a month. Pity he had no knowledge of
the scandal that underlay Kitty's exclusion from the family. Not that it mattered. It was enough that Aunt Silvia
had all but swooned at sight of the girl. Yet, curiosity
gnawed at him. What was it? Better yet, who was it?

His thoughts were interrupted. 'Dreaming, coz? What's
so absorbing that I have twice called your name to no
purpose?'

Claud's gaze focused on a tall and loose-limbed gentleman, clad in a suit of black silk relieved only by a scarlet
waistcoat, with a countenance already at nine and twenty
showing signs of dissipation. Baron Rothley's resemblance
to his sister was visible in a pair of luminous brown eyes
and a wealth of dark hair, worn in a disorder his cousin
knew to be deliberate. Until tonight, Claud had taken the
resemblance for granted. It struck him more potently now,
when he recognised in Ralph Rothley's features not his
sister Kate, but the unknown Katherine Merrick.

'Good Gad!'

Ralph's brows shot up. 'I beg your pardon? You haven't
shot the cat thus early in the evening, dear coz?'

Claud waved a dismissive hand. 'It ain't that. Scarcely
touched a drop, as it chances. Only I never realised—'

He broke off, abruptly remembering that he must not
mention Kitty. Unless his aunt had confided in her eldest
son? Unlikely, he decided.

'If you are going to talk in riddles, dear coz,' pronounced his cousin languidly, 'I shall take my leave of
you.'

'No, don't do that,' said Claud quickly, feeling the need
to talk. To *someone*—if he could not speak of the matter

uppermost in his mind. 'To tell the truth, old fellow, I'm a trifle up in the boughs.'

Ralph grinned sympathetically. 'So I supposed when I heard you grinding your teeth. My aunt Lydia again?'

Claud set his jaw. 'I tell you, Ralph, if I don't end by murdering her, it won't be her fault! How m'father has stood it all these years I shall never know.'

'By dint of avoiding confrontation and keeping himself out of range,' said his cousin sapiently. 'And who shall blame him?'

'Not I, for one.'

He could wish it had been possible for him to follow his father's example. Lord Blakemere, as his son had now and then had cause to ponder, was either a weak man or a prudent one. No match for his wife, he had early abrogated all control over his family, preferring to absent himself from contention in favour of pottering about—as the Countess mockingly phrased it—among his vast collection of ancient objects.

It had often been remarked that the Earl's trips abroad had grown both lengthier and more frequent after his marriage, but Claud had been less aware of his absences than his returns, which had afforded a degree of relaxation in the severity of the household. The arrival of his father, laden with all manner of coins, statuary and bits of stone or pottery, could not but upset the rigid routine imposed by the Countess. Some of the happiest hours of his childhood had been spent by the side of his sire, while Lord Blakemere expounded upon the virtues of his finds and the archaeological sites from whence they came. Claud did not boast much of an interest in the objects themselves, but the peaceful serenity of his father's society had been soothing, and a welcome respite from his constant battles with the creature that ruled the lives of all who were nominally harboured under the Earl's banner.

'Seems to me you'd best marry Kate and have done with it,' Ralph suggested. 'You'll get no peace otherwise.'

Claud tossed his head. 'I ain't going to marry Kate. She don't want it, and nor do I.' He glared at his cousin. 'And why must you needs turn traitor, I should like to know?'

'I haven't,' Ralph said briefly. 'But I know my aunt. I don't think there's a more determined woman alive. And it's no use thinking my mother will withstand her either.'

'So much for Babs' theory, then,' said Claud gloomily. 'Seemed to think your word would carry weight with Aunt Silvia.'

'Of course it would,' grinned his cousin. 'But I have no illusions, dear coz. My mother is more frightened of her sister than she is fond of me. Aren't we all?'

'Not me,' declared Claud stoutly. 'At least, I may be, but that won't stop me from facing her down!'

Ralph sighed. 'No, I have observed that in you for several years. I foresee a delightful summer! I wonder if I should repair to Italy?'

'No, you don't! You'll stand buff with Kate like a good brother should.'

His cousin groaned. 'Must I?'

Claud drew a breath and took hold of Lord Rothley's shoulder. 'Ralph, I'm going to need your support. Can't tell you why, but you may take it from me that, come a se'ennight or two, hell's foundations will be quivering!'

'You appal me.'

Detecting amusement as well as interest in Ralph's brown eyes, Claud half-regretted the words. But it occurred to him forcibly that in taking the step he intended, it would be as well to have at least one member of the family on his side. Dared he take Ralph into his confi-

dence? No, too risky. Baron Rothley was in many ways
as reckless a man as his father before him, and disinclined
to face up to tricky situations. Did he know the truth, he
would undoubtedly counsel his cousin to abandon a course
calculated to set the whole family in an uproar. Instead
Claud clapped him on the shoulder.

'I've had enough of dancing. Care for a rubber of
whist?'

He did not reach the sanctuary of the card rooms, however, before being once more caught by his cousin Kate,
who lost no time in requesting her brother to leave them.

'Ralph, pray go away! I need to speak to Claud alone.'

But Claud was not disposed to be spoken to in private.
He grasped Rothley's arm to prevent his moving. 'Wait a
bit, old fellow!'

That faint amusement crept into the Baron's fleshy features. 'Now this becomes interesting. Kate anxious to converse, and you reticent, Claud? And now I think of it, our
mother has been oddly distracted today. What have I
missed?'

'Oh, the devil!' Claud released him and turned on his
young cousin. 'Now see what you've done!'

Kate flushed. 'What was I to do when you will keep
avoiding me? I only want to know what transpired after
you left us.'

'So there is something.'

Claud was drawn by his cousin Ralph's firm but gentle
hand, and found himself presently situated in an alcove off
to one side of the relatively empty dining room, both cousins barring his passage out. He groaned inwardly as Kate
began to give her brother a fluent account of the morning's
events. What was he to say in answer to the inevitable
questions? He was distracted from thinking up an innoc-
uous response by Kate's further words.

'Ralph, you are older than both of us. Do you know of any such scandal in the family? I could not question Mama, you understand, for she was so distressed.'

Baron Rothley was looking both amused and astonished to learn of the existence of Miss Katherine Merrick, but he shook his head.

'Must have been while I was at Eton. How old is the girl?'

'Almost one and twenty,' answered Claud before he could stop himself.

Kate exclaimed. 'I would not have supposed her to be older than myself. Poor thing! Did you deliver her safely back to the Seminary, Claud?'

The moment had come. Thoroughly discomposed, Claud prevaricated. Not that he would hesitate to lie, only a fellow needed to be prepared for this sort of thing!

'She's safe enough, never fear.'

'Yes, but are we?' demanded Rothley. 'What sort of a girl is she? Can she be trusted to keep mum? For all we know, she may take it into her head to try blackmailing us or some such thing.'

Such a resentment blew up in Claud that he was hard put to it to keep his tongue. Flighty she might be, but he would stake his oath that such a base endeavour would never so much as cross Kitty's mind. He was glad that Kate answered for him.

'I am sure she would not, Ralph. She did not wish for anything from us, except to know that she belonged to the family. Indeed, she struck me as a trifle meek.'

'Meek!'

'Is she not, Claud? She was very quiet when I saw her.'

'Because she was distressed, confound it! Who wouldn't be, with Aunt Silvia swooning all over the sofa at sight of her?'

Ralph laughed. 'Did she, indeed? I wish I had seen it!'

'You could have had my place for the asking!' retorted his sister. 'It was dreadful, and I did not know what to do. Poor Mama was utterly confounded.'

'If the girl was your double, I'm not surprised. It's enough to confound anyone.'

'It wasn't only that, Ralph. I believe there really must be a dreadful scandal attached to the girl.' Her brown gaze veered to Claud. 'Mama could not stop talking of it for hours after you left. Though she said nothing to the purpose—or nothing that I could make sense of—except to reiterate how much Aunt Lydia would dislike to have it known. But it is my belief that Mama would dislike it just as much, which makes me wonder if that girl is not indeed to do with our family. I mean the Rothleys, not the rest.'

'Only too likely,' remarked her brother in a cynical tone. 'She wouldn't be the first female to bear my father's stamp.'

'Ralph!'

Incensed, Claud intervened. 'No need to say so in front of Kate, old fellow!'

But his cousin was unrepentant. 'Nonsense. She's old enough to know the truth. I'm not in favour of keeping girls in ignorance. Ten to one she'd hear it from another source if she wasn't already aware that our father was a rake.'

'Of course I know that. Only I—'

'Only you don't like to think that his by-blows are littered all over the country. No, nor do I, but it's a fact. And if that's what this girl is, I'll lay you odds I know exactly what happened. Her mama tried to come the ugly with my mother, who panicked and went bleating off to my aunt, and Aunt Lydia bought the woman off.'

'Oh, do you think so indeed, Ralph?'

Kate sounded relieved. Claud was frankly appalled. If that was the way of it, his union with her would certainly serve his mother out. But it was forcibly borne in on him that he would be doing Kitty a great disservice by marrying her. There was no possible way such a history could be glossed over. In Society's eyes, Kitty would be damned. And he with her, for the matter of that.

For the first time, he regretted his hasty proposal. If his servants had carried out his instructions, then Kitty was at this moment safely tucked up in the spare bedchamber at his lodging, ready to start tomorrow morning for Gretna Green. Hang it, but he had landed himself well and truly in the suds!

Chapter Four

A sixth sense dragged Kitty from a confused dream, and her eyes fluttered open. They fell upon features that had taken part in the wanderings of her sleeping mind, and which were frowning down at her from behind the light of several candles. Kitty started up, and the face shifted back.

'Didn't mean to startle you,' said Claud apologetically.

With an automatic gesture, Kitty brushed back the tumble of her hair. She pulled herself up, and discovered that she had been lying at full length on the sofa in Claud's parlour. She was attired, moreover, in the silver spangled gown. Kitty caught folds of it into her fingers, recalling that she had tried it on in the hope of assuaging her loneliness while her affianced husband was off on an evening of pleasure. She had not meant him to find her thus clad. She fended off a feeling of consciousness.

'What time is it?'

'I don't know exactly. Past one or two, I dare say.'

Kitty watched him cross to the mantelshelf and lay down the candelabrum. There was another on a table near the windows, and the light diffused between them, lending a softer sheen to Claud's countenance as he turned to look at her, and a glow to his hair. She became aware of a chill in the atmosphere, though the night was warm. Kitty felt his withdrawal, and experienced an unaccountable sensation of sinking. Without conscious thought, she played for time.

'Was it enjoyable, your party?'

'Not in the least. To tell the truth, wish I hadn't gone.'

A faintly bitter note sounded in his voice, and Kitty's feeling of alienation intensified. 'What—what happened there?'

'My cursed family saw fit to fill my head with questions.'

'About—about me?'

'Who else?'

He shifted restlessly, moving to the window and twitching a curtain there. Kitty eyed his profile in dismayed silence. Into her mind floated the recollection of her earlier annoyance with him. She remembered deciding that she would not marry him. Had she meant it? If she had not, she was undone, for it was abundantly plain that Claud was regretting his decision to wed her. Unable to bear the suspense, she said it outright.

'You have changed your mind.'

Claud turned. He could see her features only dimly, but the hurt in her voice was all too clear. The play of light on that preposterous gown was oddly disturbing, as it captured a gleam of silver here, and there a twinkle of glass. Just as the cloud of the girl's dark hair about her features— alarmingly pretty in repose—had caught at something in him that he barely understood. She had an ethereal quality, sitting there in the semi-darkness. He answered not at all what he had intended.

'I still wish to marry you, Kitty.'

There came a hushed response. 'But perhaps you know you should not.'

It was uncannily perceptive. He could not bring himself to the cruelty of agreement. Instead he came to a chair set opposite the sofa and seated himself. It occurred to him that Kitty might have answers to those questions. It was not possible, if her parentage were suspect, that she would have no inkling of it. Had she not mentioned believing in a destiny wholly different from that for which she was intended? He opened without preamble.

'Who were your parents, Kitty?'

He saw her frown, and a look of withdrawal entered her face. 'Why do you ask me? If you mean to find out how I am related to your family, you are wasting your time.'

Claud curbed an impatient retort. 'But we might establish something. Mean to say, you said you had no guardians, so I must suppose you to be an orphan.'

'We are all orphans at the Paddington Seminary. It is a charitable institution.' There was resentment in her tone, and Claud could not blame her. He persisted nevertheless.

'Yes, but your parents? You must know who they were.'

'I know who they *said* were my parents!'

Kitty had thrown it at him, convinced that these enquiries were but the preliminary to his being rid of her. Not that she wanted to marry a creature who had evidently come to despise her! She sighed.

'What use is this, Claud? We both know that the truth of it is cloaked in secrecy. You had better address yourself to your aunt.'

'Yes, but she won't talk, will she?' he snapped. 'And if I'm to be your husband, I'm entitled to know everything you can tell me.'

Kitty's chin went up. 'You are not going to be my husband! I am grateful for the things you have bought me, and tomorrow I will be perfectly satisfied if you will only arrange for me to be taken back to Paddington.'

'Well, I ain't going to!'

'Then I shall take the stage.'

Claud leaped up, and flung over to the mantel again, bringing his fists crashing down upon its edge. 'Hang you, Kitty, you are enough to try the patience of a saint!'

She did not respond, and the flare of annoyance died. When he turned, he found her rigid in the sofa, her fingers clasped tightly together, and her features set.

Cursing under his breath, Claud moved to the cabinet to one side of the fireplace, and seized one of the decanters that Mixon always kept ready for his use. He filled one of the crystal glasses and tossed off the wine. Then he poured himself out another and upturned a second glass. Giving this a much smaller measure, he brought it across and held it out to Kitty.

'Here, drink this.'

She looked at the glass, but she did not reach out to take it. 'What is it?'

'Only Madeira. Take a sip or two at least,' he recommended. 'It'll mend your temper.'

A giggle escaped Kitty despite herself, and she took the glass and lifted it to her lips. It was strong, but sweet. And Claud was right. A few sips made her feel a degree better. She looked across to the chair where he had reseated himself and was nursing his own glass between his fingers. He caught her eye, and a smile abruptly lit his face.

She remembered the engaging look from earlier in the day. Only she had not noticed how the smile warmed the blue eyes in a captivating way. She found herself responding to his first question, as if it had taken his warmth to loosen her tongue.

'The Merricks were supposed to be my parents. Only

there was so much that I could never explain. I don't remember them much, for I was only six when I came to the Seminary.'

'*Six?* Shouldn't think you'd remember anything at all.'

Kitty sipped her wine. 'But that's just it, Claud. I remember excessively strange things. There was a house, for instance, but I think it didn't belong to my—to the Merricks. There were often people staying there—gentlemen, and ladies sometimes too. I used to serve them at table. At least, the Merricks served them, and perhaps I helped. I must have been often in the room, for I remember seeing them at dinner—laughing and exceedingly merry. And sometimes the gentlemen would take me on their knee and teach me rhymes and songs.'

Claud watched the play of expression in her features. There was puzzlement there, and yet a poignant hint of sadness, as if there were a nostalgia of pleasure in the memories. And she was right. It sounded an odd type of life.

'They would dance, too, on occasion,' Kitty went on. 'But in the day, I think the gentlemen went to hunt, for I can still see the picture of them gathered on horseback outside. I used to watch from a window above stairs.'

The implication hit Claud. 'What were you doing living in a hunting box?'

Kitty jumped. 'Goodness, I never thought of that! Do you suppose it might have been a hunting box?' A faint breathlessness attacked her. 'But that would not explain the lady who came to visit when there were no others there.'

'What lady?'

'I cannot tell you her name.' Kitty fortified herself with another sip of Madeira. 'I know she was a lady, for she arrived in a coach. She was the only one to come into my room, and she always brought me a gift. I remember a fan once, and a doll another time.' Her stomach was churning, but she resolutely pressed on, unaware of how tightly her fingers held to the glass. 'She used to sit and talk with me—I can't recall of what. We played games, I think. And if she gave me a book, she would read to me. I remember her voice particularly. It was full of music. I have been reminded of listening to her voice when I play the piano-forte.'

Almost Claud had guessed it by the time she looked up.

'At the time, I made nothing of it, save that I looked forward to her coming. It was only when I grew older, when I had sense enough to work it out, that I thought she might have been my mother.'

The velvety eyes were luminous, and the wistful quality of her tone drew a shaft of compassion from Claud's breast. And more. If Kitty's conclusion had any validity, her story hardly squared with Ralph's sordid theory. He let it lie for the present, his curiosity now thoroughly aroused.

'And your father?'

Kitty shook her head. 'There was once a gentleman who came on his own. I only remember him because Mrs Merrick took me down to the parlour. The man stood me on a table and—and looked at me. I remember that well for it frightened me. He kept shaking his head and laughing.' She shivered. 'The memory is but vague, and perhaps because I have gone over it so many times, it has changed and I think more of it than it deserves. But I always thought that man must be my father.'

'Yes, but you've no evidence of that,' objected Claud. 'Could have been any one of a dozen fellows. But didn't you think the Merricks were your parents?'

A flush overspread Kitty's features. 'Everyone said so,

including Mrs Duxford. Only I cannot remember to have called them so—ever. Nor do I recall any instance of affection from either of them.'

'That ain't no proof,' Claud put in on a cynical note. 'I don't say m'father ain't fond of me, but to hear the Countess, you'd suppose I was a changeling! As for affection, I might whistle for it.'

Kitty said nothing, the evocation of the memories of her remote childhood having cast her into a mood of depression. Or was it the present circumstances?

Claud brushed his own words aside. 'All beside the bridge. What else do you remember?'

'I have said it all.'

For no consideration would she speak of those other memories, dreadful memories that had given her nightmares. She had once brought herself to confide them to Nell. Her friend had been unsympathetic, pointing out that it was a judgement upon her for having sneaked around in the night, watching and listening in places where she had no business to be. It was true, but Kitty had derived no comfort from it, protesting that she had been too young at the time to be aware of what she did.

'Then you were too young to make sense of what you heard and saw,' was all Nell had to say. Kitty had been left wishing she had confided instead in Prue, who would at least have sympathised with her troubled thoughts. But Prue had been altogether too innocent to be privy to such things. She was distracted by Claud's protest.

'But you must remember more! What of your schooling? Who nursed you when you were ill?'

'Why, Mrs Merrick, of course. And she taught me such schooling as I had, which was not very much, the Duck said.'

Claud was dissatisfied. 'Well then, who brought you to

the Seminary when these Merricks died? Were you in this hunting box at the time? How did they die?'

Kitty laid her empty glass down on the little coffee table beside the sofa. 'That is just it, I don't know. It was said that they suffered an accident. I can recall nothing but that a lady and gentleman came one day and took me away in a coach. I know that I said no farewells to the Merricks, so perhaps they had died.'

'Who were these people? Was it the lady you think was your mother?'

'No, for this woman had few words for me. She was dressed in black, and the gentleman too, which I found frightening. He was kinder, I think. It's the oddest thing, for I can remember little of them, nor of the journey. Prue always said she thought I must have been in shock. However it was, I found myself at the Seminary, with the name of Katherine Merrick, and there I have remained ever since.'

There was a flatness to her tone more poignant to Claud than if she had wept. He finished his wine at a gulp and set the glass down. 'Have you never heard from these persons, or seen them again?'

'Never. All I know is what I have told you, and until this morning—or rather, yesterday I must call it now—I had no expectation that I would ever run into anyone remotely connected with my past. Or indeed, my real family.' She added, with a faint note of rising anger. 'And I wish very much that yesterday had never happened!'

It had been a good deal more comfortable to imagine everything, and to know nothing. Now, with images rising in her head like so many spectres, she was left with more questions and the certain knowledge that those who knew the answers would never be brought to reveal them. And she had foolishly been seduced into the notion of forcing herself upon them willy-nilly.

She got up from the sofa, automatically shaking out the spangled folds of her petticoats. Claud rose too, and they faced each other in the glow of the candles.

'A pretty history, is it not?'

The warming smile appeared. 'A sorry one, rather.'

Kitty swallowed. 'Pray do not pity me, sir. I ask only that I may be allowed to keep the things you bought for me, for I will have no other opportunity—'

'You'll keep them,' he interrupted, 'and add to them. Can't have my Viscountess sporting nothing but a muslin gown or two.'

Kitty's lip trembled. 'Claud, I wish you will not! We can't be married, you know we can't.'

'I know nothing of the sort. Fact is, I couldn't take you back to Paddington after what you've told me if I wanted to.'

'But why? You know you had changed your mind!'

He shrugged. 'It's true, I had. Only I've changed it back again now.'

Kitty waved agitated hands. 'Oh, this is mad! What will your mother say? And your aunt Silvia—all of them?'

'Let them say what they like!' He possessed himself of her unquiet hands. 'Kitty, don't you want to know the truth?'

'After what has passed? No, I don't.'

'Well, I tell you, I'm on fire to know it! What, leave it alone and let the Countess win, after all? I can see myself!'

'I don't know what you mean,' said Kitty, vainly trying to drag her hands away.

Claud pulled them to him, bringing her closer. His face echoed the sardonic look she had seen him wear before. The blue eyes were fairly blazing.

'I'll lay you odds she had a hand in it all! Don't you remember Aunt Silvia's words? She spoke of having it all dragged up again, of the Countess being as mad as fire. I thought I'd got an explanation tonight, only it don't fit with what you've told me. There's something in this, Kitty, and I'm hanged if I let it go until I know what it is!'

To her mingled astonishment and delight, he leaned forward and dropped a light kiss on her brow. 'Go to bed now. Should think you must be dropping with fatigue. I know I am, and I mean to make an early start.'

'Yes, but we have not settled this!'

Claud turned her round bodily and gave her a shove. 'Bed! And don't argue, or I'll be forced to carry you there myself!'

Reluctant and not a little bewildered, Kitty crossed to the door that led to a hallway and so to the bedchambers, and halted there. Turning, she made one last attempt at an appeal.

'Claud, pray—'

'Kitty, I'll count to three. One—'

'*Wait!*' begged Kitty desperately.

Claud paused. 'Well?'

She hesitated, an uneven heartbeat making her breathless. He stood there in a pose of unconscious arrogance, slim and almost handsome in his evening dress of a green that became him well. That inflexible look was in his face, and Kitty's will died. She did not know how to fight him. And how it came about she had no notion, but she no longer wished to. But the question nevertheless emerged.

'Are you sure you want to do this, Claud?'

He strolled up to her, but he did not touch her. It was darker at the doorway, but Kitty clearly saw the stubborn jut of his chin.

'If you must have it, Kitty, there ain't a choice. For a

man of honour, that is. Couldn't cry off now if I wanted to. Not that I want to, but you'd best hear the truth of it. And you don't have a choice either. You're a gentlewoman born, and I've compromised you. Therefore we start for Gretna in the morning, like it or not.'

There were moments when Kitty became convinced that she was dreaming. She was at last growing used to the speed of the curricle, learning to relax in her seat so that she swayed with the movement. Wrapped in the woollen cloak she was warm enough, despite the unaccustomed lightness in the feel of her new plain muslin gown. Since the sky had been overcast from the morning, the carriage hood was up, which kept out the worst of the wind. She was sorry for Docking, and had said so, only to discover that the groom, instead of clinging on behind for dear life as his master rattled over uneven roads, had developed a trick of sitting on his perch facing backwards, with a leather strap caught about him and fastened to the vehicle for safety.

'Usually find him asleep when it's time to blow up for the change,' Claud had informed her. 'Dratted fellow can sleep through anything!'

It might have been more comfortable to make the journey in a post-chaise, but her betrothed had announced that he had no intention of spending more time on the road than he had to and would therefore drive himself. Not much to Kitty's surprise, her own wishes in the matter had not been consulted. No doubt she would eventually become accustomed to having her feelings disregarded. Even Mrs Duxford, who had previously had the ordering of her life, had not been so high-handed about it.

The remembrance of the Duck set Kitty thinking about the letter she had with difficulty written. Come the morning—which had begun much later than one might have anticipated from the Viscount's asserted intentions!—it had been borne in upon Kitty that she had been absent for nearly four and twenty hours with neither explanation nor contact. However little her preceptress thought of her, Kitty knew she would be frantic with worry. The Duck had ever taken as a sacred trust the welfare of the girls in her care. It behoved Kitty to write and set her mind at rest.

Having partaken of breakfast while his lordship slept on undisturbed, Kitty had asked Mixon for paper and a pen so that she might set about this duty, and use up the time until Claud should deign to rise. The valet had categorically refused to awaken him at Kitty's request.

'His lordship's standing instructions, miss, are to let him have his sleep out.'

'But not today! We have a long way to travel.'

Mixon had bowed. 'So I understand, miss. But failing any specific instructions from his lordship, I cannot take it upon myself to vary his accustomed routine.'

Kitty was obliged to possess her soul in what patience she could muster, and content herself with sitting down to the trying task of writing to Mrs Duxford. To explain her predicament had proved altogether too complicated. Three separate attempts to describe her present circumstances were screwed up and consigned to the wastebasket. In the end, she had achieved a simple note that merely stated that she was both safe and sorry to have occasioned any disturbance or concern.

'I shall come to see you presently, ma'am, and explain it in person,' Kitty had added. 'You need have no apprehension on my behalf, for I am well taken care of.' She had almost sealed the letter, when a further thought occurred and she had been obliged to open it again to add a conscientious postscript. 'I shall return the three pairs of white hose, but I have made use of the toothbrush and toothpowder and will give you back the money for them.'

When Claud had at last emerged from his bedchamber, it had been past eleven. Clad for the road in top-boots and buckskins, together with a serviceable frock-coat of brown fustian over a mustard-coloured cassimere waistcoat, he had remained wholly unchastened by Kitty's protest.

'I thought you meant us to make an early start.'

'Eleven is early. Dash it, you couldn't expect me to scramble up at the crack of dawn!'

Kitty had rapidly gone beyond expecting anything from Lord Devenick. Except contrariness! She had presented him with the letter, requesting him to have it sent through the post. He had glanced at the inscription, and then handed it on to his valet with a brief instruction to see to it, and then addressed himself once more to his breakfast.

'Have you told her we're going to be married?'

'No, for I could not think how to explain it all in a letter. I have not even mentioned you.'

'And how d'you suppose she will react when you walk in with your husband in tow, silly chit? You'd better not have written at all.'

'But then she would be wondering what has become of me.'

'Well, she won't know that from your letter, by all accounts.'

'She will know I am safe,' Kitty had argued. 'Are you not going to let any of your family know that you are going away?'

'Gad, no! Not that any of them will trouble their heads over it. They'll suppose I've gone off to visit a friend or some such thing. They know my habits.'

Kitty had laid down the coffee cup Mixon had given her—upon his lordship's command, not her request. 'Well, it is not my habit to disappear from the Seminary without trace, and the Duck certainly knows that!'

Claud had looked struck, pausing with a forkful of beef halfway to his mouth. 'Something in that. Good thing you wrote that letter. Mixon, remind me to frank it before I go, and have it sent off this very day.'

It was all of a piece! Kitty would hardly have been surprised had he woken up that morning with a new determination not to wed her after all. She had never known a person so changeable. As the day progressed, she had leisure to observe that the Viscount's disposition was nothing if not impulsive. And all to service his own desires. His movements were wholly dictated by whether *he* had need of food or rest. Kitty would have been glad of a respite when they stopped at Baldock for another change of horses.

'Are we to have a luncheon here?' she asked hopefully.

'No, I'm not hungry,' came the callous reply. 'Besides, I want to push on to Stilton today.' He then turned to the groom who had jumped down. 'Docking, isn't it Stilton where Mendoza fought Gentleman Humphries years ago?'

For several indignant moments, Kitty was ignored while Claud engaged with his groom in several reminiscences about prize fighting. When Docking went to confer with the ostlers, she seized her chance.

'If we are not going to eat here, when will we stop for food?'

'Huntingdon.'

'And how much longer will it take us to reach there?'

'No more than a couple of hours.'

The thought of another two hours before she could eat again was enough to have drawn the strongest protestations from Kitty. Except that the curricle was on the move again and she dared not distract Claud's attention from the road.

His madcap progress made the hair fairly start upon the back of her neck. He drove at breakneck speed, hardly slowing even when the press of traffic in a town demanded it, and cursing at slower vehicles. It was a while before Kitty got used to his shocking pace.

The promised break for luncheon proved all too short, although the food was more than welcome. They were away again within the hour, Claud asserting his intention to reach Stilton before nightfall. Having no notion how long this might take, Kitty sighed and refrained from asking. She already felt as if she had been travelling all her life, and the motion of the carriage at length lulled her mind into a disbelieving stupor.

She reminded herself that she was partaking of an adventure as good as any fairy tale. Yet, try as she would, she could not persuade herself that it was anything but a fantasy. Her senses told her that she was in a curricle on the Great North Road, and that the man beside her was destined to become her husband within a few days. It was all the dreams she had ever dreamed, and more. But under that apparency sat a horrid knot of truth that Kitty had been doing her best to blot out of her mind.

This stranger was prepared to marry her, Kitty Merrick, who threatened to bring him only scandal and disgrace. Why? *Why?* So that he need not marry his cousin Kate? For honour? Claud had said as much. Kitty did not know enough of the rules of Society to be sure, but she found it hard to believe that an unknown creature, a prospective governess, could be so compromised. The conviction of doing wrong grew upon her. Only how to right it now that she had taken the plunge was beyond her. There seemed to be no way back.

By the time they finally drew into the yard of the Angel Inn at Stilton, night had overtaken them and his lordship had been driving for more than six hours, with a short respite for luncheon, and had covered over sixty miles. Kitty, herself utterly exhausted despite having been merely a passenger, was astonished to hear him as enthusiastic as when he started out.

'Pretty well, for one day,' he said, as he shifted around the curricle to her side. 'If we can keep this up, we'll make Gretna in two more days.'

'Two days? But you cannot mean to travel tomorrow!'

He frowned up at her. 'Why not?'

'It is Sunday. Have you forgot?'

'I had, as it happens,' said Claud, reaching up his hands to help Kitty to alight, 'but it makes no odds. Sunday or no Sunday, we'll make as much time on the road as I can contrive.'

Kitty, whose adherence to religious precepts had been more enforced than chosen, accepted this decision blithely, and stepped gingerly down from the curricle on to unsteady legs. She was awed by Claud's boundless energy.

'Are you not tired?'

Claud released her, yawned and stretched. 'A trifle, perhaps. Probably sleep like one dead tonight. But what I chiefly need is a wash and dinner!' He turned to a maidservant hurrying across the yard. 'Ho, there! Where's your landlord? Fetch him to me at once! See the horses bestowed, Docking. Not a bad team, that. We'll take them on in the morning.'

With which, he walked into the inn, leaving Kitty to follow in his wake as best she could. It struck her forcibly that this treatment scarcely accorded with the courtesy due to the lady he was intending to marry. Had the brute no thought for her at all? It did not augur well for her future wedded life, and Kitty sighed as the golden dreams she once had entertained receded further into the realms of fantasy.

She found him negotiating cheerfully with the landlord, and was soon following the man's wife upstairs and into a neat chamber where one of the lads deposited the portmanteau loaned to her by Claud's valet. Unable to contemplate the effort of opening it and searching inside for her night attire, which she had fortunately remembered to purchase along with other necessities, Kitty contented herself with washing her face and hands, and rummaging for a hairbrush. The muslin gown was crushed, but it would do. But her hair was dusty from the roads, and it took time to repair the damage. She had just rethreaded the ribbon through her dark curls when a maid knocked at the door to call her to come down to dinner.

Presently she found herself in a well-lighted parlour, where a fire had been made up in the grate against the cool of evening, throwing a cheerful warmth into the room. A table in the centre was being laid with covers for two, and Claud was in close colloquy with the landlord on the subject, as it turned out, of the quality of the wine in his cellars, of which his lordship was anxious to partake. He had discarded his driving coat and his hat, and the short fair hair was freshly combed, but he had not changed, except perhaps his cravat, which was clean and neatly tied.

'Been thinking,' announced her betrothed, when the waiter had served them with slices of pie and a chicken fricassee and departed.

'What about?' asked Kitty cautiously.

'Where it is you fit into the family.'

It came as a welcome surprise to Kitty to learn that his attention had been directed towards her, even obliquely. Had he spent the past hours in the curricle pondering on it? She wished he might have spoken of it and assuaged a little of her despair.

'Did you work out a conclusion?'

'No, but I've got a notion or two worth trying. Seems to me I'd best acquaint you with the ramifications of the family first, or it won't make sense. As well you know who they are before you run into them lock, stock and barrel.'

With this sentiment, Kitty was in complete agreement. 'Must we run into them?'

'Bound to,' said Claud, piercing a generous portion of pie with his fork. 'Most of 'em are to be found at Brightwell through the summer months. The Rothleys have one of our houses there, a few miles east of Brightwell Prior, which is the estate the Countess chooses to live at. The principal Blakemere estates are in Hereford, but she can't be persuaded to remove there for more than a week or two in the year, more's the pity.'

'Why is it a pity?'

'Because my own place is at Shillingford, and it's a deal too close to Brightwell for my liking. Can't get away from her—or the family, come to that.'

Kitty began to feel a trifle apprehensive. 'Is it a large family?'

Claud helped himself to more of the chicken. 'Depends which side you mean. We've Cheddon cousins and an uncle and three aunts on m'father's side. Two of my cousins are in orders and another in the Navy, and all the females are married and scattered around Hereford, so I don't see much of them, thank the Lord!'

Kitty was inclined to echo him. She was about to ask if Claud suspected she came within the Cheddon side, when she recalled it was Kate Rothley she resembled.

'And on your mother's side?'

'Yes, that's where we should be looking,' said Claud thoughtfully, as if he had read her mind. He reached for his wine. 'You've met Kate. And Aunt Silvia, come to that. She's the youngest of the Ridsdale sisters, and the Countess is the eldest. They were all three daughters of a duke, which is what made my mother so deucedly high in the instep. It's my belief she's never got over being born into the purple.'

The more Kitty heard about the Countess of Blakemere, the less she wanted to meet her. And this woman was to be, however reluctantly, her mother-in-law? She sought to deflect Claud's explanations.

'You mentioned a sister of yours, I think?'

'A sister? There are three of 'em! M'sister Kath is married to Wilkhaven. She's the eldest. Then there's Mary, who was carried off to the North by a fellow a dashed sight too old for her, but that's the Countess all over. Peel has a title that goes back to the Conquest, and that was enough. That, or riches, as it turns out. Seems she's pressing Babs with a younger son with expectations.'

'Babs?'

'Barbara. Youngest sister, just out,' explained Claud through a mouthful of chicken. 'Only seventeen.'

'And have you no brothers?'

He shook his head, and downed the chicken with a draft of wine. 'Which is why the Countess is so set on my marrying. She don't want the Cheddon cousins stepping in.'

Kitty ate in silence for a while, burdened by a horrid realisation that to her would fall the loathsome duty of producing an heir for the Blakemere title. It was an aspect of the situation that had escaped her until now. The thought of it turned the food in her mouth to rubber. She laid down her fork and reached out a trembling hand for the tumbler of water she had opted to drink.

'That's my siblings accounted for,' said Claud, pushing away his plate and leaning back in his chair. 'Then there's Kate, who is third of the Rothleys. Both the fellows are older. Ralph took the title years ago. My cousin George is a redcoat—Captain Rothley now. And then there's Tess, but she don't count as she's only fifteen.'

'And that's all? I shall never remember the half of them!'

Claud laughed. 'You will, once you've met 'em all. But wait a bit, for there's more.'

Kitty blinked. 'Yet more?'

'There's the Hevershams. At least, strictly speaking there's only young Harry, for he was born to my aunt Felicia. Don't remember her too well, for she died in childbed when I was at Eton. My uncle Heversham married again, and there's a boy since then, but we don't count him as family. Fortunately they're further off in Berkshire.'

A trifle bewildered, Kitty tried to unravel the puzzle, and singularly failed. Perhaps she was overtired. 'Did you mention another aunt before? What was her name?'

'Felicia. She was the middle sister, Lady Felicia Ridsdale.'

'Oh, your *mother's* sister.'

'And Aunt Silvia's too. Only children of my grandmother's that survived. There was Lydia, who is my mother, Felicia followed her, and then Sylvia, who is Kate's mother. Three girls only. Title went to another branch of the family when m'grandfather died. Estates are in Derbyshire and Grandmama Litton moved to Buxton for her health. She's a Katherine, which is why the eldest daughters of my generation were all—'

He broke off abruptly, and Kitty saw a look of disbelief spread across his features. A vague premonition sent a riffle of apprehension through her veins.

'Oh, what is it?'

Claud was staring at her, the blue eyes roving her face as if he sought there for the truth of whatever it was that had entered his head.

'It can't be,' he said slowly. 'There ain't a particle of evidence. Only it would explain the dust kicked up by Aunt Silvia! Or would it?' He shook his head, as if this did not fit. 'No, it don't make sense. But you said a female came to visit—a lady. Only why in the world should it make you look like Kate? She favours my uncle—or so I've always thought. Wonder if it ain't so, after all?'

This was more than Kitty could endure. She clutched the edge of the table with fingers that felt as numb as the hollow in her chest.

'Claud, what is in your head? Pray *tell me*.'

He drew in a breath and blew it out again. 'It's the maddest notion, Kitty, but it just might fit.'

Kitty nearly screamed. '*What* notion?'

'Don't you see? You were named Katherine.'

'What of it?'

'Think about it! There are three daughters of Katherine, Duchess of Litton. Lydia, Felicia and Sylvia. Now look at the next generation.' He counted off on his fingers. 'There's Kate, the daughter of Silvia. There's Kath, born to Lydia. And there's you, also named Katherine. Can it be coincidence?'

The implication was sinking in. Kitty could only stare at him, the vision rising in her head of an unknown lady who had visited a lonely little girl.

Chapter Five

Oh, if it was so! Kitty thrilled to the thought, for of all her memories this only was sweet. Only why had she then to be concealed? Had not this Felicia been married? What was the name Claud had said? She could not remember, but there had been a marriage. She recalled the belief she had ever held, and was hardly aware of speaking.

'I had always worked it out that I was the outcome of an unfortunate liaison between a high-born married lady and a gentlemen equally high born. Yet if it was your aunt, then who was the gentleman?'

Claud had been refreshing himself with a draught of his wine, but at this, he laid down the glass. Forgetting his company, he brought it out flat.

'According to my cousin Ralph, you must be my uncle Rothley's by-blow. Only he'd no thought of my aunt Felicia, if that was the case. Thought it must be some impossible female who threatened to make trouble for Aunt Silvia, who had then gone to the Countess for help.' Missing the stricken look in the eyes of his betrothed, he went on blithely. 'Only too likely, for my uncle was the deuce of a rake. Must have fathered dozens of progeny on any number of females, both high and low born, for by all accounts he wasn't too particular. More than one female is said to have passed my uncle's offspring off upon her own husband.'

Horrified, Kitty quailed at what was an all too likely scenario. Her voice was taut. 'It would explain everything, would it not? How dreadful if it should be so! Oh, Claud, do you indeed think it was he?'

'No, I don't,' he replied unexpectedly. 'For one thing, your mother couldn't be my aunt Felicia if that was the way of it, and for another, the Countess wouldn't have put my uncle Rothley's bastard to school.'

An alternative presented itself to Kitty's questing mind. 'She might perhaps have paid someone else to do it.'

Claud frowned. 'The Merricks, you mean? It's a thought. Wouldn't think the Countess would let herself be bled through the nose on that account, however.'

'But she would not have been. Paddington charity cases are supported by donations to the Seminary. There is a Board which gets in the money and arranges everything.'

The blue gaze settled upon Kitty's face. Was Claud pondering this last just as she was herself? Any payment to the Merricks could only have been made until she was six years old. And if her mother was a vulgar creature who had harassed a peeress, who was that lady Kitty's memory could by no means explain? What of those persons who had fetched her to Paddington? They could have been anyone, agents of those who had decided her future. Which brought her squarely back to the Countess of Blakemere.

'Hmm,' mused Claud at length. 'This ain't going to be as simple to unravel as I'd hoped. After what you told me last night, I made sure it wasn't my uncle Rothley. Now I'm almost as certain that it ain't my aunt Felicia. Dashed if I know what to think! Wish I could remember whether Kate and you—and Ralph, come to that, for he's in the same mould—are like the Rothleys or the Ridsdales. Can't recall my aunt Felicia, and my aunt Silvia has put on so much flesh one can't tell any more if Kate and Ralph resemble her.'

A worse thought struck Kitty. 'It could not have been your aunt Silvia who was my mother, could it?'

Claud's eyes popped. 'Gad, I never thought of that!'

'She was so very disturbed at seeing me, and perhaps that was why.'

But Claud was beginning to shake his head. 'Don't see it, Kitty. She'd two children already by then—Ralph, and George, who's my age. Even had she played my uncle false, she'd only to pretend the child was his. Who would have known? No need for her to ferry you off to these Merricks.'

Relief swept through Kitty as the common sense of this reasoning took hold. 'Yes, and the same would be true of your mother.'

Claud jumped and the wine spilled from his glass. 'My mother! For the Lord's sake, what put that into your head? Jupiter, that would put paid to the marriage, sure as check!'

Realising what she had just said, Kitty stared at him in growing alarm. 'We would be brother and sister! Lord, are you *sure* it is not so, Claud?'

'Sure? Of course I'm sure! At least—' He broke off, setting down his glass and wiping the traces of wine off his fingers with his discarded napkin.

'You see! You are not sure at all!' Kitty rose hastily to her feet. 'We can go no further! You must take me back to the Seminary, Claud. I *knew* I was doing wrong!'

Claud was also on his feet, throwing down the napkin. 'Wait a bit, Kitty. Let me think!'

'Of what use is thinking? If there is the slightest chance of such a thing—'

'Well, there ain't!' uttered Claud in triumph. 'Knew you couldn't possibly be m'sister.'

'*How* do you know?' uttered Kitty desperately.

'Mary.'

'Mary? What in the world do you mean, *Mary*?' she mimicked him.

'M'sister Mary. She's coming up to two and twenty, which means the Countess must have been heavily pregnant when you were conceived. Or giving birth? One or the other at any rate. Can't have been your mother too.'

Kitty did a frantic calculation in her head, and concluded that Claud was right. She sank back into her chair and dropped her head in her hands.

'I feel quite sick.'

'Not surprised. Made me a sight queasy myself!'

He poured himself a measure of wine and drank it down. Noting Kitty's bent head, he upended her unused glass and half-filled it.

'Here, drink this. It'll put heart into you.'

Kitty raised her head and took the proffered glass, sipping at it gingerly. She was unused to wine, a single glass on Sundays being about all she had ever drunk. But the liquid warmed her and the shock began to recede.

'I don't think I care to probe any further, if this is to be the result.'

'Don't be a nodcock, Kitty. Must pursue it. You want to know, don't you? Got to look at all the options.'

'It is all very well for you,' uttered Kitty aggrievedly. 'You are not going to discover that your mother abandoned you and your father was a hateful rake!'

'Yes, but we don't know my uncle Rothley was your father,' Claud pointed out, correctly interpreting this embittered pronouncement. 'For my money, he might well not have been. He was so bloated and disfigured through his excesses by the time he died, that I have no notion what he looked like at the start.'

Kitty could bear no more. Setting down the glass, she got up and shifted away from the table. 'I am too tired to discuss the matter further tonight. I shall go to bed.'

Claud had risen automatically. 'Very good notion. Hanged if I won't be close behind you. Like to get an early start tomorrow, for if we can make Newark, we'll be better than halfway.'

Kitty left him in no very comfortable frame of mind. But although she felt as if she could sleep for a week, the discussion of her antecedents so haunted her that her recalcitrant brain refused to compose itself for slumber.

Worst was the hateful—and all too probable!—idea propounded by the unknown cousin Ralph about his father. Of all things, Kitty longed to have that disproven. She searched her mind for another explanation. That she had originated with remote cousins, for instance, who had been forgotten by one and all. Had not Claud spoken of having innumerable cousins in various parts of the country? Could it not have been a fluke that she so greatly resembled Kate?

But it would not serve. Of one thing only could they be certain, and that was her embarrassing likeness to Kate Rothley. Which gave most in favour of the late Baron Rothley being her father. Was it unreasonable to suppose that Lady Rothley should swoon at the sight of one of her husband's by-blows? No, it was not. Particularly if someone—Kitty's mother?—had thought to capitalise upon the uncanny resemblance. One could sympathise with the family for ensuring such a skeleton was securely locked in the closet. And here she was, rising up to haunt them!

Guilt and despair engulfed Kitty, and if she slept, it was so fitfully that she had no recollection of having done so.

* * *

Except that she did wake, starting up in shock, to find the chambermaid leaning over her and shaking her at the shoulder.

She blinked dazedly. 'What—what is it?'

'You're to get up at once, miss. His lordship is awaiting you this age, and anxious to be gone.'

Kitty sat up, though her head swam from lack of sleep. 'Lord Devenick? He is up already? What time is it?'

'Past ten, miss.' The girl moved to the stand that held the basin and ewer. 'I've fetched up hot water. Will there be anything else, miss?'

Unable to think beyond the frantic necessity to hurry, Kitty shook her head, throwing aside the covers and scrambling out of bed.

'No—or stay! Will you tell his lordship I shall be but a moment.'

The girl curtsied and withdrew, and Kitty stumbled to the basin and splashed water into it. Her head felt thick, her legs unwieldy, and it was difficult to be obliged to prepare in a state of semi-sleep. She dragged off her nightgown, and washed as fast as she could, trying to gather her wits. If only she had extracted clean underclothing from her portmanteau last night. Only she hadn't, and it did not help that she could not, in her frantic state, recall what she had bought during her shopping spree and what she had forgotten. There was nothing for it but to delve among the collection of brand-new items, disarranging them unmercifully as she did so.

Managing to extract a clean shift, she threw it on, and struggled with her stays, the laces having become unaccountably knotted. Her fingers were all thumbs, and she could have wept with frustration. At length she undid the knot, and was able to complete the remainder of her toilet without undue delay, once again putting on the plain muslin gown. But the moment she had brushed her hair and was threading a ribbon through it, she remembered that she must also pack. A knock at the door heralded the entrance of the maid again.

'His lordship says as how you must come now, miss.'

Kitty glared at her. 'Come now? How in the world can I come now, when I have not had time to pack my portmanteau? Pray tell his lordship that I am almost ready, and if he had wished to leave thus early he should have said so last night!'

She flung across the room and hefted her portmanteau on to the bed with hands that had begun to shake—as much with anger as frustration. Out of the corner of her eye, she saw the girl curtsy and move to leave the room again, and quickly put out a hand.

'No, don't tell him that, if you please! Just say that I will be down directly.'

The maid nodded and withdrew again. But the instant she was gone, Kitty wished that she had not changed the message. Really, Claud was the limit! Yesterday he must needs keep her waiting while he rose at his leisure and only appeared at eleven. But today, she was in the wrong for remaining in bed no later than an hour before that!

Seizing her belongings from all about the room, she thrust them pell-mell into the portmanteau with unnecessary force, wishing that she might instead have thrown them at his lordship's head.

Leaving the bulging receptacle on the floor, Kitty grabbed up her cloak and hat and sped down to the private parlour as speedily as she might for the lightness pervading her head. Throwing open the door, she was chagrined to find Claud marching up the room with his pocket watch in his hand. He turned as she entered.

'At last! What took you so long? Should have thought you'd have been ready hours before this!'

Kitty exploded. 'Had I known that you wished to leave hours before you are used to rise, I might well have been! How was I to guess that you might get up out of your bed at an unearthly hour?'

'Where is your portmanteau?' he demanded, ignoring everything she had said, as he ripped the cloak and hat from her hands and flung them into a chair to one side.

'I left it upstairs,' Kitty answered, staring in disbelief as her cloak slid halfway to the floor and her hat rolled away down the carpet. 'Have you run mad?'

Claud pushed past her without responding and into the doorway, shouting for a waiter. Kitty went to retrieve her belongings, placing the cloak neatly back on the chair and tweaking the hat into shape. She heard Claud give an order to someone outside to fetch her portmanteau down to his curricle, and wished she might refuse to accompany his lordship, who was undoubtedly the most infuriating creature in the world. Then he was back, the blue eyes sweeping the room and settling upon her where she was laying the hat neatly upon her cloak.

'Leave that, and sit down,' he urged, moving to the table and pulling out a chair. 'What do you want to eat? I warn you, I won't stay long for you, so you'd best choose something easy.'

'Then go without me!' Kitty flung at him, sailing across the room and throwing herself down into the chair in a manner that did little to improve the already uncertain state of her head.

'Don't talk such flimflam! How can I possibly go without you?' rejoined Claud, seizing upon the coffee pot. 'Do you want some of this?' He upended a cup and began to pour. 'Take one of those wigs. Landlady says they're fresh baked this morning, and I found 'em tasty.'

Kitty began to feel harassed beyond endurance, as she took the coffee with which he had served her and sipped at it, watching in growing dudgeon as Claud chucked two of the spiced buns on a plate and proceeded to cut them open and butter them. As if he were a nursemaid and she a schoolgirl!

'Do you intend to stuff them into my mouth as well?' she demanded wrathfully.

'What d'you mean?' responded Claud in an injured tone. 'Only trying to help.'

'"Only trying to help." You are trying to rush me!'

'Of course I am! Don't you realise that it's past ten already? And don't copy me, devil take it! Here, eat this.'

A plate landed in front of her, set with two buttered halves of a wig. Kitty lifted one automatically to her lips, as Claud lavishly spread butter upon the second one. She bit into the soft bread, but she had chewed her way through less than half of it before the oppression of her betrothed hovering over her destroyed all vestige of appetite. She threw the thing down again.

'If you mean to stand there brooding, Claud, I shall not be able to eat a thing!'

Grudgingly he moved to one side. 'Well, I wish you will get on!'

'How can I when you are so impatient?'

'Dash it, Kitty, stop making such a fuss!'

'I like that! If anyone is making a fuss, it is you. Why can you not leave me in peace for five minutes?'

Claud flung away from the table, and went to stare fretfully out of the window upon the gardens below. Having risen betimes himself, it was galling to be obliged to wait. Kitty had on the same clothes as yesterday, just as he did himself, barring a clean shirt and cravat, so how hard could it have been? Why, he did not know, but he felt restless and fidgety. Likely it was the tedious length of this journey. He wished it had been possible to avoid it, but it was no use thinking of that. Had Kitty's birthday been only a few days away, it might have been worth waiting. As it was, she did not attain her majority until July, and there was no sense in stewing that long. He wanted it over, so that he might confront the Countess and watch her burn.

Little did my Lady Blakemere know, as she made her preparations to return to the country for the summer months, that all the pleasure of her sojourn there was to be utterly destroyed. He had played the scene over in his mind a dozen times, there being little else to occupy him when the roads were clear and his attention had leisure to wander. Except the vexed question of Kitty's parenthood, which chafed him only because it gave the Countess an advantage in the anticipated war. How would he outguess her and counter any attacks?

For attack she would. After the first assault—which must assuredly bring her down!—she would do all she could to outwit him. But he would be ready for her. Let her do her worst. Let her plead, pray, scold or upbraid, he would be as a rock. Once he was married, there was nothing she could do.

The delay became unbearable, and he turned to find that his wretched betrothed had barely touched the repast he had prepared for her. His patience snapped.

'What the devil are you doing? I thought you were hungry!'

Kitty glared at him. 'If I was, you have ruined my appetite!'

Claud strode forward. 'Well, if you're not going to eat, for the Lord's sake, let's go!' He seized his caped driving

coat from the back of one of the chairs and shrugged it
on. Clapping the beaver on his head, he turned to find that
Kitty had only got as far as standing up in her place.
'*Move,* can't you? Where's your hat and cloak?'

Despite every effort to do justice to the meal—her recollection strong of having been left hungry yesterday by
Claud's lack of consideration!—Kitty had been unable to
swallow more than a mouthful or two of coffee. But this
faded into insignificance as she was bundled into her cloak,
her hat thrust upon her, and fairly pulled from the parlour
and down into the yard of the inn where Docking had the
team ready harnessed and champing at the bit. Seething,
Kitty was all but thrown up into the curricle, where she
righted herself as best she could and struggled to put the
hat upon her head before the vehicle could be driven out
of the yard and on to the open road.

Wrapped in offended silence, Kitty had determined to
ignore any attempt on the part of his lordship to engage
her in conversation. But the miles fled by—the roads being
relatively empty on the Lord's Day—and he made no such
attempt, which effectually reduced her to a cauldron of
held-down fury. Compounded with a gnawing hunger and
inevitable fatigue from her sleepless night, this soon led to
an incipient headache. Kitty began to feel physically sick.
At which inauspicious moment, Claud broke the silence.

'We'll be stopping at Streeton at the Ram Jam Inn.'

Kitty did not care where they stopped—as long as they
stopped. She longed to know how far it might be, but for
no consideration would she ask, contenting herself with a
frigid monosyllable.

'Yes?'

Claud glanced round at her. 'Should think it would appeal to your romantic fancy, for Dick Turpin is said to

have stayed there with his mistress. Believe they boast a collection of relics that they claim belonged to the rogue—boots or some such.'

At any other time, this information would have enchanted Kitty. Instead, most improperly, she silently consigned the long-dead highwayman and his boots to a place of great heat—and Lord Devenick with them.

'Indeed?' she said coldly.

In the periphery of her vision, she caught Claud's frowning gaze directed upon her and deliberately looked away, over the fields. A mistake, she quickly realised, for the rolling hills beyond made the jolting of the carriage seem worse, increasing her nausea.

Hastily directing her attention back upon the road ahead, Kitty surreptitiously moved her hand under her cloak and pressed it against the growing discomfort at her stomach. Her headache intensified, and it became hard indeed to adhere to her resolve not to sue for succour.

Noting the stiffness of his companion's shoulders, Claud abandoned his attempt to bring the silly chit out of the sulks. If she chose to behave like a thwarted child, it was all the same to him. As long as this was not an augury for their future married life. It would be a confounded nuisance to be forever wheedling her out of a black mood. She was of a volatile temperament. Last thing he wished for was a domestic life that was nothing but one wrangle after another! The chit would have to learn that he would not tolerate this sort of thing.

There were other problems looming before him. His London accommodation, for a start. One parlour and two bedchambers would scarcely serve when he was married. Where would he put his friends? Servants, too. Kitty would need a maid, who could scarcely sleep in the stables in the mews around the corner with Docking. No, he would have to acquire a house. Not in the grand manner like the family home in Grosvenor Square, but a snug little place conveniently situated to his accustomed pursuits.

He was still mentally working out his needs when he entered Streeton. His attention snapped back to the matter at hand, and he reined in his cattle to a trot, his eyes sweeping ahead for the sign of the Ram Jam Inn.

'There it be, guv'nor,' came from behind where Docking had arisen in his perch. 'And not before time, to my way of thinking. Only look at miss there!'

This adjuration sent Claud's gaze jerking away from the swinging sign to be seen in the street ahead, and around to find Kitty deathly white, and holding a handkerchief to her mouth. He took in the situation without difficulty. All his earlier irritation with her was forgotten.

'Good Gad! Hold hard, Kitty. We'll be there in two ticks!'

If this was not strictly accurate, it was sufficiently cheering for Kitty to manage to keep back the threatening nausea in one last desperate effort. It was a close run thing. The carriage clattered to a halt in the yard of the inn, but for the life of her, she could do nothing to get herself out of it. Aware only vaguely of shouts and running feet, it was with real gratitude that she found Claud below her, holding up his hands.

'Come on, let's get you down!'

She made a heroic effort to rise, still holding the handkerchief to her mouth. Then she was swung through the air, a sensation that served to destroy any control she had left. The moment her feet touched the ground, she turned aside from the figure before her, and disgorged the contents of her stomach upon the cobblestones of the yard.

The retching continued for several minutes and Kitty was aware of nothing but the violent discomfort and the strong pair of hands that kept her from falling to the ground. In the hazy background, there was Claud's voice, peremptory and sharp.

'Don't stand there goggling, dunce! Fetch a female to me here! And have a room made ready for the lady.' Then something soft was given into her hand. 'Here, Kitty, use this. We'll have you lying down in a trice.'

Clutching the second handkerchief, Kitty wiped at her mouth with fingers that quivered hopelessly. The clouds were dissipating and she felt a degree less ill, but her legs were jelly and she could not help whimpering. Claud's voice came again, gentler.

'Hush, now! It's all right. Can you walk? No, you can't!'

And then she was lifted off her feet, and Claud was carrying her through a doorway and into a wide hall. Within a few moments, her cloak had been removed and she was laid down upon the cushioned softness of a bed and a bustling woman was attending to her needs.

It was more than an hour later when Kitty stepped gingerly down the stairs in search of Lord Devenick. She had vomited twice more before her stomach had emptied, and had lain exhausted upon the covers while the plump female in attendance had wiped her face and hands with a wet cloth, enquiring from time to time whether she felt a degree better. Kitty had dozed a little, and woken again, still with a raging headache. She recalled the woman who was in the room, and discovered that she was the landlady, who had caused a tisane to be made up and brought for Kitty's relief. After drinking it, she had been divested of her gown and had again fallen asleep, only to wake to the hollowness of hunger and a strong sensation of guilt.

Upon rising with caution, she had found that her legs

were to be trusted again and the headache had receded almost entirely, leaving her head a trifle thick but relatively pain free. Thankfully, she washed her face and hands and cleaned her teeth, and then donned her muslin gown— from which a thoughtful person had removed the offending debris of her illness. Feeling only a little delicate, she had braved the outside world.

Downstairs, a waiter led her past the coffee room and along to a parlour situated further down the corridor. Here she found Claud, who leaped from a seat at the table, where a collection of eatables were laid out, and came towards her, all trace of this morning's fidgeting start set aside in favour of an unaccustomed self-reproach.

'Are you sure you are well enough to come down? Shouldn't have rushed you. Should have had a proper breakfast, for it's fatal to travel on an empty stomach. Why didn't you tell me you were feeling sick?'

Dazed by the barrage of comment and question, Kitty threw up her hands. 'How can I answer you? I am sorry to have been troublesome, but—'

'Here, come and sit down,' Claud interrupted, pulling out a chair.

A giggle escaped Kitty. 'You are doing it again!'

He paused, one hand upon the chair back. He let out a self-conscious laugh. 'So I am! Must be habit. But aren't you hungry?'

'Ravenous,' Kitty assured him, coming to the table.

'Well, you'd best take it lightly. A little now and you'll be able to do better justice at dinner. No need to fill up for a journey, for we'll go no further today.'

Kitty took her seat. 'But I thought you wanted to get to Newark.'

'Only because I don't want to spend too long on the road altogether,' he rejoined, moving to sit again. 'It is

Sunday, after all. Don't make a particle of difference if we're a day or two later, and there's no sense in going on if you're going to be sick again.'

A riffle of gratitude snaked through Kitty, for she had indeed been contemplating a resumption of the journey with trepidation. But a feeling of guilt persisted, and she could not but voice a protest as she took up her napkin and spread it across her knees.

'I wish you will not be solicitous! It is not at all like you, when I had made up my mind to it that you are the greatest beast in nature, and it makes me feel terrible for having delayed you.'

Taken aback, Claud stared at her for a moment, and then burst out laughing. 'Wish I knew how to take that! Have I been so beastly to you?'

Kitty smiled. 'You know very well you have been perfectly horrid.'

He grinned. 'Well, if I have, you ain't been precisely saintly yourself. If ever I met such a shrew!' He passed her a basket of bread. 'Butter's at your elbow.'

'A shrew! I think that is most unfair.' Kitty helped herself to a soft roll and took a knife to the butter. 'I know I have a hasty temper, but—'

'Yes, and so have I,' agreed Claud, picking up a jug of water and pouring a measure into a glass set at Kitty's place. 'And it ain't what I bargained for. Nor to have my words thrown back at me the way you do in that mimicking way!'

'Well, I am sorry, but I cannot help it. I was always used to ape voices, and I don't know that I'm doing it.'

'No, I've noticed!' said Claud feelingly. 'I tell you, I'd not have had half the trouble with Kate. Biddable girl is Kate. Which makes it difficult to see how you could be any sort of sister to her.'

'Oh, don't,' begged Kitty, setting down the roll. 'Pray don't start on that subject again, Claud, for I was kept awake last night thinking of it!'

'Ah, so that's what made you as surly as a bear this morning.'

'That, and you dragging me out hours before you are accustomed to rise,' returned Kitty reproachfully.

'Well, but—'

'And pray don't tell me that you were in a hurry to be gone, because I see now that it was all an instance of your hateful selfishness. It is all of a piece!'

About to drink of the best house ale, Claud lowered the tankard. 'Selfishness? What do you mean, selfishness?'

Kitty immediately regretted her unguarded words. Only now that they were out, there was no putting them back again. Making a play of looking over the various meats on offer, she tried to mitigate the slur.

'I do not mean to say that you are not generous, for I know you have bought me all manner of clothes, and—'

'But not without you reminding me that you needed them,' interrupted Claud, with a rueful look. He took a swig of ale and set down the tankard.

'That is exactly it,' declared Kitty, pleased to find him of so ready an understanding. 'It is what you do all the time. I dare say you don't mean to be so selfish, but the truth is, Claud, that you think of nothing but your own needs.'

He sighed, dragging his fingers through his short gold locks. 'Thing is, Kitty, never had to think of anyone but myself. Can see I'll have to mend my ways.'

Kitty could not but be gratified, although she had grave doubts of Claud's ability to do so. She must suppose the habit to be so ingrained that nothing short of constant nagging was likely to change it. Still, it was something that he was willing to try.

'Hadn't really thought it through, this marrying business,' he said musingly, as he set about carving a ham.

'Thought it through? No, indeed. Nor I, if it comes to that.'

'Have to make a few changes in my way of life.' He laid a couple of slices on Kitty's plate, and shifted his attention to a large bird that flanked the ham. 'Would you like some chicken?'

'A little, if you please. What sort of changes?'

'Was thinking about the London place, for a start. Ought to move. Find a little house in a good part of town.'

The words brought Kitty hurtling back to reality. The remembrance of the painful wonderings of the night came in on her, and she spoke her mind without pause for thought.

'What is the use of thinking of it? Once the scandal has broken, I will not be able to show my face in town!' She laid down the knife and fork she had but just taken up. 'Claud, you said you had not thought it through and that is nothing less than the truth. It is just what kept me awake last night. We are making a terrible mistake!'

'No, we ain't. Best thing we could do.'

'How can it be the best thing? If the horrid notion you had of me last night has any foundation, there is nothing but shame and scandal ahead of us.'

Claud remained unmoved, merely laying a couple of chicken slices on to her plate and adjuring her to eat. 'No sense in fretting in any event, Kitty, for there ain't nothing to be done about it now.'

'Yes, there is,' Kitty insisted. 'You may still take me back to Paddington, and no one will be the wiser.'

'That's flimflam, Kitty. Besides—'

'No, hear me out! I know that you are supposed to have compromised me by my staying in your lodging, and that it is not at all acceptable to have been unchaperoned in your company for two days—'

'Three.'

'Three, then,' conceded Kitty, too urgent to argue. 'But apart from your servants, no one knows of it. I am sure they will not betray you, and I shall say nothing at all of the matter for it would not serve me to do so. And if you are thinking of the Duck, I shall make up a tale that will satisfy her, just as you suggested.' She smiled a little uncertainly. 'I have had occasion to invent tales before, you know, and it will not be so very difficult to devise a reason for my absence—and for the things you have given me.' She noted that inflexible look about Claud's mouth, and knew that she was making no impression upon him. 'Claud, pray don't look like that! You must see that this escapade is impossible. Let us put an end to it—now, before it really does become too late.'

That chin was jutting dangerously. 'And what will become of you, Kitty? With all that you now know—and don't know—can you really want to go back?'

'I must,' she said resolutely. 'I shall become a governess, just as they intended, and who would care?'

'I would.'

Kitty gazed at him dumbly. A faint tattoo disturbed the rhythm in her veins. 'Why, Claud?'

He uttered a short laugh. 'Use your head, Kitty! How could I rest easy in my conscience if I returned you to Paddington with nothing said, after all that has passed?'

'But why should it matter to you? You scarcely know me!'

'Matter of fact, I probably know you better than I might a débutante I'd met half a dozen times at parties through the season. All too often the case in my circle. In any event, no point in discussing it, for I ain't going to change my mind. Besides, we are practically halfway to Gretna already.'

For a few moments, Kitty said nothing more, partaking almost without noticing of the chicken Claud had laid upon her plate. Why could he not see how impossible this union was? She was mad to have agreed to it. And now it did indeed seem to be too late, if they had really come so far upon the journey. How could Claud take so lightly the possible hideous nature of her past? It was apparently of no importance to him. Yet he was insistent upon the marriage. She could not understand it.

'I've been thinking, Kitty,' announced Claud abruptly.

'What about?' she asked listlessly.

'Your background, of course.'

Kitty gave an inward sigh. Must he begin upon that? It was hardly worthwhile to protest, for she had no doubt it would make no difference to him that she did not wish to talk of it.

Shoving away his plate, Claud looked over the other dishes for a sweet. 'Have to face it that it may have nothing to do with either of my aunts. You might be out of cousins on my uncle Rothley's side, which could account for Aunt Silvia being upset.'

It was an idea Kitty had already discarded. 'Surely your mother would not then have troubled herself to hush it up?'

'Oh, wouldn't she?' Claud picked up a glass dish and inspected its contents. 'Anything that smacked of scandal, as long as it touched on any member of a family that had to do with her own, would be enough for the Countess to interfere. You don't know her, Kitty. Trust me, she'd not let one of us cross the line if she had breath left to expostulate!'

Kitty's little appetite had left her. She moved her plate to one side, the chicken hardly touched. All the dread of her future crowded in upon her, and the thought of her nuptials at the end of this journey oppressed her unendurably. She shook her head when Claud offered her the fruit bowl, and watched him partake of a syllabub as if he had not a care in the world. She was hardly aware of speaking.

'It seems to me that my past is nothing but an enigma and will remain so.'

Claud looked up from the glass dish that held his half-finished sweet. A light in his eyes glittered oddly.

'Not for long. The Countess is bound to kick up the deuce of a dust when she finds out I've married you, and we are certain to discover the truth.' A note of exultance entered his voice. 'Can't wait to see her face! Kick up a dust? She's going to pull hell up from the nether regions and loose it upon the earth. And, by Gad, I'll enjoy every moment of it! If I'd thought till Domesday, I couldn't have come up with a more perfect revenge.'

A weight of depression settled upon Kitty's spirits. At last she understood Claud's fixed resolve. The scandal that she feared was for him a weapon. A tool to serve his lust for vengeance. That was his only reason for marrying her. She was to have her wish. She would marry a lord and achieve her ambition. But at what price?

Arrayed in the new spangled gown, in which all her pleasure had been destroyed, Miss Katherine Merrick vowed herself to Claud Cheddon, Viscount Devenick, on a sunny Thursday afternoon, three days into the month of June. The bridegroom graced the ceremony in black breeches and a blue cloth coat that admirably set off his eyes and lent a vibrancy to his golden locks that induced in the bride an unaccountable desire to weep. The wedding was celebrated in the parlour of the Queen's Head in Springfield, a mile or two short of Gretna Green village, before one David Laing, one of the dubious priests that abounded in the area.

The ceremony passed in a haze for Kitty, and after a quick glass of wine to celebrate her nuptials, she found herself once more in the curricle, heading back towards Carlisle. Reckoning up the days, Kitty discovered that almost a week had passed since Claud had encountered her on Paddington Green. It was hardly possible that she was now Viscountess Devenick, and she started when Docking addressed her as *my lady*. The golden band upon the third finger of her left hand—which Claud had had the forethought to purchase in Doncaster—was the only thing that gave her new status reality, and Kitty kept feeling for it under her glove, as if to reassure herself that she truly had taken this fatal step.

If she was indeed Lady Devenick, there was no change to convince her in the treatment she received from the man whom she must now call husband. Would she wake up in her narrow bed at home in the Seminary and discover that it had all been a dream? Home! The word caught at her. Where was she to call home now? Claud had spoken of houses in Oxfordshire. Were they headed there? Or to London? No, for had he not said that the season was ended? If he was to confront his mother, he must travel to her. She sought enlightenment.

'Where are we going?'

Claud cast her an indifferent glance. 'Brightwell. We'll take the same route back, and turn off at Stamford. Shouldn't take more than three days to make Oxfordshire. Mind you, that would get us there on Sunday and I've no wish to run into the vicar. Countess often invites the fellow round after church. Four days then, and we'll aim to be at Brightwell Prior on Monday.'

Four days! And then she must face Lady Blakemere. The horrid thought struck her that the Countess was now her mother-in-law. Oh, what had she done? But it was useless to bewail what could not be mended. She must make the best of it. And to say truth, if she must be married to someone who only wished for it for selfish reasons of his own, then it was better to have found a peer of the realm. Claud had said she might spend as she chose, and there would be comfort in acquiring pretty gowns.

But her attempts to find things to be thankful for ended abruptly when the curricle drew into the yard of the Kings Arms at Temple Sowerby and it suddenly came to Kitty that, if she was married, she would be expected to inhabit her husband's bed.

Chapter Six

Kitty's stomach knotted, and she could barely find strength to climb down from the vehicle. She released Claud's guiding hand at once, and walked ahead of him into the inn, gripped by rising terror.

'Two bedchambers, if you please. And have the lady of the house take my wife up to hers at once.'

The relief at hearing Claud order separate chambers was so intense that Kitty completely missed his allusion to her married state. It was only after a meal during which he was markedly silent, but in no other way different, that it was recalled to Kitty's mind. And that only because of the chambermaid whom she found turning down the bed in her room.

'Will your ladyship be requiring anything further?'

Kitty stared at her. *Your ladyship.* How did she know? And then it came to her what Claud had said. In a sudden rush of realisation, all vestige of hope died. She was not dreaming. It was real. She was Claud's wife. She had been spared tonight, but for how long? Sooner or later, he must wish to beget heirs, and she could do nothing to save herself from the inevitable ordeal.

The thought of the intimacy brought the blood rushing

to her face. She remembered those occasions during the
last two days when Claud had given over the reins to his
groom and taken a rest from driving. He had squeezed up
to make room, quite crowding Kitty. To be pressed so
close to him that she could feel the warmth of his body
all down one side had proven intensely disturbing, sending
unaccountable waves of heat rippling up and down Kitty's
veins. She had been conscious throughout of the hardness
of his thigh against her own, and had been at pains to
introduce topics of discussion that might deflect his attention from her dangerous emotions. Difficult though it was
to converse with that dryness affecting her tongue!

Fortunately, Claud had easily been drawn into reminis-
cence about his father, to whom he was obviously attached. Kitty learned of the Earl's addiction to all things
ancient, and was almost diverted from her physical dis-
comforts by tales that Claud relayed of Lord Blakemere's
visits to foreign climes. It appeared that he was away more
than he was at home, and it was not difficult to divine,
from Claud's utterances, that this was in a measure due to
the coldness in the character of the Countess. A reflection
that only added to Kitty's apprehensions.

She dismissed the maid, who had flitted about the room,
drawing the curtains and tidying away the cover she had
taken off the bed, and began to ready herself for the night.
The spangled gown, its lustre undimmed, yet failed to raise
a spark of comfort in her breast as she removed it and laid
it in the portmanteau. With automatic motions, she brushed
out her long black locks until they gleamed. She dallied,
preparing the white muslin gown for tomorrow, and finding excuses to prolong her toilet.

But the inevitable climb between sheets brought the
memories to the surface. Long-buried, they rose up to taunt
her now, with their dreaded groans of agony, the writhing

bodies that had accompanied the hateful coupling in the bedchambers of that place where she had spent her earliest years.

She remembered creeping along the corridors where the ladies slept, and finding half-open doors and stealthy sounds within that drew her like a magnet. And then she saw them. Entangled in the bed with a gentleman atop, who punished and pummelled and shunted, emitting angry grunts, while the suffering female cried out in agony, begging in vain for mercy. She had fled that day, and passed another room where, by the movement and noise that came from within, exactly the same thing was happening.

Thereafter, when the sounds had come in the night—the cries of agony, and the horrid squeaking of the bed-springs—Kitty had buried her head under the pillows so that she need not hear. But the sounds had echoed down the years, until she had learned that this was how a man would treat his wife to come by his children.

The shock had been severe. Kitty's ambitious dreams had faltered for a time, cursed by the horrid punishment of the marriage bed. Only she had allowed herself to forget! And here she was, uncompromisingly a wife. And married to a man who had shown himself on occasion a merciless brute. Kitty had no notion why he should delay, but she was desperately thankful. Only for how long could it last?

The final leg of the journey was to Claud interminable. With each mile that brought him closer to the culmination of his scheme, the knot of anticipation within him tightened. He developed a trick of touching the broadcloth coat of sober blue—worn over his buckskins in a half-conscious attempt to lend a note of solemnity to the frivolity of his elopement—where that inner pocket safely concealed his marriage lines, the incontrovertible proof with which he would confound the Countess.

Driving through the familiar Oxfordshire country by a route he had frequently taken required little of his concentration. Which left his thoughts to turn constantly upon what awaited him at Brightwell Prior. By this time the family would be firmly entrenched, disturbing his father, who had not once come to London during the season, sending first one excuse and then another. Poor Papa! His peace was at an end.

For the first time it occurred to Claud to wonder what Lord Blakemere's reaction might be to his son's unorthodox marriage. Not that his opinion counted for anything. But Claud would be sorry to grieve his sire. Only he did not think his father would care one way or the other, provided he was not dragged into the brouhaha that must infallibly ensue. A lost cause. When the Countess found her son adamant, she would put the screws on her husband to try and force his hand.

But what could his father do, after all? He could scarcely disinherit him. Nor could he put him under a financial squeeze, since Claud's income derived from the Shillingford estates, and was considerable. The turnover had been done with all legal entitlements, and there was no retrieving it to Lord Blakemere's use. A factor which might have weighed with Claud in other circumstances. As things stood, he had been independent from the day his father had turned Shillingford over to him. Much to the Countess's chagrin. But her emotions then, he recalled, were as nothing to what she was about to experience!

The exultance rushed up again, until he could barely contain it. He owned himself thoroughly affected, to a point where his appetite had deserted him when they made their last stop for luncheon. He noted that Kitty was also having trouble eating. Indeed, she had been looking peaky since the wedding. He had been too wrapped up in his own thoughts to see it. Was that what she meant by selfishness? He would make it up to her, once the initial blast at his mother was over. For now, he was too wound up to be capable of seeing to her needs. Kitty must wait.

The approach to Brightwell Prior took him past the village of Brightwell, where the Rothley cousins lived, and he had a mild instant of sympathy for his aunt Silvia. Would she swoon all over again when she heard of it?

And then all speculation was swallowed up by the heat of anticipation that almost overwhelmed him. Despite all his loathing of the Countess, he could not repress a resurgence of that dreadful feeling that had attacked him whenever, as a child, he was sent for to her private sitting room. He slowed the curricle for the turn past the small lodge where the gatekeeper dwelled, and felt his heart begin to hammer in his chest as he picked up speed again and started up the long drive towards the mansion.

The grey stone building came into sight behind the trees, its familiar outline thrusting high and wide. It was one of the more considerable of the Blakemere mansions, and its many rooms had been home to Claud for most of his childhood. He swallowed painfully. Glancing at Kitty, he saw his own inevitable apprehension magnified in her set, white features. Seeing it, his trepidation abated.

'Don't look so terrified! I won't let anyone harm you, never fear.'

She looked round at him, a wavering smile on her lips. 'I suppose they cannot kill me, but that is the best you can say.'

Claud found himself laughing, and exhilaration swept through him. This was his moment! 'We'll beat her yet, Kitty! She can't win this one!'

The great front doors were soon within sight. Claud slowed the curricle, and with all the business of alighting and helping Kitty to come down, he lost track of his triumph for a few moments. But all too shortly, his mother's butler was opening the door to him, the little smile of welcome fading at sight of the female at Claud's side. He drew Kitty into the massive hall, with its cumbersome stairway leading to the gallery above, and lost no time in throwing his news at the fellow's head.

'This is Lady Devenick, Vellow. You'll be surprised, no doubt, but we were married a few days ago.'

The butler was bowing to Kitty, his astonishment, if he felt any, swiftly concealed. 'May I welcome you to Brightwell Prior, my lady.'

'Vellow has been with the family forever, haven't you, old fellow?' Claud announced carelessly to Kitty.

'With the Littons, my lord,' the butler reminded him. 'I came to Lady Lydia when my mistress became the Dowager Duchess of Litton, my lady.'

'He means my grandmother. Countess at home, Vellow?'

The butler turned back to the son of the house. 'Indeed, my lord. Also Lady Silvia and Lord Rothley, together with—'

Claud cut him short, consternation gripping him. 'The devil! Both of them together? And my cousin too?'

'Most of your cousins, my lord. It is quite a family party.'

'You don't mean it! Confound it, who else is here?'

He cast a harassed glance at Kitty's face. She looked aghast, as well she might. The last thing he had expected was to introduce her to the family at large!

'The Hevershams, my lord, along with your lordship's

sister, Lady Katherine, together with Mr Wilkhaven. Lady
Mary has not yet arrived.'

Claud exploded. 'Hang it, why the deuce must they all
come now?'

The butler's brows rose, and then comprehension appeared in his eyes. 'Your lordship having been otherwise
occupied, you may not yet be aware that Lady Barbara's
betrothal was announced this week.'

'Was it, by Jupiter?'

'The gathering is by way of a celebration, my lord.'

Claud found Kitty at his side, an imploring look in the
brown eyes. 'Pray, Claud, could we not go away again?'

It was tempting, but it would not do. He had not come
all this way to be thwarted at the last moment! Besides,
he did not think his emotions would stand any further delay. It was unfortunate, but it could not be helped.

'No sense in that,' he said, catching her lightly about
the shoulders. 'You'll do, Kitty, never fear. Probably a
dashed good thing, now I think about it. She can't ring a
peal over me with the whole family watching. All got to
know sooner or later. Might as well be now.'

Kitty looked as if she might run away. Her voice was a
thread. 'I don't think I can do it, Claud.'

He hugged her to him. 'Yes, you can. I'm with you.
And they can't blame you, after all.' He put her away from
him and looked her over. Apart from her pallid skin, she
looked devilishly pretty. She had shed her cloak and hat
into Vellow's hands, and the muslin gown with its dainty
black spots became her well, showing off a comely figure.
The black hair, which she had tidied at the last halt in
preparation, fell in ordered curls down her back. Claud
gave her an encouraging smile.

'You look well enough, if it weren't for your white face!

No one is going to notice that, though, so don't fret yourself into flinders over it.'

Kitty had no thought to spare for what she looked like. It had been bad enough to be obliged to face Lady Blakemere. To walk in on the whole of Claud's family—her family!—was a nightmare. Her knees were shaking and she could barely walk as Claud led her inexorably towards the door of the drawing room where the butler had said most of the family were assembled.

She wished with all her heart that she'd had the courage to reject Claud's proposals; that she had never begun upon the business of the spangled gown that had landed her in this mess. Indeed, she wished that she had not been sitting on the fence that day in Paddington Green when fate had shown its ugly hand and dragged her into the mire. For mire it was. Whatever awaited her on the other side of that closed door, no dreamed of expectation could have prepared her for the worst moment of her life.

The door opened. Upon a background of overwhelming blue, swam a sea of faces. Already there was shock and bewilderment spreading rapidly across them. Kitty distinctly heard the voice of the butler who had let them in.

'Lord and Lady Devenick, my lady.'

Clinging for dear life to Claud's arm, all thought swallowed up in fright, Kitty stepped into the room.

There was a moment of utter silence. And then a shrill scream rent the air, and pandemonium broke out.

It felt like one of those dreams where one was powerless to move as everything turned in a whirlwind about one, when the mind was fogged and all it contained was both real and unreal at once. Kitty was aware of being in a small room where the furnishings were shabby and worn, but the twittering of the young ladies who had accompanied her up the stairs was meaningless. Time seemed to have frozen, leaving her mentally back in the mass of silver and blue that was the drawing room, in the centre of a maelstrom.

There were people in motion, crossing and re-crossing before her eyes, while the hubbub of sobs, bewilderment and protests in many voices made it impossible to make out a word. She had taken in the fat aunt she had once seen, whose noisy weeping perhaps added most to the cacophony, and there had been the other woman, sheet white and staring—a woman of imposing stature with grey hair whose eyes had made her shiver. Claud's voice had come close at hand, in hot argument with an older man standing nearby. Kitty had clutched his arm the more strongly, fearful of losing the only hold she had upon familiarity.

And then the mirror of her own features was before her and she recognised Kate. Claud was turning, speaking in an earnest undervoice.

'Get Kitty out of this! Babs, go with her. Find somewhere quiet.'

He had prized her fingers from his arm, and Kitty had been ushered between two whispering females out of the hideous crowd, away across the wide hall and up an imposing stairway. In no condition either to prevent this abduction or to mark the way, and feeling utterly bereft at the loss of her one support in this dreadful place, Kitty had traversed willy-nilly several corridors and another back stair before ending up in this place of relative calm.

'This used to be our nursery,' announced the girl Kitty did not know, releasing her and leading the way into the cramped room. 'Sit down, do. Poor thing, I should think you must be wholly overset!'

An understatement. But Kitty had not strength enough yet to say so. Only when she was seated, with Kate beside

her and the other female plonking down into a chair opposite was it borne in upon Kitty that there was yet another
girl with them, hovering by the door as if she was not sure
of her welcome. Kitty's directed gaze drew the attention
of her companions.

'Tess, what are you doing here?' demanded Kate.

'Well, I did not know where else to go,' uttered the other
in a hushed tone, moving forward into the nursery, her
eyes moving from Kate to Kitty and back again, alive with
curiosity. 'With Mama crying all over Ralph, and everyone
screeching so, I thought I had best come away.'

'Yes, but there is no need to come in here. Claud wants
the poor thing to have quiet—at least until the hoo-ha has
died down.'

'Oh, let her stay,' interrupted the fair girl sitting opposite, who was drinking in the amazing likeness with just
as much interest. 'It is useless now to try and keep anyone
out, and I am sure Tess is dying to know just as much as
I am.'

'Oh, very well,' agreed Kate grudgingly, 'but you are
not to start questioning her. I am sure nothing could be
more horrid than to be confronted with all of us at once.'

With this Kitty found herself to be in complete agreement. The sensation of clouds in her head was abating a
little, and she roused herself to ask a pertinent question of
the fair girl opposite.

'Pray, which of Claud's relatives are you?'

'How stupid of me,' uttered Kate. 'I am so sorry, Miss
Merrick—' She broke off, her brown eyes round. 'Oh,
dear, but you are not Miss Merrick any more! Had I best
call you Katherine then?'

'I am Kitty. Call me Kitty.'

'Of course, yes, I had forgotten. Kitty it is.'

The fair girl stared. 'But how is it that you know her at

all, Kate? Why did Claud turn to you? I knew you had a secret between you! Fie, Kate! It is no use keeping it now. You must tell us everything.'

'Babs, pray hush a moment. Let poor Kitty catch her breath at least. Why don't you send for tea?' Kate turned to Kitty again. 'You would like tea, I dare say. It will revive you, I'm sure.'

The fair girl had risen, showing to advantage a gown over gown of exquisite cut, perfectly fitted to her trim figure. The round gown was of the ubiquitous white muslin, while the overgown was made up in a clear blue with a pleated bodice and a short train. Kitty eyed the ensemble with envy as Babs tugged upon the bell-pull by the fireplace.

'You need not think, just because I'm ordering tea, Kate, that I won't press Kitty for the whole story, for I could not bear not to do so. Besides, since she is clearly my sister-in-law, I have every right to demand to hear it.'

The fair locks, prettily caught up at the back and curling about a face that became abruptly familiar, impinged upon Kitty's consciousness. She spoke without thinking.

'You must be Claud's sister. You are very like him.'

'Not as like as you and Kate,' retorted the girl.

'Babs!' chided Kate. 'Kitty, forgive my tardiness, but this is Babs. Lady Barbara, if you must have her proper title. And that is my sister Theresa—Tess as she is known.'

Kitty's eyes turned to Tess, who stared back unselfconsciously. She had uttered no word since she had explained her appearance, but she did not look to be of the retiring type. She was attired in the demure frock of a schoolgirl, but the white muslin was of fashionable cut and style. Only vaguely alike to Kate, Tess had hair of a much lighter brown and eyes of grey, or perhaps a light blue. But there was a mischievous look about her, which Kitty, experienced in the ways of girls in their teens, immediately recognised.

Her attention was drawn back to Babs, who had reseated herself and was leaning eagerly forward. 'Now, pray tell! How is it you come to look just like Kate? It is an extraordinary likeness, but why did everyone react in such a mad fashion?'

Kitty shrunk back in the sofa, loath to begin upon explanations that could only lead to more questions.

'Kate, did you know they were to be married, you sly thing?' chimed in Tess.

'I most certainly did not,' declared her sister, 'and if you wish to remain in here, Tess, you had best hold your tongue.'

'Fie, Kate, you can't blame poor Tess,' protested Babs. 'Here is Kitty—another Katherine, if you please!—looking exactly like you, and turning out to be my sister-in-law, when it's plain as a pikestaff she is already related to us in another fashion.'

Kitty swallowed. It was out. They had held back from saying it. But was it not exactly what was being said in that big drawing room downstairs? She drew a breath.

'The truth is I don't know any more than you do. It was—it was all an accident, you see.' Two pairs of eyes gazed at her expectantly. Only Kate, who already knew this history, looked on with a silent frown. 'Claud saw me sitting on a fence in Paddington, and he took me for Kate. He insisted on bringing me back to London. But when—when we arrived at...'

She could not go on, and only looked imploringly at Kate, who, to her intense gratitude and relief, reached out and squeezed her hand, and then took up the tale.

'You may imagine how astonished I was, but when I

saw the effect it had upon Mama, it all became at once very serious.'

'What effect?' demanded Babs.

'She nearly swooned. And then she said that Aunt Lydia would be horrified, and there would be a dreadful scandal, and she insisted that Claud must take Kitty back to Paddington to the Seminary.'

'Seminary?' queried Tess.

'It's a school for orphans, I believe. They turn them into governesses.'

Babs blinked. 'Why didn't Claud take her back there? Why marry her instead?'

Kate shook her head. 'I know nothing more. Except that the same evening, at the Chale ball, when I tried to ask Claud whether he had taken her back, he evaded the question. Now I can see why, but at the time I just assumed he had done so.'

'Then he must have already made up his mind to the marriage,' guessed Babs. 'I recall that he was secretive that night.'

'As for why he married her, you must ask Kitty,' stated Kate, 'if she will tell you. If I had to guess, I can only suppose he did it to prevent Mama and Aunt Lydia from forcing him to marry me.'

The other two stared, looking from Kate to Kitty and back again. Kitty could not help glancing round at the girl who wore her face. Despite the likeness, it was incredible that she had ever been mistaken for the elegant creature beside her. In a chemise gown of delicate yellow, with sleeves to the elbow criss-crossed by ribbon, Kate looked a deal more fashionable than Kitty in her spotted muslin. Indeed, she felt distinctly out of place and was relieved when Babs broke the silence.

'But what would be the point of avoiding marriage with you, Kate, when Kitty is the living spit of you?'

'Especially as he didn't wish to marry you in the least,' piped up Tess.

'Nor I he, if it comes to that.'

'It doesn't sound like Claud to me,' Babs objected. 'He is so stubborn, and he said he would not let Mama make him marry you, Kate, remember? I particularly asked him about it, too.'

Tess's features abruptly lit with excitement. 'Perhaps he *did* wish to marry you, Kate. And finding you set against him, he married Kitty as a substitute!'

Babs poured scorn upon this frivolous suggestion, and her sister begged her not to put forward nonsensical suggestions. Kate then glanced at Kitty, apology in her face.

'I beg your pardon. This must be painful for you, but perhaps you know more?'

Kitty perceived that all three young ladies had now turned back to her for enlightenment. She was feeling a degree less disorientated, but she did not know if she was up to giving them the history of her elopement. Nor could she feel that Claud's true motive would meet with approbation. Besides, she had no means of knowing what he would counsel her to do. She did not know where he was at this moment. Nor when she would be reunited with him. Or if perhaps the lady of the house would find a means of keeping them apart.

This last thought proved so unpalatable that Kitty stood up. 'I must find Claud!'

Kate pulled her down again. 'You had best stay here. One of us will presently go in search of him. Ah, here is the maid come in answer to the bell.'

Babs jumped up. 'Fetch us a tea tray, if you please. Three cups.' She turned and counted. 'No, four. Oh, and bring cakes or some such thing. Are you hungry, Kitty? I should think you must be.'

The maid withdrew, and Kitty found herself once more under scrutiny.

'Now, then,' said Babs.

Kitty spread helpless hands. 'I don't know what to tell you.'

'Fie, Kitty, everything! How you are related to us and why Claud was so mad, and—'

'Hush, Babs,' protested Kate. 'Tell us only what you feel you can, Kitty.'

Kitty sighed. 'The truth is that I don't know how we are related. Claud and I have gone over the possibilities, and they are all of them horrid!'

'I should imagine they are. That is the sport of it!' exclaimed Babs delightedly. 'I wonder how we could find out more? Still, even if we are related in some other fashion, I at least welcome you into the family, Kitty, if you are indeed Claud's wife.'

'Well, we did make our vows at Gretna, so I suppose I must be.'

'Then no one can dispute that!' said Tess with satisfaction.

'Yes, and I know Claud has the certificate,' averred Kitty, gaining confidence, 'for he means to show it to the Countess.'

'Capital!' approved Babs. 'If he has proof, the matter is beyond even Mama's power to change.'

Lady Blakemere would not have agreed with her.

Claud faced his mother across the large expanse of carpet that separated them in her sparsely furnished sitting room. There was a *chaise-longue* in the window, a desk against the inner wall, and a few straight chairs judiciously placed. The walls were plain, adorned with one portrait, of Lady Blakemere's mother, the Dowager Duchess of Litton, and two landscapes taken from the Earl's principal estate. Its simple severity was, and—so Claud believed— was intended to be, intimidating.

The Countess had taken up a commanding position by the mantelpiece, as had been her invariable habit whenever one of her offspring was called before her for the purpose of chastisement. The unfortunate victim was made to stand in the middle of the carpet, in a position exposed and vulnerable, while the homily was read that preceded the infliction of the rod.

Well aware of her tactics, Claud had refused to co-operate, firmly planting himself at the other end of the room between two chairs where he had the wall behind him. He folded his arms and awaited her pleasure, triumph hot within him.

The moment had been all he had anticipated and more. He was persuaded that it had been fully a minute while the Countess had been struck dumb. The blood had drained visibly from her face, leaving it with an unaccustomed pallor that would remain forever etched in his memory. But the supreme victory had been the utter incredulity in her eyes. Those bleak and loveless eyes, whose contempt had filled his soul with hatred.

They were no longer unbelieving, and she had recovered her poise. She had lost it only briefly, but it had been enough to give Claud the most profound satisfaction. What was more, it had dispersed the entirety of his apprehension. In five and twenty years, he had never seen her remotely disconcerted until that moment. The blow had struck hard, and her vulnerability, however ephemeral, gave him strength. He felt ready for anything she might throw at him.

The dumbfounded look had turned to cold fury, but the recognition had not dented Claud's courage. Rather it had elevated it. He was ripe for battle! He had watched her first turn to speak to his aunt, and then lost sight of her as his uncle Heversham had come up to him, his voice an undertone of annoyance.

'What the devil have you done, you young fool? Have you taken leave of your senses? You crass idiot, Devenick!'

Claud had turned on him. 'Save your breath, sir! It has nothing to do with you. And I'll thank you to keep your insulting remarks to yourself!'

His uncle had looked nearly as astonished as his mother, and Claud had almost been betrayed into a laugh. Heversham had moved away, heading purposefully for the Countess, and it had been borne in upon Claud then that the whole family was in uproar. Discomfort in the region of his forearm pulled his attention round to Kitty, and he saw the bewilderment in her face. Looking about in an unconscious bid for assistance, he had caught Kate's eye and jerked his head to bring her over.

With Kitty out of harm's way, he was able to turn his attention to the havoc he had wrought, and had found the Countess moving in on him.

'You will attend me in my sitting room immediately, Devenick.'

He had bowed, and he hoped the irony of it had not escaped her. 'As your ladyship pleases.'

She had swept from the room, and Claud had cast a glance around the place. The various relatives remaining were engaged in hot discussion in little clusters throughout the room. A gloating satisfaction engulfed him. He had put the cat among the pigeons! Let them try and find a way out of this. For himself, he felt upheld by having justice

on his side. Kitty had been made outcast by persons in this
room, along with his mother. Let them take the consequences!

Outside, he had nevertheless thankfully closed the door
upon the hubbub and had paused as he saw the Countess
check by Vellow in the hall ahead.

'Request his lordship to join me in my sitting room, if
you please. As a matter of urgency, Vellow. You may say
as much.'

Only then had it occurred to Claud that his father had
not been present. Had he had time to think about it, this
would not have surprised him. Such a gathering was exactly what Lord Blakemere most disliked. But the Countess had called upon him! Reinforcements? That was a rare
occurrence. His sense of triumph intensified as he climbed
the stairs. It must mean that the Countess knew not how
to tackle this affair.

He reached Lady Blakemere's sitting room but a bare
moment behind her, but long enough for her to establish
herself in her position of avenging motherhood. She was,
as ever, immaculate, the dove-grey silk enhanced by an
expensive Norwich shawl retied twice and fastened below
the bosom. A neat cap half covered her abundant grey
locks and about her throat were twisted the pearls her husband had brought back from one of his expeditions.

Claud took up an opposing stance and thrust out his
chin.

The opening volley was tame. 'Well, Devenick?'

'Well, ma'am?' riposted Claud.

'I am waiting for you to explain yourself.'

'Don't follow you, ma'am,' said Claud in a puzzled
tone.

Her eyes narrowed. 'I think you follow me very well.'

Claud met the steel gaze and waited again. There was

a thankless pause. Lady Blakemere shifted her ground and regrouped.

'Am I to understand that you have married this girl?'

He was ready for that. 'Perfectly correct. Would you care to see my marriage lines?'

'Issued at Gretna Green, no doubt?' There was scorn in her voice. 'I think not.'

Claud shifted one foot over the other and leaned back at his ease. He saw rage flicker in the Countess's eyes and revelled in it. She straightened up abruptly, abandoning her accustomed affectation.

'You will oblige me, Devenick, by informing me exactly where you met the girl and the circumstances that led you to taking so disastrous a step.'

He pretended blankness. 'Disastrous? Don't take your ladyship's meaning. In what way disastrous?'

Balked, Lady Blakemere shot him a look that would have withered him in the past. Claud met it blandly. She turned away from him and moved to the window. He could scarcely believe it. Never had she turned her back upon him in an interview such as this. She did not know what to do!

The hiatus proved only momentary. She turned her head, her features set. 'You have not answered me. Where did you meet her?'

Claud said it with all the deliberation at his command. 'Paddington.'

A muscle rippled in her cheek, but her gaze did not waver. 'Go on.'

He shrugged. 'Well, that's it, ma'am. Took her for my cousin Kate and brought her back to the Haymarket.' He permitted a faint frown to crease his brow. 'Can't think why my aunt Silvia didn't mention it to you.'

This proved too much for her. 'Can you not indeed?

Don't fence with me, Claud!' She swept round and crossed halfway towards him, spitting fury. 'How dared you do this? How *dared* you! You may cease this ridiculous pretence. If you took the girl to the Haymarket, you must be all too aware of the precarious nature of her position. It is inconceivable to me that Silvia would not have instantly given herself away, just as she did downstairs. Of course she did not tell me! Fool that she is. Else I might have nipped this in the bud.'

Claud watched her parading up and down, her poise shattered. It was evident that she was barely able to speak for the fury that choked her. Unholy glee enwrapped him. How much it made up for those all too frequent occasions, here in this room, when she had utterly routed him. How good it was to watch her stew! If his marriage proved indeed disastrous, he would compound with fate for a lifetime of misery just to have experienced this moment. And Kitty had given it to him. His heart swelled with gratitude.

The door opened and Claud looked to find his father's features peering around it, bespectacled, the blonde wisps of faded hair about his head awry as usual. When he saw his son, his face lit and he entered the room. A spare man, Lord Blakemere was habited in the country attire he favoured, in a mulberry frock-coat over buckskins, a striped waistcoat his only concession to fashion—and that outdated.

Claud crossed to him and put his hands into the ones held out in welcome.

'My dear boy! It's good to see you.'

Claud returned the pressure of his fingers. 'And you, sir.'

Lady Blakemere's icy tones cut across the reunion. 'I trust you will still think so, Blakemere, when you hear of Devenick's lunacy.'

The light died out of his father's face, and a pained expression entered it. 'Lunacy, my dear? Surely not.'

It was, Claud knew, his defence against his wife to be ever mild in manner. If his son suspected that Lord Blakemere was not always as bewildered by events as he appeared, he kept it to himself. He watched his father's leisurely progress across the room with affection in his breast, hardly hearing the indictment that issued from the Countess's lips.

'He has defied every precept of common sense, and married—'

'Married? Do you say so, indeed? *Married*, Claud?'

'Yes, sir, I was married last Thursday.'

'He was married at Gretna Green, of all vulgar things, and to a female with neither birth nor breeding, who is, as you will readily discover the moment you look at her, the subject of an episode in this family that I had considered closed beyond recall.'

Blakemere appeared unmoved. 'Which female, my dear? Should I know her?'

His wife had difficulty in controlling herself. 'I must request you, Blakemere, to have a little sense! Of course you do not know her. But that is neither here nor there. You must intervene, Blakemere. I assure you, it will not do.'

The Earl blinked under his spectacles, flicking a glance towards Claud and back to his wife's face. 'But if he is married, my dear, I fail to see—'

'Believe me, he will not be married long!'

Claud strode forward. 'Believe me, I will, sir!'

'Be quiet, Devenick! Blakemere, the marriage must be set aside. You will arrange it.'

The Earl blinked again. 'Set aside? My dear, I think you mistake me for the Archbishop of Canterbury.'

Claud was obliged to bite down upon a laugh. For one gleeful moment, he thought the Countess was indeed going to succumb to an apoplexy. Her features grew crimson, and she was clearly choking on hot words that had risen to her tongue. Would she break the habit of a lifetime and annihilate her spouse in public? Such an exhibition was of all things what she most despised. Discretion was all in all to her.

It was evidently a severe struggle, but Lady Blakemere managed to get the better of her spleen. Abandoning her spouse for worthier prey, she turned on Claud again.

'Leave us, Devenick! But do not imagine for one moment that this is the last you will hear from me on this subject.'

Claud bowed. 'I have no such sanguine expectation, ma'am.'

His mother glared at him. 'Get out!'

He bowed again, and strolled to the door in as nonchalant a fashion as he could, where he turned and addressed himself to his father. 'I will seek out my wife, sir. Later, perhaps you would care to be presented to her in form?'

'Dear me!' uttered the Earl. 'Yes, we had better meet her. Don't you think so, my dear?'

Claud left the room, hearing the Countess explode into speech before he had properly shut the door. Not for the first time, he experienced a pang of sympathy for his sire. Yet he knew the Earl had his own armour. For himself, the whole situation had paid undreamed-of dividends. He had vowed to confound the witch, and he had done it. She was by no means at a stand. But he had won the first encounter—and with ease.

He bethought him of Kitty, and went off to find her with an odd leap of delight at his chest. To the victor the spoils!

* * *

The tea, over which the young ladies chattered without cessation, proved efficacious. Kitty began to revive, and was able to answer the pelting questions more in her usual manner. Babs and Tess would have probed deeper into the mystery of her identity had Kate not prevented them, but the circumstance of Claud mistaking her for Kate was entered into, and Kitty was drawn into describing the abduction. Babs and Tess most improperly hooted with laughter—especially at her almost exact imitation of Claud's vocal delivery—but Kitty cut short Kate's chidings.

'To tell you the truth, although I was excessively dismayed at the time, I am happy to be shown that there is a funny side. Indeed, I think I might have ended by laughing over it myself had things not progressed so rapidly in quite another direction.'

'Yes, and how came you to decide to marry Claud upon so short an acquaintance?' demanded Babs.

'Tell us, pray,' begged Tess.

Even Kate could not conceal her curiosity, though she said nothing. Kitty eyed Babs, to whom she felt drawn. Perhaps because she had a look of Claud? And something of his temperament, she thought, as well as his warmth.

She smiled. 'You will laugh, I am afraid, but it all began with a spangled gown.'

She was in the middle of relating this history, which proved too much even for Kate's gravity, when the door opened and Claud himself erupted into the room. Wholly ignoring everyone else, he fastened his eyes upon Kitty.

'There you are! Been looking all over for you.'

A spark leaped in her chest, and she was on her feet, and making her way between the furniture before he had shut the door. 'Claud, thank goodness!'

'Come here to me, my lucky charm of a wife!' he called exuberantly, advancing into the room and holding out his arms. 'You will not believe how I triumphed and it's all thanks to you!'

Kitty reached him on the words, and was astonished to find herself caught up in a convulsive embrace that lifted her right off her feet. The breath was crushed out of her and she experienced a sensation of the most exquisite pleasure that deprived her of all power of thinking. When he put her down, she could only gaze up into features transformed, blue eyes blazing with excitement, strong hands gripping her shoulders.

'She was *appalled*, Kitty! She could barely speak to me! If you thought Aunt Silvia was shocked, you should have seen the Countess. Thought she was going to explode with spleen! Never enjoyed anything so much in my life! Hang it, Kitty, I couldn't be more pleased I found you if I tried till I was blue in the face!'

Dazed by his eloquence, Kitty found herself nevertheless catching his enthusiasm. 'Then you won?'

'Won? I crushed her under my heel!'

Kitty searched the sparkling orbs. 'Do you think she will receive me?'

Claud's grip relaxed, and he laughed. 'Won't have a choice. She don't believe that, mind, but she'll find it ain't a particle of use trying to set the marriage aside, for she won't be able to.'

'Set it aside?' cried Kitty, aghast. 'Is that what she said?'

He nodded, grinning. 'Told m'father he must arrange it. M'father said he ain't the Archbishop of Canterbury. The Countess was as mad as fire. Thought she was going to expire from an apoplexy, but she got over it. Pity, but there it is.'

At this point, they suffered an interruption from Kate. 'Claud, that is a dreadful thing to say!'

In the intense relief of being reunited with Claud, together with the exuberance of his mood, Kitty had forgotten the presence of others in the room. She flushed as he released her and turned to his cousin.

'No, it ain't,' he argued. 'The woman's a she-devil!'

'She is still your mother, and you ought not to speak in such a fashion.'

'Fie, Kate, don't be so stuffy!' begged Babs. 'If you had married Claud and been subjected to Mama's strictures, you would say the same.'

It was borne in upon Claud that the place was packed with the young females of the family, and he bent a severe frown upon them. 'Hope you haven't all been plaguing the life out of Kitty!'

'Of course we have not,' said Babs indignantly. 'Have you forgot that you enjoined Kate and me to take care of her?'

'So I did,' said Claud, unabashed. He shifted to where they were all seated, bringing Kitty willy-nilly behind him by the simple expedient of taking her by the hand. 'And I'm grateful to you.'

'I should think you might be,' put in Kate. 'And to Kitty, since it is perfectly clear why you chose to marry her.'

'Oh, is it?'

'Yes, it is, Claud,' said Babs, frowning. 'Now, at any rate. Indeed, I don't know why I did not think of it for myself, for it is just like you! Only you might have thought of Kitty's comfort when you decided to use her in your battle with Mama.'

A ridiculous sense of loyalty compelled Kitty to intervene. 'Pray don't say so, Babs. It is just as much my fault as his.'

'No, it ain't, Kitty. Most triumphant day of my life, and

I won't have you girls taking the gilt off my gingerbread!
This is my affair, and I'll see it through.'

Both Kate and Babs answered this, talking together so
that neither could be understood. Kitty was relieved when
Claud called a halt.

'Quiet, the pair of you! Both missing the point.'

'Which is?' demanded Babs.

'He means Kitty's likeness to me,' guessed Kate.

'Did Mama tell you—'?

'Don't be a nodcock, Babs! The Countess wouldn't tell
me unless there was no choice. But I'll find it out, never
fear.'

'How?'

'I don't know yet, but you may be sure I'll get it out of
someone, by hook or by crook. Seems to me there's more
people than Aunt Silvia know about it. My uncle Heversham for one. First thing he did was go for me.'

'Did he, indeed?' asked Kate, awed. 'Then it must certainly be a family skeleton.'

'Does Papa know?'

'If your mama does, then he must, Babs,' Kate pointed
out.

'How frustrating it is not to have an inkling!' exclaimed
Babs. 'I declare, the mystery alone might have been
enough to make you marry her, Claud!'

'Only it wasn't, was it?' objected her cousin. 'He married her only to get back at Aunt Lydia, and I think it is
horrid of him.'

Kitty, who had been thoroughly depressed upon recog-
nising this, only a few days since, surprised in herself a
rise of indignation at this censure. Why in the world she
should want to defend Claud she had no notion. Merely
because she was married to him did not change his character. Glancing at his face in the awkward silence that had

fallen, she was dismayed to see that all his earlier effervescence had dissipated in favour of a sulky look.

But young Tess, suddenly entering the lists, threw Kitty's emotions into utter disarray. 'I can't think why you are being so mean to Claud. Why, it is the most romantic thing imaginable!'

'Oh, do be quiet, Tess,' begged Kate. 'You don't know what you're talking about.'

'I know better than you,' averred the fifteen-year-old.

'What can you know of romance at your age?' demanded Babs scornfully.

The mischief was alive in Tess, as she swung round on the newly-wedded pair. 'While you have all been talking, I have been using my eyes. See, they're holding hands. They must be in love!'

Chapter Seven

No two people could have sprung apart more swiftly. At the instant Kitty tried to disengage herself, she found her fingers released as if they were red hot. And the gale of laughter that followed did nothing to relieve her feelings.

'Confound you, young Tess, I could willingly throttle you!' growled Claud.

'Well, but—'

Tess's protest was lost as the door once again opened. Claud turned, still in no little annoyance, to find Lord Rothley on the threshold. Relief swept through him. A more timely entrance could not have been desired! Before he could speak, Kate was up and crossing to her brother at the door.

'Ralph! Has Mama recovered? What is happening down there?'

The Baron entered in a leisurely way and closed the door behind him. 'Mama is closeted with Aunt Lydia in her boudoir. Our uncle Heversham has captured Uncle Blakemere and dragged him off to the library. Aunt Heversham is prostrate upon her bed, I understand. And the rest have sensibly made themselves scarce in double-quick time.'

A trifle of Claud's earlier triumph resurfaced, and he heard the excited exclamations of the girls with growing pleasure at the havoc he had wrought. The greater the uproar, the more the Countess would bring up her batteries against him. But he would be ready for her!

Claud absently watched his sister and cousins huddle in the space between the furniture, their chattering voices subdued for the moment. His attention was claimed by his cousin Ralph, who lifted an eyebrow at him.

'You promised me hell in a tea cup, dear coz, but I never dreamed you meant it! Won't you present me to your bride?'

Claud looked to Kitty, and found her eyes shifting from the female coterie in close conversation to Ralph's remarkably similar features. He almost went to her, but in time recalled that ridiculous assertion made by his young cousin Tess.

'Kitty!'

The brown gaze met his warily. 'Yes?'

'My cousin Ralph. He's Kate's brother and the head of the Rothleys.'

Kitty found herself looking into a face that seemed all too familiar. There was a gleam at this man's brown eyes, which she saw with a little shiver of remembrance, though she could not have met him before. Then he smiled, and the cynical look gave way to one of amusement.

'Well, well. Had I met you as Claud did, I'd not answer for it that I wouldn't have taken you for my sister too.' He held out a hand. 'How d'you do? Not that I need ask. You'd have to be a saint not to sink under the shenanigans Claud has unleashed in this house!'

She took his hand, but was prevented from replying by the expletive issuing from Claud's lips.

'Hang it, Ralph, I'd have thought you at least would

have appreciated the beauty of it all! Am I the only one to wish to see the Countess served in her own coin?'

'She is not, I thank God, my mother,' returned his cousin. 'It has a certain appeal, for all that. If only I had not been chosen for the role of general comforter. Do you realise that I have had my own mother weeping all over my coat? I have no doubt I shall be obliged to listen to no end of wailing and complaint! And this, dear coz, is undoubtedly to be set to your account.'

'Well, I don't care,' said Claud, his chin jutting. 'If she didn't want me to marry the wench, she shouldn't have swooned all over the sofa that day. All she had to do was pretend it was an honest mistake and I would've thought no more about it.'

Such a speech was scarcely designed to afford Kitty gratification. But her reception at Lady Rothley's hands had been so distressing to her that she was inclined to agree with Claud. Only the thought that, instead of being at the centre of a dreadful family upset, she might now be ensconced at the Seminary, forever unknown, had curiously little attraction. The worst of this uproar was better somehow than the best she had known in her lustreless past.

'I suppose you realise,' she heard Ralph drawl, 'that you have stolen your sister Barbara's thunder?'

Consternation spread through Kitty and her eyes went to Babs, who was talking hard with the others. She tried to think of a way to apologise for having ruined her betrothal celebrations, but Claud was before her.

'Babs!'

His sister's pretty features came frowningly over her shoulder. 'What is it, Claud?'

'Ralph has just reminded me that this is supposed to be your betrothal party.' His voice changed and he strode a couple of steps into the room. 'I've just realised what that means! Don't tell me you accepted Chale's youngest after all? Babs, how could you give in so tamely?'

Babs bounced out of the feminine circle. 'You need not be censorious, merely because you have rocked the house to its foundations! As it happens, I changed my mind about him.'

'But you said he had a face like a frog and was tedious beyond words!'

He was pleased to see that his sister looked a little conscious. 'Well, yes, but I discovered that he is dreadfully shy and did not know what to say to me. And I like frogs! Besides, it seems that Lady Chale is nearly as strict as Mama, and this fortune Francis has inherited means that he has an independence *and* an estate. We shall be living miles and miles away from both our families!'

Of all things, Claud could appreciate this. He felt the proximity of Shillingford to Brightwell Prior the more acutely at this moment. There would be no getting away from the Countess's attempts to destroy his marriage. He wondered how long it would be before she was forced to unearth the skeleton and tell him all.

'Oh, and by the way,' cut in Ralph, looking at the girls. 'I forgot to mention that Mary has arrived. Kath asked me to tell you all.'

This intelligence had the effect of breaking up the gathering, all three females shrieking in unison, hot against the oldest of the cousins for not telling them before. In a few moments, the room had emptied, and Claud found himself alone with Kitty. For a moment, he said nothing, feeling all the embarrassment attendant upon that nonsensical notion voiced by Tess. He could not doubt but that Kitty felt it too, for she could scarcely look at him. Impatience threw him into speech.

'Dash it, Kitty, this won't do! You must not mind Tess. She is chock-full of mischief and as silly as a peahen. Can't let her prattle come between us just when we were getting along famously.'

Kitty's large brown eyes came up. 'Were we?'

'Of course we were! Bound to take a bit of getting used to, this business of being married. But I give you my word, it won't make a particle of difference to the way I think of you.'

She was not sure how to take this. How did he think of her? But she was not going to ask him that.

He grinned, a trifle sheepishly. 'Won't be long before you're throwing it at my head again that I'm a selfish brute! I'll try not to be, and I won't let anyone else bully you, on that you may depend.'

A smile wavered on Kitty's lips. 'You may not be able to stop them. Indeed, once you know the truth, you may not wish to.'

'That's flimflam.' He came up to her and groped for one of her hands. 'Whatever happens, I can't be sorry I married you. Told you, I owe you something for today alone. Believe me or believe me not, this has been the best day of my life!'

He dipped his head and his lips touched her fingers. A sliver of emotion whipped about her bosom. But she knew that Claud's triumph had nothing to do with her. She was only the catalyst. Then her hand was released and he was opening the door.

'Come, wife. I'll present you to my two other sisters. Mary and Kath ain't high in the instep and like the rest of the younger element, you'll at least get a welcome from them.' It was a pleasant thought, but was unfortunately followed by one immediately depressing. 'And then we'll beard the Countess and run upon our fate.'

In the event, Kitty was spared a confrontation with Lady Blakemere. Whether the manner of its being denied her was worse than the interview would have been was a moot point. It was certainly humiliating. And it served to set up Claud's back, strengthening his determination.

The ladies Mary and Katherine greeted her pleasantly enough, if with a little reserve. But Kitty did not know whether to be glad or sorry when Claud, choosing a moment when the attention of his sisters had been reclaimed by the younger girls, suggested they should slip away and drew her out of the parlour where the introductions had taken place.

'Ralph says my aunt Silvia is laid down upon her bed, and my uncle Heversham has gone to see his wife,' he said, drawing her towards the stairs. 'The Countess must be in her sitting room, and I'll lay any money she has m'father in there with her. So now is our chance. She won't come the ugly if my sire is present.'

This was scarcely comforting. There was nothing in the world Kitty wanted less than to confront her mother-in-law, especially after what Claud had said about her wishing to set the marriage aside. Her nerves had settled a good deal, but the imminence of the meeting now caused them to surge up again, rendering her breathless and causing a tremor to start up inside.

Her heart was jumping as they traversed a long corridor. Glancing up at Claud, she saw the thrusting chin was well out, and her spirits sank. He had the bit between his teeth, and meant to rout his mother if he could. Kitty felt like a pawn in a chess game.

Claud halted at a door and grinned down at her. 'Beginning to feel as if making startling entrances is my mission in life!'

Curiously, this remark gave Kitty a little courage. It could not be worse than their first entrance this afternoon, for all was known already. And had not Claud promised that he would let none bully her? Devoutly trusting that this included his formidable mother, Kitty followed him into the room. She felt an immediate atmosphere of coldness, which might have been attributable to the wealth of empty space.

Two people were present. A woman of commanding stature with grey hair above a high wide brow, dressed in a grey silk gown of fashionable cut, and a spare-looking man, whose resemblance to Claud was marked both by the pleasantness in his face and the faded blonde hair—such of it as was left to him. He wore spectacles, but as he turned to see who had entered, a hand came up and he lifted them slightly, peering in an uncertain manner.

'Trust you will excuse this interruption,' said Claud in a voice of formality that chilled Kitty. 'Wished to present you to my wife.'

She saw his gesture towards her, and automatically made her curtsy.

'Name of Katherine,' stated Claud, 'but she prefers Kitty.'

There was a brief silence. Lady Blakemere, for the woman was evidently she, stared straight at Kitty's face for the space of a moment with a gaze cold as blue steel, thin lips tight with disapproval. It felt an age while that gimlet eye seemed to sear straight into Kitty's soul. And then the Countess turned, crossed to a door at the back of the room, and exited through it without uttering a single word.

A more comprehensive snub Kitty could not have imagined. She felt wholly crushed, and a weight of despondency gathered, ready to descend, held in check for the moment only by shock.

Beside her, Claud, equally shocked, but thrust through instead with murderous rage, was within an ace of tearing after his mother. An utterance from his father brought him up short.

'Hold a moment, my boy!'

Unable to trust himself to speak, Claud directed his gaze upon his sire and found there all the sympathy he could have wished. But Lord Blakemere was not looking at his son. It was evident that his whole attention was taken up by Kitty. He crossed the room to her, and held out a hand.

'My dear Kitty, allow me to do the honours of the house. I am Blakemere.'

A rush of gratitude swept through Claud, dissipating his rage. He might have known Papa would make all right! He watched as Kitty was drawn gently to the *chaise-longue* in the window and made to sit down. The Earl brought another chair close and seated himself beside her. Claud hoped that the warmth and kindness of his smile would serve to mitigate the worst effects of the insult. He gave his attention to what his father was saying.

'You must not mind, dear child, if all is not quite as it should be.'

'A masterly understatement, sir,' put in Claud savagely.

A gesture silenced him. 'I will not insult your intelligence with platitudes, my dear Kitty. You cannot be unaware of the difficulties attendant upon your marriage, and I have no doubt that my son in some sort forced the matter upon you.'

'I did not, sir!'

The Earl's mild gaze turned to him. 'Dear boy, a female does not engage upon a Gretna Green affair without a deal of encouragement from the party of the second part. You will not, I hope, pretend that it was this child's notion and not yours that you should embark upon a clandestine marriage.'

Claud shifted his shoulders. 'No, of course not, but—'

'Sir, it was my fault just as much as Claud's,' Kitty piped up.

The blue eyes, gentle under the spectacles, came back to her face. 'How so?'

'You see, I must otherwise have been a governess, and I confess I was dazzled by—by his wealth, and—and the thought of becoming a viscountess, though I knew I should not have consented—especially with the threat of the scandal hanging over us. But although I tried to stop it once or twice, it just seemed to—to roll on!'

She faltered to a halt under a gaze in which there was not the smallest vestige of judgement. Yet it was a gaze that made her feel obligated to reveal the truth. She had not meant to say as much—nor anything indeed. The Earl's slight smile encouraged her.

'Claud had his own reasons for marrying me, my lord. But had I shown myself averse to the notion, I know he would not have persisted.'

'I would hope not,' uttered the Earl, a touch of amusement in his voice. 'An unwilling female would be the very devil, especially if one meant to drag her all the way to Scotland.'

A giggle escaped Kitty, and Claud's laughter warmed her. 'Well, we did quarrel once or twice. But for the most part I went with him willingly.'

'Despite the threat of scandal.'

It was said gently, but there was a disturbing note in the Earl's voice. Kitty felt herself go hot, but she met his eyes boldly. 'I did want to know about it, sir. I still do. You see, I have such odd memories. And when Lady Rothley…' She petered out, unable to continue, her eyes going to Claud in an unconscious plea for assistance.

He did not fail her. Crossing to stand beside the *chaise-longue*, he faced his father. 'Aunt Silvia nearly swooned at the sight of her, Papa. She intimated that there would be a scandal, and the worst thing in the world would be if my mother were to hear of it.'

'And so you naturally decided that the best possible solution was to marry the girl,' said his father.

Dismayed by the flatness of Lord Blakemere's tone, Kitty longed to have an excuse she might put forward to mitigate Claud's culpability. Put that way, all the disaster to which she had been trying to blind herself sprang up anew. And then she saw the stubborn jut of Claud's chin, and the glitter at his eyes.

'My motive, sir,' he uttered, almost through his teeth, 'must be as well known to you as it is to me. If you think it was wrong of me, then so be it! I stand by it, and I will do so until hell freezes over!'

He strode to the door. 'Come, Kitty.'

Kitty's uncertain gaze went from Claud's stormy face to his father's mild one, and she was startled to see a look of sadness in the older man's eyes. Kitty could not bear it. Reproach sounded in her voice.

'Claud!'

For a moment he stood irresolute, warring with the unwilling guilt and a burning sense of injustice. Of all men, his father knew what he had suffered! And the Earl had stood by and allowed matters to take their course. Now he chose to upbraid his son for an act that had given him his vengeance!

Fighting his conscience, Claud strode restlessly across to the mantel, unconsciously taking up a pose that all too closely resembled the stance of his mother. He heard his father's voice, and looked round.

'Kitty, my child, would you be very kind and allow us a little moment to ourselves?'

Claud watched his wife jump up with alacrity. She cast him a glance in which he read both reproach and uncertainty. His father had risen too, and she turned to clasp the hand he was holding out.

'Thank you, sir, for your kindness to me.'

'Kindness costs nothing, my dear.'

With which enigmatic remark, he escorted her to the door. Claud called out before she could leave, 'Find Babs or Kate. I'll be with you shortly.'

Kitty nodded, and withdrew. Claud eyed the Earl as he came slowly across to the mantel. The hand that was laid upon his shoulder was gentle.

'Believe me, my boy, I do understand. I am less troubled by your motives, than by the consequences. Especially as they concern that taking little thing you have taken to wife.'

Claud turned, suddenly eager. 'She is taking, isn't she?'

'Very. But that does not help with who she is.'

Abrupt frustration overcame him. 'Then who is she, sir? I feel sure you know!'

Lord Blakemere turned away. 'I am not at liberty to discuss that.'

'I see.'

One of those world-weary smiles was directed at him. 'I doubt it, my boy.'

'Well, it makes no matter. The Countess will tell me eventually.'

'I doubt that too,' said his father frankly.

'Then if I am not to know, why in the name of all the

gods should I give it the time of day?' demanded Claud, exasperated.

The Earl reseated himself and crossed one leg over the other in a relaxed manner that was to Claud supremely irritating. He shunted to the window behind the *chaise-longue* and looked out without taking in anything of the expanse of lawn below. His father's calm tones reached him.

'My boy, I do not think you appreciate the delicacy of the situation.'

'Delicacy?' Claud thought he understood, and flushed, shifting out into the room. 'I see what you would be at! Did you suppose me a creature devoid of sense or feeling? I will force nothing on Kitty, if that's what you fear. Time and to spare for that side of things. Besides, we're as yet too little acquainted to be climbing into bed together!'

There was a brief silence. He looked round and found his father's gaze upon him, an odd look in his face—of surprise? Or puzzlement perhaps?

'Why do you look at me so?'

Lord Blakemere apparently shook off his abstraction. 'I thank you for your confidence, my boy, and I am glad to learn that you are possessed of so fine a delicacy of feeling, but that was not what I meant.'

'What, then?'

'I was thinking rather of the immediate future. You have made your gesture, but what happens now?'

Claud turned to face him. 'You underestimate me, sir. There's more to it than a gesture. As for the future, I'm married and intend to stay that way. Or d'you ask how Kitty's relationship to this family is to be resolved? For my money, that's a matter for Lady Blakemere.'

'And what of Kitty?' persisted his sire.

Claud became impatient. 'What d'you mean, sir? She is my wife!'

'And who else?'

'You know better than I!'

His father tutted. 'You are missing the point, my boy. It is not you, who will be subject to gossiping tongues. It is not you, who must dredge up her courage—she has a deal of it, I'll warrant!—and face the world. It is not you, Devenick, who will be *hurt*.'

Claud stared at him, the final word ringing in his ears. Emotions surged up. Protesting, pleading to be heard. He had every right! He was vindicated by all possible judgements! Anyone must see that. The end justified the means—it had to.

Only an image of Kitty's pallid features intruded into his mind. Today, and earlier when he had taken her to the Haymarket. There at least he had not been at fault. But what he had put her through today, all for his own gratification, did not bear investigation. She had been *terrified*. With the memory of Aunt Silvia's unkind reception, how fearful must she have been to be subjected to the judgement of the entirety of his family? And he had given it not the slightest consideration.

He flung away, striding restlessly up and down his mother's sitting-room carpet in much the same way that she had done in their earlier interview. All the meaning of his father's words hit him with stunning force. He had pursued his goal with single-minded dedication, caring nothing for the consequences. Well, they meant nothing to him, why should they? He could—and would!—take anything the Countess threw at him. But it had not been he who had been cut dead in this very room!

Halting, he turned to face the Earl. 'Kitty herself called

me selfish. Was I ever so? I thought that role was reserved for my mother!'

Lord Blakemere's mild expression did not alter. 'It is not the only point in which you resemble her, my boy. I have been reminded of nothing so much as two deer with their horns locked in battle.'

Claud was betrayed into a laugh. '*Touché*, sir.'

The Earl smiled. 'But I fear I must share in the blame for your self-obsession. Perhaps I left you too much alone.'

It was too near the bone to be denied. Claud remained silent. He felt the more responsible. He had dragged Kitty into this. It behoved him the more to see it through. He would have said as much, but that the inner door opened and Lady Blakemere re-entered the room.

Claud braced himself, clamping down on the instant rise of spleen. For a wonder, she was smiling at him!

'Devenick, I am glad you are alone.'

She meant, of course, that he no longer had Kitty with him. Though it was scarcely new that she should dismiss her husband as of no account! The Earl was once more wearing his habitual bland expression. Claud tried to keep his tone even.

'What is your pleasure, ma'am?'

She moved into the room, heading once more for her favourite position. But she stood comfortably before it, rather than in her pose of the *grande dame*.

'I had been desirous of an interview with you since speaking with Silvia. From what she told me, I am forced to realise that your error was perfectly innocent. I have midjudged you, Devenick.'

Taken aback, but wary, Claud remained aloof. 'Indeed, ma'am?'

'If only you had come to me, you need not have felt yourself obliged to offer the girl marriage.'

'*Obliged?*'

The cordiality faded a little. 'I must assume that was your motive. There could be no other, Devenick.'

'Oh, couldn't there?'

He caught a slight movement in the Earl and glanced across. His father's eye was upon him, and Claud compressed his lips. If his sire supposed he was going to be persuaded to run with this horse, he was very much mistaken!

'You were deluded, my poor boy,' continued his mother.

Claud almost ground his teeth. When had he ever been 'her boy'? She was up to something. It was a ploy. She must be mad to imagine he would fall for it!

'There was no necessity for you to marry the girl at all. If you were aware of the circumstances, you would know that nothing could be more unnecessary.'

'D'you mean to tell me the circumstances?'

She hesitated, a touch of her old manner returning. 'You know me better than that.'

'And you know me, ma'am! What's this all about? You ain't in the habit of cajoling me. What do you want?'

Winter returned to her eyes. 'Very well, if you must have it. There are grounds enough for annulment. Whether or not you co-operate in this, I intend to see to it that the marriage is put at an end.'

'You interest me exceedingly, ma'am,' sneered Claud. 'But how?'

'That you will learn in due course.'

A heady laugh escaped him. 'You ain't got a notion, have you? This is all bluster. You are utterly at a stand!'

The glitter at her eyes told him he had read her accurately. But she would never admit as much! Instead, she turned to the Earl.

'Blakemere, compel him!'

Her husband eyed her. 'With what means, my dear? He is of age, and wholly independent. I wish you will trust in his integrity.'

'Integrity? When he has committed so rash an act?' She came away from the mantel towards her husband, addressing him as if Claud's presence was of no account. 'He had best be sent to Shillingford until we can find a solution. We will keep the girl here and under my eye.'

'The devil you will!'

Turning on his heel, Claud left the room precipitately, filled with a new determination. It did not take him many minutes to find Kitty, who had gone to earth in the nursery again, accompanied only by Tess on this occasion. He marched in and seized her arm, dragging her up.

'No time to waste, Kitty. We're off.'

She did not argue, allowing him to drag her out of the room, and wholly ignoring the popping eyes of his young cousin.

'But where are we going?'

'To Shillingford. I'll barricade all the doors and post sentries with rifles at the windows before I let the Countess take you away from me!'

The establishment, which Kitty was to make her home, was a charming seventeenth-century house, built with the traditional mullioned windows and steep gables. It was rambling rather than imposing, although its many rooms were bewildering at first to one who had grown up in a four-square red brick utility, built for its purpose and devoid of character. The Duxfords had inhabited an adjacent building, relatively small, if pleasant enough, into which only the older girls had been invited to partake of wine on Sundays.

Upon their approach in the curricle, the mellowed stone walls of Shillingford Manor had glowed in the setting sun, and Kitty was at once enchanted. Having been erected upon the site of an ancient baronial hall and inheriting its name, the Manor was situated in one of the oldest of the family estates, she learned from Claud.

'Believe the original manor had been here since the Normans or some such thing. Wouldn't have done for us had it not been knocked down and this place put up in the last century. I've seen the plan of the old place and it must have been confoundedly draughty. But you'll find the present house cosy enough, I believe.'

Which Kitty did, appreciating the relaxed atmosphere in rooms of comfortable size with invitingly solid and deep-cushioned wing chairs of gently curving style. The woodwork decoration was ornate, with carvings of flowers, fruit and animals, with paintings and hangings on block-printed wallpaper attached to the panelling. There was a general air of untidiness, perhaps due to Claud's hitherto bachelor status, which Mrs Papple, the bustling housekeeper, was prone to deprecate.

The servants, with the exception of Mixon, who Kitty had already met, were uniformly at one with the faintly chaotic air in the house, and—no doubt due to a fore-knowledge gleaned from the valet who had joined them from London—fully primed for her arrival. A late dinner was in preparation, announced the butler, a round and smiling individual of a chatty disposition. He welcomed Kitty in an avuncular fashion, as if he had nothing more to wish for than the advent of an unknown mistress who had been obliged to travel to Gretna Green for her marriage.

'Time and past this place had the feminine touch, my lady. Many's the time I've said to his lordship as he should up and get himself to the altar. That way we'd see more of him, my lady, than in a few short weeks of summer.'

He cast a provocative glance at his master as he spoke, and was instantly taken up. 'If you imagine I'm planning to settle here from one year's end to another, Hollins, you old rascal, you're wide of the mark!'

The butler disclaimed, and was peremptorily ordered to hold his tongue and allow the housekeeper to take her ladyship in hand. Kitty was then led up a handsome wooden staircase to one side of the hall, and shown into a pleasant bedchamber with a set of windows that gave on to the front gardens.

'You won't see much now, my lady, but it's a fair prospect. There's plenty of land, and a good surrounding of woodlands for your privacy.'

Kitty peered out into the gathering dusk, and was able to make out the shapes of trees about a spacious area of green.

'I've aired the sheets against your coming, and Biddy will pass a warming pan over them before you sleep tonight.'

Turning back into the room, Kitty inspected the bed. It was an old-fashioned solid structure, all of oak including the tester, with carved and inlaid decoration and fluted balusters on the front posts, and hung with damask drapery in a rich veined red. It looked enormous to Kitty and could not but dredge up those deeper fears, which had been swallowed up in the harrowing events of the day. The question begged to be asked.

'Where is Lord Devenick's room?'

The answer soothed her as nothing else could have done. 'He has the chamber as matches this one, across to the other side of the stairs.'

Her panic eased. If Claud proved content to be situated

at such a distance, perhaps he did not intend to pursue his marital rights in the immediate future. The Duck had spoken of that practice obtaining among members of the peerage of occupying separate rooms, when she prepared her pupils for the habits and customs of any great house they might inhabit as a governess. Kitty could only be grateful for it.

She returned her attention to Mrs Papple, who was busily engaged in demonstrating the accoutrements of the bedchamber, opening doors and drawers as she talked.

'There's laying space for your gowns here in the trays of the press, and two drawers at bottom besides. You'll be able to set oddments in the cupboard of the dressing stand. It ain't a deal of accommodation, but if you wish for it, my lady, there is a small chamber next to this, which you may appropriate for a dressing-room. Unless you would prefer your maid to occupy it?'

'I have no maid,' Kitty told her ruefully. Nor did she know what she would do with one if she had. Although she and her two friends had helped each other with strings and buttons, or an occasional dressing of hair for a special event, they had been encouraged—nay, ordered!—to be self-sufficient in all things. None was going to assist the governess to dress!

Only she was no longer a governess, would never be one. Despite the hideous reception accorded her by Lady Blakemere, she was married to a peer of the realm who had avowed his steadfast intention to withstand any attempt to set her aside.

For the first time, the reality of the event sank into Kitty's brain. She sat down plump upon the bed, drawing the concerned eye of the housekeeper.

'Why, what is the matter, my lady?'

'I wish you would not call me that!' uttered Kitty impulsively.

Mrs Papple blinked. 'But, my lady—'

'Pray don't!' She drew a breath, holding unconsciously to the edge of the mattress either side and disarranging the red patterned bedspread. 'It is all so new and—and bewildering, Mrs Papple. I believe I have only just this moment taken it in that I am indeed Lady Devenick.'

A comfortable laugh came from the housekeeper, and she bustled forward. 'Indeed, and you are, my dear ma'am, and mistress of the house to boot. But if all I've heard is true, it don't come as no surprise that it's hard for you to adjust.' Kitty found herself being patted upon the shoulder. 'Never you fret, ma'am. Just leave all to me. Time enough for you to worrit yourself over housekeeping and such when you've learned your way about.'

'Thank you.'

Although Kitty knew not whether she was more or less cheered by the discovery that her escapade was common knowledge in the house. It was immediately evident that Mrs Papple had opted to mother her, for she found herself under instruction to rest quietly upon her bed until dinnertime, when the housemaid Biddy would be sent up to help her to dress. The housekeeper assisted her to remove the spotted muslin gown, and inexorably ushered her on to the bed with the down coverlet drawn over her.

Presently Kitty found herself alone, and at liberty to engage upon her own thoughts. They were not uniformly happy.

While she was warmed by the kind reception accorded her by the younger members of Claud's family and his father, this did not wholly outweigh the enmity of the Countess. That she ruled the roost in the household was self-evident, even had Kitty not understood it previously from her spouse.

Her *spouse*.

How odd it sounded! Claud was her *husband*. How many times had he called her wife? Had he assimilated the relationship so readily? Was it indeed more than a full week since he had first encountered her? So much had happened that Kitty felt it as if months had passed.

How foolish had been her dreams! She had prattled of marriage with a lord as easily as she had prattled of that dratted spangled gown, never once considering the realities of the wedded state. It had little to do with parties and balls! Housekeeping? Scarcely a subject the Duck had thought necessary to include in her education! Kitty was prepared to be entertaining and to dance. She could chatter in French and show off her sketches. But her duties did not end there. She must decide upon menus and see that guests were comfortably bestowed. Ensure Claud's comfort—and his happiness. And bear his children, cost her what it might in that painful necessity. Kitty shivered and turned her face into her pillows.

There was no escape. Like him or loathe him, she was bound to Claud for life—unless the Countess succeeded in separating them. Kitty recalled Claud's avowed intention to hold on to her, come what may. But could he? And if he did, and the scandal broke, would he still wish to?

Chapter Eight

The arrival on Friday of both Babs and Kate was a profound relief to Claud's growing restlessness. He had kept his impatience in check, convinced that it was better to await what the Countess might do than to risk going to Brightwell Prior to engage in verbal battles. But inaction was driving him demented. Having dragged Kitty to Gretna Green at speed in order to hasten the moment of confrontation, he now found time hanging heavy on his hands.

There were estate matters demanding his attention, but Claud entered into them without enthusiasm, mentally occupied with the question of how his mother might counter him. An occasional enquiry satisfied him that Kitty was settling in, and he told off Papple to keep an eye on her. They met at meal times, but his days were spent out of doors. Prevented from beginning his investigations into Kitty's history while the family were congregated at Brightwell Prior, he rode or drove about his acres at his agent's urging, in a bid to dissipate the restless energy possessing him.

When he came in from an excursion to check upon outlying farms, he was delighted to discover his sister Babs and his cousin Kate taking a dish of tea with Kitty in the big front parlour.

'I'm deuced glad to see you both! Why couldn't you have come before? It's all of four days since we came back. What's happening at home? D'you know what the Countess has been up to? Has Papa said anything?'

'A fine catechism, I must say!' declared his charmingly bonneted sister from a wing chair by the window. 'Which question would you like us to answer first?'

'All of them!' He glanced at the tea things at Kitty's elbow, and crossed past her to the mantelpiece where he tugged on the bell-pull. 'Wait while I have Hollins fetch me a tankard of ale.'

Kate, who was placed opposite Kitty on the other side of the fireplace, laughed. 'Now he will have us wait.'

'Fie, Claud! We have been here this age, and have told it all to Kitty.'

He turned. 'Well, you ain't leaving until you've told me too!'

'If you only knew how tricky it was to slip out,' objected Babs. 'Besides that my betrothed is at home, together with Lady Chale.'

'And Mama has been in such a state of nerves,' added Kate, 'that I have been almost constantly in attendance on her.'

A giggle escaped Babs. 'I must say it has been excessively exciting. We had to bribe the groom to drive us, and—'

'Bribe the groom?' Claud blinked. 'What for? Why in Hades shouldn't you go out whenever you wish to?'

The two visitors looked at each other, but it was Kitty who answered. 'They have been forbidden to come here, Claud.'

He experienced an immediate rise of chagrin. 'Forbidden? By the Countess?'

'Who else? And if we had made an excuse for our going, she would instantly have guessed at our purpose. You know what Mama is.'

'None better,' snapped Claud. 'Does this prohibition apply to everyone?'

Kate rose from the chair and moved to him, laying a hand on his arm. 'I am so sorry, Claud, but Aunt Lydia told us all that you had been banished to Shillingford—'

'Banished?'

'—and that no one in the family must be seen to come here so that the news of your being in residence does not spread to our neighbours.'

'Not that one can place the slightest dependence upon that,' put in Babs sapiently, 'for there is no doubt that the servants will gossip in every tavern from Brightwell to London. How Mama supposes she can keep the matter secret is beyond me!'

'Banished!'

Claud found his cousin's gaze upon him, those brown orbs—so like and yet so unlike Kitty's—frowning in question. 'Why do you keep on saying it?'

The door opened to admit his butler, and Claud swung away from the fireplace and marched towards the fellow, bottling his spleen as best he could. 'Hollins, fetch me some ale. No, make it brandy!'

'At this hour, my lord?'

'I don't care what hour it is! Fetch it at once!'

A startled expression overspread the butler's features, but he bowed and withdrew. Claud found Kitty at his side.

'I wish you will strive to be calm, Claud! It won't help matters to be losing your temper.'

He eyed her with resentment. 'Is it now your mission in life to soothe me?'

'Yes,' stated Kitty frankly, 'because when you flare up, you don't care what you do. I have never known anyone so impulsive! Besides, I believe you have been spoiling for a fight since we came here on Monday night, for you have been prowling about like a caged beast, and now you seize upon the first excuse—'

'D'you realise,' he interrupted, 'what that she-devil has done? Taken advantage of my walking out of the place. I *walked*, Kitty. She thought to separate us by sending me to Shillingford, and keeping you at Brightwell Prior. That's why we left the place in such a hurry and came here. Now she's telling the family she's banished me!'

'Well, you knew she would fight you. You said so yourself.'

Claud was silenced. It came to him that Kitty had noticed his restlessness. Had been watching him, been troubled by it perhaps. His mood swung, and hardly realising what he did, he caught her about the waist.

'Have I been beastly again? Beg your pardon, Kitty! Had my mind on the Countess and what she might do.'

Kitty managed a smile. 'I know. And here is your chance to find out, Claud. Only they cannot stay long, so you had best save your rage for when they have left us.'

To her relief, Claud grinned. 'What a sensible wife you are, Kitty.'

He released her, and presently, fortified with ale—for his butler, wise in his master's changeable ways, brought him both ale and brandy—Kitty was able to relax while he took a seat near her and listened to what the girls were able to impart. She did not know why she had leaped into the breach in that way. Herself apprehensive of the immediate future, it had not helped to see her husband impatient and restless. Had it to do with the Countess? Or was his dissatisfaction with his marriage? The thought could not but obtrude. He had wedded her on a whim, and perhaps he was now regretting it when the consequences began to bite.

Kitty had not been thinking of that, though, when she intervened. To see Claud upset had distressed her. Which was mad. Why should his mood affect her? At a loss, Kitty glanced across at him, and heard what Babs was saying.

'They have got into a habit—whenever they can escape from our guests—of going off into locked rooms, and excluding the rest of us. Either it is Uncle Heversham and Mama, or Aunt Silvia and Mama. And once it was the three of them together.'

'What of Papa?' asked Claud. 'Has he been involved?'

Babs snorted, but Kate responded. 'You cannot suppose that my uncle Blakemere would not make himself scarce while such a crisis was in progress?'

'And with my prospective in-laws on the premises too,' agreed Babs. 'Papa slips away whenever he can to his collection. He says he is cataloguing. If Mama insists upon his presence, he just disappears the moment her back is turned. You know how he is.'

'None better,' agreed Claud, but with a feeling of flatness in his breast.

Could not his father this once have supported him? He had shown himself sympathetic, and the only reproach he had for his son had been on Kitty's behalf. Why could he not stand firm against the Countess? But neither his liking for his new daughter-in-law, nor his undoubted affection for his heir, would make him pit himself against the Countess. Though his sire never did her bidding! With an inward sigh, Claud recalled that Lord Blakemere never battled for his rights. His time-honoured tactic was to turn his back on the Countess and do exactly as he chose.

'Besides, what could Papa do, when all is said?' came from Babs, as if she had read his mind. 'Or any of us, come to that.'

'You at least have not been idle,' put in Kate, smiling. 'She has been behaving in the most reprehensible fashion, Claud, listening at keyholes.'

'Have you, by Gad?' he asked eagerly, wholly unmoved by the dubious ethical nature of his sister's actions. 'Did you manage to glean anything by it?'

'Very little.' Babs fidgeted oddly with her skirts, evading his gaze. Was there something she did not wish to tell him? Then she was speaking again. 'They must be alert to the possibility that they might be overheard, for they always speak in low tones so that it is very difficult to make anything out.'

'But is it not odd,' said Kate, 'that it seems always to be Uncle Heversham involved?'

Claud pounced. 'Ha! It ain't odd at all, if Kitty was born to our aunt Felicia.'

Both girls exclaimed, but Kate jumped to the obvious conclusion. 'You mean rather than my father?' And then consternation spread across her face. 'I do beg your pardon, Kitty! I never meant to say that.'

Kitty reassured her. 'It is not a new idea, Kate. I know about your father, and it seems to me the most likely conclusion that I am one of his bastards.'

Babs burst out laughing, much to Claud's obvious annoyance. 'Fie, don't be cross! It is only the way Kitty said it that amuses me.'

'If we are honest, Kitty,' Kate said apologetically, 'we have been discussing it openly, when our elders are absent.

Ralph sticks to it that you and I have a look of Papa, just as he does.'

Claud jumped in. 'Then it is my uncle Rothley you resemble. I could not recall just what he looked like. Thought perhaps your looks came from the Ridsdale family.'

'Not according to Ralph. And he should know, for he is old enough to remember. Only we never thought of Aunt Felicia.'

'Yes, but there's nothing to say it was her beyond a memory of Kitty's,' said Claud.

The two girls begged for enlightenment, and Kitty reluctantly spoke up. 'There was a lady who was used to visit me when I was but a small child. I have no reason to think it was your aunt Felicia, but it might have been.'

'How disappointing,' pouted Babs. 'Fie, this is the most famous mystery! I wish we might get to the bottom of it.'

'Fie, Babs!' Kitty copied her. 'You cannot wish for that more than I!'

Babs burst into laughter. 'You have me exactly!'

Realising what she had done, Kitty made haste to apologise.

'She's always doing it,' put in Claud. 'Don't take it amiss, for she don't mean anything.'

'Indeed I don't. It is only when I am impatient or cross that I do it without realising.'

'Poor Kitty,' Kate soothed. 'I for one can't blame you for that. It must be hard for you not knowing the truth.'

'We'll find it out,' said Claud bracingly. 'Only I can't pursue the thing right under the Countess's nose. You girls keep your ears open, and advise me the moment the party breaks up. Then I can investigate the matter without the Countess breathing down my neck.'

Both girls promised to do what they might, and then rose to leave.

'For if we are to escape detection,' said Babs, automatically shaking out her muslin petticoats, 'we must sneak back in before anyone misses us.'

They bid a friendly farewell to Kitty, and Claud escorted them out to the open carriage that was awaiting them in the drive. He assisted Kate into the vehicle, and as she began to unfurl her sunshade, turned to help Babs. To his surprise, she drew him a little away from the carriage and leaned close.

'I could not tell you before Kitty,' she whispered, 'but I did overhear something.'

Claud seized her elbow and pulled her further away. 'I knew it! Thought you were holding back. What is it?'

Under the straw bonnet, his sister's blue gaze was troubled. 'It was quite by accident, when I happened to be passing Mama's sitting room and heard her voice raised in anger. Then I heard Papa.'

'Well, what?' demanded Claud impatiently.

Babs leaned closer, lowering her voice the more. 'I heard him tell Mama that you had confided to him that you had no intention as yet of—well, not to beat about the bush, Claud—of *bedding* Kitty.'

'Hang it, he didn't tell her *that*?'

'But he did, Claud. And from what Mama said, I very much fear that she means to use it to arrange an annulment on the grounds that your marriage has not been consummated.'

Claud cursed fluently. How *could* his sire have betrayed him? It was all down to his confounded habit of letting the Countess do exactly as she chose. The Lord knew one expected little of him by way of support, but he might at least have refrained from handing her live ammunition!

'Should I not have mentioned it?' asked his sister anxiously.

Controlling himself, Claud reassured her, gripping her hand. 'You're a good sister, Babs. Only hope you may find happiness with this Francis of yours.'

She giggled. 'I hope the same for you. But to be truthful, I suspect your choice is far more likely to make you happy than is mine—provided Mama does not succeed in putting a spoke in your wheel. Kitty is delightful!'

'Babs, do hurry!' called Kate from the carriage.

'I had better go.' She leaned up to kiss her brother's cheek. 'Take good care of her, Claud. And for heaven's sake, take her to bed!'

He was relieved that his sister did not wait for any response, but dashed up to the carriage and jumped in. He followed and closed the door upon her. Goodbyes were said, and he instructed the coachman to set off. Claud stood, watching the carriage rolling down the short drive until it turned out of the gate and was lost to sight, his mind on the ramifications attendant upon Bab's final admonition.

Several days went by before Claud acted upon his sister's confidence. He had meant to do so at once, and had been fully prepared to march into Kitty's bedchamber that very night. Having donned his night gear, he had dismissed Mixon, and sallied forth into the dark corridor, his candle held aloft. And then his nerve had failed him.

Whether it was the sudden remembrance of Lord Blakemere's words to him about Kitty being hurt, or the awkwardness attendant upon the whole proceeding, Claud could not have said. He had stopped short well before reaching Kitty's door, and had stood irresolute for several moments of indecision while the quiet of the house closed in on him. All manner of arguments against proceeding roved through his head.

She was likely already asleep. To wake her only to thrust himself upon her could but serve to reinforce her opinion of his brutishness. A gentleman ought to lead up to these things with more finesse. He had not so much as kissed her! It would be better to woo her in form, prepare her a little. Only how to begin? Touch her? Snatch a kiss? She might welcome his attentions, were he to go subtly to work.

He had retreated to his own chamber, there to pace the floor, his imagination boggling at the formalities necessary in the course of making love to his own wife. Nothing in his amorous experience had prepared him for this cold-blooded approach. His various mistresses had been uniformly of his choosing—one for her comely figure, another for the delectable honey in her lips, and yet another for her virago rages that had unaccountably inflamed his passion. There had been nothing mechanical to these liaisons. His urges, when they came, had been satisfied by whichever of the creatures had happened at the time to be in favour. He was not one for the stew pots of Covent Garden and the dubious pleasure to be found in the arms of a wayfaring harpy. Warned off these dangers by his father— who had taken at least these measures to ensure an education that could not be forthcoming at his mother's hands—Claud had abided by his wisdom. It had never been a point with him to flout his sire.

But flouting the Countess had rapidly become a problem. The longer Claud dallied, the worse it was. He could not face Kitty across the table at meal times without the matter jumping into his head. He caught himself eyeing her in a manner that clearly disturbed her, for she began to fidget and shy away from his glance. It did not augur well for his wooing!

But at length Claud's patience deserted him. He calculated on Tuesday night that he had wasted four days. It would not do. He had been married near two weeks, and there was no real reason to delay. Taking up his candle, he nerved himself to brave the unknown.

The knock at her door threw Kitty's heart in her mouth. Was it he? Then her growing fears were not groundless. There had been something in his look! She had seen it with dread, hoping against hope that it was her imagination. What might have prompted him to precipitate this side of the marriage was as nothing, when all her attention was reserved for the frightful moment when her fears might prove true. Now it had come!

She kept quiet, hoping that Claud would think she was asleep and go away again. It was craven, but she could not help it. The haunting memories from the distant reaches of her childhood had been heavy in her mind these many days. The door hinge creaked, and she held her breath in the darkness, wishing she had drawn the curtains about the bed despite the heat of the night. A light appeared, and then he was there. She could see that he was clad in a dressing gown, which hung open over a long nightshirt. There could be no doubt of his intention! Fright swallowed up all Kitty's common sense.

'You awake, Kitty?'

It was a piercing whisper. Had she been asleep, it must have woken her. Nevertheless, Kitty held her tongue, hardly daring to breathe.

The light came closer, and she could see Claud's features peering from behind it. All she had to do was close her eyes and pretend to be asleep. But like a petrified animal, she could only stare up at him, watching his approach. As he reached the side where she lay, and was close enough to touch her, instinct took over. Kitty rose up like a hunted bird from its concealing bush, and shot out at the other side of the bed.

Claud reeled back, his candle dipping. Wax spilled onto his hand. He uttered a grunt of protest and hastily put the candlestick down on the bedside table. Leaning to the light, he inspected the damage, scratching away the residue of the wax, and hissing a breath against the pain.

'Confound you, Kitty, I've burnt myself! What the deuce did you do that for? Thought you were asleep!'

Across the bed, he could see her face, ghostly white in the shadows. There was a tremor in her voice.

'What are you d-doing in my room?'

The sting at his hand drove Claud into irritation, and he forgot caution. 'Don't be a nodcock! You must know what I'm doing here!'

'Oh, Lord!'

Claud watched her seize a robe draped across the back of a chair and drag it on. Devil take it, she was afraid of him! He broke into speech.

'It's all right, Kitty. There's nothing to frighten you. I admit I may have startled you, but—'

'Claud, please go away! I can't—it is not possible to— pray, just *go*!'

She was clutching the robe about her, and in the half-light, he could see that she was shaking. Dismayed, he began to move around the foot of the bed. Kitty retreated to the head. Claud checked.

'Kitty, wait! At least let us talk it through.'

'Talk? You don't wish to talk!' she threw at him. 'You came to—to do *that* to me, and I can't bear it! I know I ought, but I can't. I *can't*, Claud!'

Baffled, and with the stirring of resentment inside him—a dashed insult to be rejected in such a fashion!—Claud hesitated. He thought of denying his intention, but what was the point? He must have signalled it in his musings and hesitation. Then why had she not prepared herself for the inevitable? The resentment burgeoned, and he advanced towards her.

'Hanged if I see why you should carry on like this! Must have known it would come eventually when you married me. I admit it's a thought sudden, but—'

He broke off, and checked again, realising that Kitty was not listening. She had bent down and was opening the door to the bedside cabinet. With startled eyes, he saw her withdraw the chamber pot.

'What the deuce—?'

Kitty scrambled on to the bed, and stood up, holding the thing aloft, both hands tightly gripping the handle. 'If you come one step closer, I shall hit you with this!'

Claud gazed up at her open-mouthed. 'Have you taken leave of your senses? You can't mean to brain me with the chamber pot!'

'Yes, I do, for I know you will otherwise easily overpower me!'

For a moment he was nonplussed, hardly able to take in the rapid change of circumstance. Was she mad to threaten him? It would not do. He asserted his authority.

'Kitty, put that thing down!'

'*No!*'

'Kitty, for the Lord's sake, stop being such a nodcock! Give me that!'

But Kitty did not intend to yield up her weapon, which was fortunately empty. She retreated to the centre of the bed as Claud made a swipe towards it. There was nothing in her head but the necessity to protect herself. Her voice was thick with distress.

'You may have been able to abduct me, but you will not take me by force!' She brandished the chamber pot. 'Brute! I hate you! I hate you!'

Claud fell back, gazing in utter disbelief at a wife transformed. This was not the Kitty he had come to know. Come to that, it was not the Kitty he had married. She was like a child fighting an imaginary monster. He held up a hand.

'It's all right, I'm not going to touch you.'

'Then go away!' shrieked Kitty.

'I'm going.' He shifted further towards the foot of the bed, and remembered his candle. 'Just let me get my candlestick. Can't grope about the corridors in the dark.'

The chamber pot was lowered a little, but Kitty kept it at the ready, turning on the bed so that she faced him all the time as he circled down to the bedside cabinet at the other side. Retrieving his candle, Claud backed to the door, seeing how Kitty watched him warily, though he would swear the fear was dying out of her eyes.

'We'll talk of this tomorrow,' he ventured.

No response. She remained in exactly the same position, staring across at him, he thought, though her eyes were scarcely visible now that he had removed the light. A rush of warmth came over him, and he suddenly wanted desperately to stay. If only to reassure her, calm her fears, show her that he was not the monster she thought him. But it would be foolhardy. It was clear she needed time. He would have to think again. Swallowing an unexpected rise of disappointment, Claud left the room.

The door closed, and the bedchamber was once again in darkness. Kitty sank slowly down in a huddle in the middle of the bed, clutching the chamber pot to her bosom.

* * *

The breakfast parlour at Shillingford was a cosy apartment, with a relatively small table set near a pair of French doors that gave on to the back lawns. Besides an oak court cupboard where the crockery was stored, there was a mahogany serving table, invariably laid with silver dishes of a morning, where Hollins hovered, ready to supply his lordship's wants. Mrs Papple had told Kitty that it was the master's preferred spot—on those occasions when he came down rather than partaking of breakfast in bed—especially in summer. On a hot morning, the housekeeper told her, with the doors open, it made a pleasant venue for the first meal of the day.

The cosiness oppressed Kitty today. Her proximity to her husband, who had buried himself behind the morning paper within seconds of sitting down, made it almost impossible to partake of the lavish spread of ham and coddled eggs supplied by the cook. She felt at once sheepish about the absurdity of her conduct last night, and excessively indignant with Claud. A while after his departure, when her frozen brain had once more shunted into gear and she was able to think, Kitty had recalled his assurance that he would try not to be a brute. And at the first chance, he had turned into one! Without warning, too.

Had he gone about the matter in a less secretive fashion, perhaps she would not have been startled into being so foolish. Instead, he had said nothing, only staring at her in that horrid way and leaving her to imagine the worst. It was his own fault that she had threatened him. Only she wished it had not been with the chamber pot! It had come so readily to hand, and only afterwards did she realise what a ridiculous figure she had cut. It was too bad of him to drive her into making a fool of herself.

But her stomach churned with butterflies for all that, and she could hardly swallow a thing. She felt as if the air itself was charged with unsaid recriminations. For there could be no doubt that Claud was angry with her. The ease of communication that had become habitual between them was at an end. Kitty knew not what to say to him.

Claud was not as absorbed by the day's news as he appeared. Several times he ordered himself to speak, and as many times found himself unable to. What was there to say? He had determined on initiating his marital rights, and had been thwarted. Almost he had forgotten the reason he had begun upon this course. Just as he decided it was better to abandon it for the time being, his butler inadvertently refuelled it.

'My lord?'

Claud lowered the paper, taking care to avoid Kitty's eye. 'Yes, Hollins?'

'There was a messenger come this morning, my lord, from Brightwell Prior.'

Claud's attention snapped in, and he sat up sharply, setting the newspaper down. 'Did he bring a note?'

'No, my lord, but he gave me it verbally.'

'Well, what did he say, man? Was it from Lady Barbara?'

'Sorry to say, no, my lord. From Lady Blakemere.'

Alarm gripped Kitty, and her eyes flew to Claud's face, which was tightening horribly. The blaze at his eyes was only too familiar.

'Oh, what was it?' she uttered involuntarily.

Hollins coughed. 'It was to my address, my lady, and to Mrs Papple.'

'*What?*'

The thought that the Countess was bypassing him and sending orders to his servants shot Claud through with fury. Hollins had called it a message, but he knew his

mother better than that. She had misjudged it, by Jupiter!
Did she think there was no loyalty to him in this place?

'Well, Hollins?'

The butler's unaccustomed manner deserted him. 'I
hope you know, my lord, as neither Mrs Papple nor me
would think to take our instructions from anyone but your
lordship. I trust as it won't result in no unpleasantness that
I'm passing it on to you, as I know wasn't expected, my
lord.'

'Cut line, Hollins! No fear of you being turned off, if
that's what troubles you. Her ladyship don't rule the roost
here!'

'As I know, my lord, only one can't be too careful.' He
threw an apologetic glance at the mistress of the house.
'It's to fall to Mrs Papple and me, my lord, to do what we
may to prevent her ladyship from showing herself abroad.'

'The devil!'

'Nor you nor her ladyship ain't to be at home to visitors,
should any come, my lord. Not that they will,' added the
butler sapiently, 'if my lady Blakemere has warned them
off.'

It had needed only this! Claud went off like a rocket.

'What in Hades does she mean by it? Dictating what I
do in my own house! Does she imagine she can keep me
from parading my wife to my neighbours if I choose?'

He was up, pacing the confines of the breakfast parlour,
muttering fury. Kitty watched him in breathless dismay.
The Lord send he did not now determine to do just that.
She had kept close in the house, but not for any reason
other than having nowhere to go. Would Claud now force
her abroad, all to demonstrate to his mother that he was
not to be dictated to? How humiliating to be forced to
show herself to people who had been primed against her!
She would not do it.

But when Claud's rage at length dissipated, and he re-seated himself, the stubborn determination had quite another portent. He summarily dismissed his butler, and bent a frowning gaze upon Kitty.

Fearing the worst, she broke instantly into speech. 'Claud, pray don't say I must go visiting when your mother has put people against me, for nothing will induce me to do it! You may say what you please until you are blue in the face, but—'

'I ain't going to say that,' he interrupted.

Kitty eyed him with a good deal of trepidation. 'What, then? I can see you mean to spring something horrid upon me!'

He thrust out his chin. 'Horrid it may be, but there's no help for it, Kitty.'

Her stomach caved in. 'Oh, *what?*'

She watched him straighten his shoulders, as if he braced himself for what he was to say. A pulse began to beat overloud in her chest.

'There's a reason for last night, Kitty.'

She swallowed, but could say nothing. She thought the blue eyes softened just a trifle, and held her breath. The words jerked from him in spurts.

'This ain't easy. But I don't have a choice. Never meant to do it—not yet awhile. But I have to.'

The vision of him entering her bedchamber floated into her mind. She hardly knew that she spoke, nor was she conscious of the desperation in the one word.

'Why?'

Claud drew a breath. Confound it, but it wasn't easy! She was starting to look scared to death again. But it had to be said. She must understand why she could not fight him. He *had* to do it.

'Babs told me that the Countess means to use it against me, if the marriage ain't consummated.'

Kitty knew it was futile, but she uttered the plea nevertheless. 'Then tell her it is! How is she to know if—if—?'

Claud uttered a bark of mirthless laughter. 'If I know the Countess, she'll bring a posse of lawyers and doctors and have them attest to it!'

Horror swept through Kitty. If there was one thing she had taken in from her education at the Duck's hands, it was the gory details concerning *marital conversation*, as she had termed it. Not that any female at the Seminary had been in the expectation of needing such information on her own account. But it had been a point with the Duck to underscore the afflictions of childbearing and all that went with it. 'She does it,' Nell had observed to her two friends, 'to warn us off falling victim to an amorous male whose roving eye might chance to fall upon the governess.' For Prue had been shocked, while Kitty had found it morbidly fascinating. It abruptly lost its fascination now.

'You mean the Countess would make me endure an examination?'

'That's exactly what I mean. And if any bloodsucking leech is brought in by my lady Blakemere, you can stake your last penny he will examine like the deuce until he can't refute the evidence!'

'Evidence?'

'That you're no longer a maid, Kitty. Surely you know what that means?'

In graphic detail! She well remembered that part of Mrs Duxford's lecture. Any doctor could tell in a moment that the fatal deed had been effected. And his methods had sounded wholly unpleasant. Kitty felt as if the entirety of the blood in her body had slid to her feet. She could not utter a word, only staring at the stubborn tilt to her husband's chin as he pronounced sentence.

'I'm sorry for it, but it has to be done. I'll do my best not to hurt you too much, but you'd best steel yourself to it. And no more chamber pots!'

The day had dragged. It had been like those horrid periods incarcerated in the Seminary attic, knowing that, after the loneliness and dreadful diet of bread and milk, there was still to come the unpleasant recital before the Duck of one's wrongdoing and the lessons one should have learned through reflecting upon it. Kitty had never been able to think of any lessons—other than what the Duck would not have accepted as salutary—and the interview had always been distressing and humiliating as she desperately tried to find *something* at the prompting of her preceptress, for fear of being sent back to the attic for a further time. She had often thought she would have preferred the rod.

It was not just the fear of the inevitable pain—she clung to Claud's promise that he would try not to hurt her too much. There was also the required intimacy of the proceeding to which she was wholly a stranger. Fleeting remembrances chased through her mind of sensations she had experienced when she had found herself in close proximity with Claud. How was she to cope when her body was separated from his only by the thin cotton of a nightgown? The thought made heat rise up inside her so that she felt as if she were stifling. And this in addition to the agonies she must endure at Claud's hands, only to thwart the Countess!

By the dinner hour, Kitty's apprehension had deadened to a dull apathy of terror that would not let her eat, nor glance up in the horrid expectation of discovering the monster Claud had become in her mind seated at the other end of the dining table. She picked at the meal, uttering no word throughout, and wishing desperately that the day might be as long again before she must retire to her bedchamber. And thereby entirely missed the fact that her husband was equally silent, and similarly unable to partake of more than a few mouthfuls of the dishes set before him.

To Claud, by contrast, the hours had raced by, bringing him all too speedily close to the point at which he must steel himself to a hateful necessity. It was not in his nature to behave in a way of cruelty that must make him too closely his mother's son! Yet if he would keep Kitty, he must deflower her. That she was terrified of the act had been made abundantly plain. Was it natural in a young wife? Or was it only because Kitty had not been educated in the ways of his social circle?

Females of his world, as he knew from his sisters, were primed for the role that awaited them as wives of England's elite, and for that principal duty of producing heirs to maintain the line and the land. Kitty was wholly lacking in this education. It was even possible that she did not know just what would happen when he presented himself in her bedchamber. Though she knew enough to be desperately afraid!

For the first time, Claud wished that he had not been so reckless as to indulge in a runaway marriage. Had he done the thing in form, as was proper in a peer of his standing, he would have had the benefit of his sire's advice—instead of being forced by Lord Blakemere's betrayal of his confidence into an act that was little better than a rape!

It was in a mood of heavy despondency that, clad in nightshirt and dressing-gown, he at length made the short journey to his wife's bedchamber. Recalling the previous night, he entered with caution. He would not put it past Kitty to conceal herself behind the door with the chamber pot in her hand!

Instead it was immediately apparent that she had taken his words to heart, for the bed curtains were open, her candle burned on the table beside her, and Kitty was sitting up in the bed. Claud let out a faint breath of relief and closed the door behind him.

He moved to the foot of the bed and paused to look at her. The loose black curls tumbled about her shoulders, her lips were slightly parted and the velvet eyes were round and staring. She would have made an alluring picture but for the fact that she was shaking so much that the bedclothes gripped tightly to her were rippling in sympathy.

Chapter Nine

A welter of emotion cascaded into Claud's chest, but the only coherent thought in his head was that he could not bear Kitty's distress.

'The deuce!'

Moving swiftly to the bedside, he set down his candle. Plonking down upon the bed, he reached for her. 'Kitty, don't look like that! It's all right. Come here to me! Come, I won't hurt you!'

He drew the shaking figure into his embrace and held her close against him, crooning as if she was little more than a baby.

'Hush, now! I won't do anything, I promise. Quiet now, Kitty, it's all right.'

She was stiff and awkward in his arms, making no sound, although her breath vibrated with her quivering. Claud uttered words that he hardly knew he was saying, the only thought in his head to comfort her.

For several moments, the unnatural state of frozen terror into which Kitty had worked herself held strong. But the soothing words—though she hardly took in their significance—and the rhythmic stroking at her back in a gentle embrace that had no vestige of amorous intent, at last began to melt the icy front. A whimper issued from her throat, and she sagged a little into the arms that tightened, cradling her.

Her breathing eased and the shaking lessened, and a few tears squeezed from her eyes and ran down her cheeks. Alerted in a moment by the sound of sniffing near his ear, Claud put her from him a little and produced a handkerchief. As he had done that very first day, he wiped the stains from her face and placed the handkerchief over her nose.

'Blow!'

Kitty dissolved into overwrought giggles, and took the handkerchief from him. 'I am not a baby!'

Claud grinned, tightening the arm he still had about her in a brief hug. 'You're acting like one, silly chit!'

Contrite, Kitty clutched the handkerchief tightly. 'I meant to be good, Claud, truly I did. Only—'

He released her. 'Only I'm a brute, and you've done nothing to deserve it of me.'

'I wasn't going to say that,' Kitty protested.

'No, I'm saying it.'

Kitty became indignant. 'But you aren't a brute, Claud! You have just shown me that you aren't. I'm the one who is behaving so very stupidly, for I knew it must come to this eventually, once we married, and you have every right to demand it of me, even if it wasn't for the Countess.'

'I know all that, but I hadn't meant to force you to it like this. And I can tell you it ain't easy for me either, Kitty. Dashed if I know how to go about it! I mean, I've never had occasion to do the thing when the female wasn't—' He broke off, realising that this allusion was hardly a matter for the ears of a young girl, be she never so much his wife. 'What I mean is—'

'I know what you mean,' said Kitty hastily. She averted

her gaze, picking at the sheet. 'Though I was meant for a governess, we were taught—told about—about *this*.'

Claud eyed her dubiously. 'Then what is it that frightens you so much? Mean to say, if you were told, surely you know that it ain't anything to be scared of?'

But Kitty could not possibly tell him about the experiences that had given her secret knowledge unknown to the rest of the Paddington girls. It was nothing for him to be scared of! He clearly had no notion what it was like for the female in the case. Which was odd, now she came to think of it. She faced him again, searching the blue orbs.

'But you said you would try not to hurt me too much, so you know you must.'

He grimaced. 'As I understand it, Kitty, it ain't much of anything to most females. The pain, I mean. Besides, they don't notice it with all the rest.'

All what rest? But she could not ask that. A sigh escaped Claud, and he shifted as if he would move off the bed. As of instinct, Kitty reached out and grasped his arm.

'What are you doing?'

He checked, frowning. 'Going back to my own bed.'

Kitty's hold tightened. 'You are leaving me? Without—without—'

His hand closed over hers, but she did not let go. 'Kitty, I'm not going to force you into this. Thought I could do it, but I can't. It ain't in me, no matter how much of a brute you think I am.'

'But what about the Countess? You said she will have me examined.' He said nothing, and Kitty suddenly released him, snatching her hand from under his. 'Do you wish for the marriage to be set aside?'

Claud caught her fingers. 'You know I don't!'

'I don't believe you!'

She was trying to wriggle free, but Claud would not let

her. 'What are you talking about, silly chit? After all I've done to face her down, do you think I want the Countess to win?'

'No, but I dare say you are sorry you married me now that you see how much trouble we are in! I don't blame you, Claud. I told you it was a mistake!'

She was struggling against him. Claud released her hand and caught instead at her shoulders. '*Will* you be still? What in Hades are you at, Kitty?'

Kitty tried to pull away, her fingers coming up and clawing at his. 'I have tried to be calm! I have tried not to plague you! But don't you think I have seen how restless you are? The only thing that catches your interest is news from Brightwell Prior. I might as well be a dog or a cat, for all the importance I am to you!'

Claud let her go, and sat back. 'If that ain't a female all over! Haven't I said how grateful I am for your part in this? Haven't I told you how much it means to me to be giving the Countess sleepless nights?'

'Oh, the Countess! That is all you care about!'

'Of course it's all I care about! That's why I married you!'

'And that's why you would bed me! Not because you wished to! Nor because I am pretty or—or— Oh, you are selfish beyond belief! I am *nothing*. My life, my past—my identity even!—is nothing, except as it is useful to you, Claud. And now you will not take me for your wife, despite the fact that I have spent the whole day in a state of high anxiety only waiting for this moment!' Her voice thickened. 'And it will be all to do again when you decide that it *must* be done, after all, and you won't care if I *die* of apprehension!'

A burst of sobs ended this speech. Aghast at her words, Claud sat irresolute, unable to think what to do. His conscience pricked him. It was just as his father had said, and he was doing it again. He looked at Kitty, all tousled hair and her face crumpled in distress, and instinct took over. The next moment she was in his arms, and his lips were buried in her neck, mouthing at the soft young flesh.

Kitty caught her breath on a sob and her tears ceased abruptly. The lipping at her skin was having an extraordinary effect upon her senses. And Claud's hands were stroking again, but in an entirely different way, caressing her curves. Heat, the sort that she had felt before at his closeness, rose up rapidly, pervading her body. Unknowing what she did, Kitty grasped at him and encountered the broad maleness of his torso over the dressing-gown. The breath hissed in her throat, and he pulled back. Kitty caught a glimpse of the blue eyes, ablaze as they stared into hers for an instant. And then her mouth was covered by his and a sensation of exquisite pleasure drowned her senses.

The tender mouthing flesh to flesh was wholly engulfing, as if her entire body became a part of it all. Her hands encountered the hardness of Claud's back, and she felt the intervening clothes as a barrier that could not be tolerated. As if she had been doing this all her life, Kitty tugged at the silken folds. How it happened she could not know, but Claud's hands left her for a moment, and lifting cloudy lids she glimpsed his frantic movement. Then the dressing-gown was gone, and Claud seized her back into his embrace, bearing her down.

Kitty slid beneath the covers, obedient to the pressure of his hands. And then her nightgown was pulling up, and a hand seared across the bare flesh of her thigh. Kitty gasped, and turned instinctively into him, needing to be close. But Claud laid her back again, and his head dipped down to find the swell of her breasts. He groaned, and buried his face between them.

Somewhere in the unreachable deeps of her consciousness, the groan rang alarm bells in Kitty's memory. But the delicious feeling, as of melting liquid within her flesh, prevented her from giving it attention as indescribable ministrations were made upon the sensitive tips to her bosom. Kitty hardly knew what was happening, so lost in sensation was she. Flaring heat from those caressing hands warred with the intensity of feeling in the depths of her being, where a well of pulsing need was growing.

Claud's mouth shifted upwards, and he caught her lips again, at the same moment working with his hands to ease her thighs apart. He was by no means as fully lost to his desires as he sensed Kitty was, and the closer he moved to the instant of entry, the more alive he became to the need to take her gently. Now that he had begun, there was no thought in his head of sparing her. All he knew was that it was happening, that it had taken him wholly by surprise to have found her so enticing to his senses, and that he could not do other than take the thing to a natural conclusion.

He mounted her, and felt her tense a little. Instinct once more came to his rescue.

'Hush, now, hush. Kiss me again.'

Suiting the action to the words, he drew the honey from her mouth, letting her feel his weight as he toyed with her lips, teasing first and then plunging in, as if with this mirror of what his invasion would do, she might sense the pleasure and forget about the pain. And then he entered her.

Kitty gasped and froze, brought wholly out of the pleasurable experience she had been enjoying up to now. The expected pain had come at last. It had been a sudden thrust, and her instant contraction made it feel three times the reality of what was there.

'Let go, Kitty, we are not yet there. Hush, now.'

The hands came up to gentle her, and his lips were there again, breathing a trifle heavily into her neck. Kitty could sense the held-in strength, and her stomach tightened. But the hands cupped her breast and his tongue worked at her nipple so that the warmth of a sudden cascaded down her veins, and her muscles relaxed.

Claud thrust again, and the advance of the invader caused Kitty to groan aloud. But without the shock, the pain was less. She did contract again, but she remembered the last time and caught desperately at Claud's face, pulling him down for the comfort of his lips. He gave them with such generosity that her frantic kisses set him on sudden fire and his control slipped a little.

With a guttural groan he surged his way to her maidenhead in one vital sweep, held there by the little shriek she gave as he triumphed through.

'It's done, it's done, it's done,' he mumbled, close against her mouth. 'It's all right, Kitty, it's done. It's over.'

But the sharp twinge of agony was gone almost as soon as it began, and Kitty came aware again to find herself tightly held against Claud, with her legs locked around his back. Her predominant sensation was one of anticipation, and his last words penetrated her mind.

'Over? You mean that is all there is?'

Claud was holding himself in with difficulty. For him, it was anything but over! Only he had no desire to unleash that passion when she must be already smarting. He made as if to withdraw, but Kitty felt it and instinctively tightened her grip. Claud began to be distressed.

'Kitty, I must move!'

But Kitty, without words to explain the dichotomy of

her need against the unknown and the lurking memories, wrapped her arms about his neck and held him the more strongly. Claud groaned, and unable to help himself, set his lips again to hers. Her response was convulsive, and he was lost.

And he did move, only within her, rhythmically, riding her as he did his mistresses, but withal in gentleness, remembering that she was new and tender, so that all Kitty's fears dissolved away as the pleasurable sensations grew and grew.

At last Claud ended it. Kitty felt him sag heavily upon her, and then he rolled away, his breath panting beside her. She was left curiously dissatisfied. There had been so much, and yet not enough. She did not know how or why, for everything he had done to her had so exquisite an effect. Apart, that was, from the short sequence that had brought her only a tithe of the pain she had expected. She knew only that she wanted more, and it was with unimagined disappointment that she heard his verdict.

He groped for her hand, and gave it a squeeze. 'There, now, it is all done, Kitty. I won't need to trouble you again.'

Listlessly, Kitty toyed with the cold meats and pickles on her plate, unable to work up an appetite. With Claud absent, she had opted to take luncheon in the breakfast parlour. The day was hot and the French windows were open to the outside lawn. Perhaps she would go there presently, hoping the fresh summer day would lighten her mood. She might as well mope in pleasant surroundings!

She ought rather to be in a state of high excitement. Had not Claud gone off to see what he could discover from his aunt Silvia about her history? Kitty could not match his enthusiasm. Did it matter who she was? It would only make everything worse, precipitating the promised scandal. And that could only destroy what little interest her husband had in her.

She could almost wish that Kate had not sent over a note this morning from Brightwell, where the Rothleys were now settled again. The party at Brightwell Prior had broken up at last, just two weeks after Claud had brought Kitty there. The Ladies Mary and Katherine had returned, with their respective spouses, to their homes, and Babs had journeyed with her betrothed and prospective mother-in-law for a visit to meet the rest of the Chales. Mr Heversham had taken his family back to Ashbury Park, and Lady Blakemere was begun upon her usual summer pursuits.

This, said Kate, in order to squash any rumour that there was trouble in the family. She presumed it must also free her aunt's time so that she might devote more energy to the business of breaking up Claud's marriage. A pronouncement that had galvanised Claud into action.

'We'll see that! I'll be off this very day to my aunt Silvia's. Without the Countess at her back, I may shake her more easily. Then I'll see my uncle Heversham—and anyone else who may have the remotest inkling of this mystery. I'll ferret it out, you see if I don't! And the Countess has opened the way at last.'

Kitty had experienced a momentary resurgence of apprehension, but it had not lasted. All too soon, her spirits had drooped into the dull apathy she had been experiencing these many days. She felt as downhearted as she had on that far-off—and never to be sufficiently regretted!—day when she had sat on the fence at Paddington Green and bewailed her unhopeful future. Had she known then what fate had in store, she would have run back to the Seminary as fast as she could!

She might as well be a governess. She was sure it was

as exciting as being a wife! And she would not have experienced an encounter that had altered her whole way of thinking about *marital conversation*—the Duck's words for it!—and then been left high and dry. She would not have lain night after night, hoping desperately for a selfish husband to come to her bed again. She would not have fallen asleep, and dreamed that he was there, so strongly that she could see the golden glow of his hair and the blaze at his blue eyes. Feel his arms around her and the tender mouthing of his lips at her throat and breast, the swelling in her depths that yearned for his invasion, only to wake again and find that it had been all a fantasy. Except for the aching need that pulsed and pulsed for long lonely moments, making her weep with frustration.

She longed for the courage to invite him back. Only how to begin? How tell a man—even a husband—that she wanted him to visit her bedchamber again and again and *again*? Kitty had no words to make herself a wanton. Nor did she know how to signal her desires. A governess in training was not taught such things. She knew how to flirt. But if she were to tease with her eyes and throw him a pert smile, Claud would just blink at her and demand to know what she would be at. Then, when she sat mumchance—as of course she would!—he would call her a silly chit and go off about his business. With no further thought of her in his head!

A deep sigh escaped her, and she pushed away her plate. Hollins stepped in to remove it.

'Was it not to your ladyship's liking? Would you care for something else? Mrs Papple will be mortified to think she's laid out nothing you can fancy, my lady.'

Kitty stood up. 'Pray tell her that it is all very good, but that I am not hungry. I am going outside, Hollins.'

'Without a hat, ma'am? It's excessively hot.'

Kitty smiled. 'Well, then, pray ask Biddy to bring out my straw hat. Oh, and perhaps Mrs Papple will also send me a glass of lemonade?'

'Indeed she will, ma'am, and bring it herself, I shouldn't wonder.'

Kitty thanked him and escaped through the French doors. If Claud did not value her, at least the servants were attentive. She had learned to allow them to look after her, despite every instinct to hold to that independence in which she had been brought up. Mrs Papple would undoubtedly bring the lemonade, and possibly the hat as well, together with a motherly remonstrance. The housekeeper had taken Kitty to her bosom, so to speak, and there was balm in it when one had no one else at all. She had begun to miss her two friends, far more than she had when she was at the Seminary. It was all of a piece. She had made a terrible mistake, and she was paying for it now.

She dared not think what would happen when Claud finally realised it as well. Inevitable that he would, once the battle with his mother was over. What would he do then, burdened with a wife he could neither love nor desire?

The drive to Brightwell was accomplished swiftly. It was good to have the reins in his hands again, and to be up and doing. The frustration of inactivity had intensified, Claud found, after that fatal night. He had accomplished what he had set out to do. But in the doing, he had unleashed a wholly unlooked-for complication. Why the chit should have put him in heat for her, he could not imagine!

He could not help comparing the situation with how it might have been had he married Kate. Made sense to think that he would have been similarly awakened to his cousin's sensuality, since they were as like as two peas in a pod. The difference would have been that he might have indulged it. As it was, he had given his word to Kitty and that was that. Made it confoundedly difficult to be around her, however, which was why he welcomed this legitimate chance to get out of the house.

It was by no means all his reason. He had chafed at the necessity to hang around doing nothing while his mother kept the family entrenched at Brightwell Prior. Bless Kate for sending the all clear! At least Aunt Silvia could not go running to her sister if she didn't like him pumping her. He hoped Ralph was at home. For if his aunt proved intractable, he had work for his cousin instead.

The house at Brightwell was a pretty establishment, situated near the centre of the village in its own grounds. It had been inhabited by one of the Earl's elderly aunts until her death, and consequently had been furnished in a manner more comfortable than fashionable, with well-upholstered sofas and chairs, convenient bureaux and a profusion of tables—card tables, wine and work tables and a plethora of occasional tables. None of the items matched, and there was little artistry in their arrangement.

The Rothleys had lived in it since the Baron's death, when it was discovered that the sum of his gaming debts necessitated the sale of the family home. The younger Ralph Rothley had no alternative but to accept the charity of the Blakemeres. The Countess had preferred him to maintain the establishment in the Haymarket and sell off his country house. The illusion, according to Lady Blakemere, would enable him to fire off his sisters successfully, although it meant Ralph was in no position to marry. Which was unfortunate. When Claud took the reins, he intended to find a way to change that.

Trading on his relationship to the family, he entered the sunny downstairs parlour unannounced, having ascertained from Tufton that his aunt Silvia was there. The room benefited from plain cream walls, for there was no harmony in the upholstery of the furnishings. He found Lady Rothley prostrate upon a hump-back sofa of cherry damask, with Kate in attendance.

In deference to his aunt, he had donned a green cloth coat instead of his habitual country frock, but he might as well have spared himself the trouble. Her greeting was not encouraging.

'Oh, heavens, it is Devenick! What does he want? Kate, you know the doctor said I must not be agitated. Send him away, I beg of you!'

Kate turned to him apologetically. 'You see how it is, Claud. Shall we go into another room?'

'No, by Gad!' he said forcefully. 'Aunt Silvia, I am not to be put off!'

A moan from the sofa greeted this, and his aunt turned her face away. Kate bustled up to him, speaking in an undervoice.

'Pray don't, Claud! You have no idea what vapours and hysterics we have to endure. Both Tess and Ralph have escaped, leaving me to cope, if you please. So I wish you will not make things worse.'

Claud fastened on the one point that concerned him. 'Is Ralph away from home?'

'No, but he shuts himself up in the library rather than—'

'Kate, what are you saying to him? Oh, has no one any consideration for my poor nerves?'

Claud watched in some dudgeon his cousin retreat to the sofa and bend over the sufferer with soothing words. Was this to be Aunt Silvia's defence? It would not do! He strode across and pushed Kate out of the way, looking down into the plump features of his aunt, blotched with patches of red.

'I have none, at any rate, Aunt! I tell you, I will be heard!'

The button eyes peered fearfully up at him. Claud was about to insist upon the long overdue explanation, when Kate intervened.

'Claud, that is enough! You cannot be so unfeeling as to press Mama. Cannot you see that she has indeed been made ill by this trouble? Look at her face!'

The matron dissolved into easy tears, sniffing dolefully into an already sodden handkerchief. His attention called to the splotches he had noticed, Claud saw now that his aunt had indeed broken out in several rashes. They were on her arms, too, which in this heat were uncovered except by a thin shawl. Frustration rose up in him.

'Well, I am sorry for it, ma'am, but my need has not changed. Why will you not tell me the truth about my wife?'

To his sudden shock, his aunt reared up at this, and let fly. 'Are you mad, Devenick? If Lydia will not tell you, do you think I can do so? Even were I minded to, there is nothing that would more surely bring her wrath down on me as well as you! I am sick of the whole affair, and I wish I were dead!'

With which, she threw herself down again and gave way to gusty sobs. Defeated, Claud backed away, allowing his cousin to move in again. Ignoring her reproachful look, he stalked out of the room and shut the door with unnecessary force.

To hell with the Countess! Had she bullied the whole family into siding with her? It was plain that he would get nowhere with Aunt Silvia. Balked, he paced the wide hallway for a moment or two, pondering his next move. Then he remembered his cousin and made his way to the library, a narrow apartment with several quiet nooks between vast encroaching shelving. He found Lord Rothley comfortably ensconced in a leather chair hidden in the very last section.

'What do you expect me to do?' asked Ralph lazily, setting down the book with which he had been passing the time. 'And don't try and inveigle me into questioning my mother, for I won't do it.'

Claud leaned his shoulders against the bookshelf running along the end wall. 'Don't worry, that ain't what I had in mind.'

'What then?'

'I want to look at your family records.'

Ralph's brows went up. 'Searching for clues?'

'I've got to find something, old fellow. And you said yourself the three of you favour your father's side of the family.'

Together they trawled through boxes containing the late Lord Rothley's papers. 'I don't know what you hope to find, coz. Most of it was burnt, to tell you the truth. There's little here but letters and accounts my lawyer thought it might be best to keep.'

'Letters! Let's start with letters.'

But everything was jumbled together, and they had to sift through the lot, a task that very soon had Ralph ringing for Tufton to bring refreshment to the room he called his study. A large term for a small apartment that boasted little more, besides a couple of chairs, than a modern satinwood tambour desk, brought in by the present occupier, and a folding card table. Ralph had little business to occupy him in reality, but it gave him an excuse, he said, to disappear when his mother's plaints became intolerable.

Working either side of the desk, the two men squinted over yellowing pages with faded print while the Madeira sank lower in the decanter. The papers yielded nothing, much to Claud's disappointment. Nevertheless, he remained with his cousins for luncheon—from which his aunt Silvia pointedly absented herself, instead taking a tray in her room—declaring his intention of studying the family tree afterwards. When he and his cousin pored over this together, several remote connections were discovered, of whom Ralph knew little.

'Nevertheless, I'll take their directions,' decided Claud. 'At least I can write to them.'

'And ask whether they happen to have mislaid a female who resembles my father?' demanded Ralph satirically.

'Hang it, what should I say then? Must act in the matter, Ralph, or I'll go mad!'

His cousin leaned across and patted his arm. 'Leave it to me. I'll find a spurious matter of business and write on that. Then I could put a question about the Merricks. If there's a family connection they will at least know the name.'

Gratified, Claud thanked him, and turned his attention to his uncle Heversham. On his return to the Manor, he gave Kitty an account of his activities, and was surprised that she did not ask any questions. She nodded, and said she supposed something would be discovered sooner or later. But otherwise, she was markedly silent.

He eyed her narrowly during dinner, and thought she looked preoccupied. He felt an urge to put his arm about her—just for comfort. But the thought of cuddling her so wrought upon his senses that he was obliged to keep his distance. Devil take it, this was all down to the Countess! Had she not pressed the matter of an annulment, he need not have approached Kitty in the first place. Though he had been bound to discover eventually how terrified she was of that side of things. She had got through it—and responded very sweetly too, which made him want her the more!

It was with relief that he left the next morning for Ashbury Park, with the intention of confronting his uncle. He had to journey into Berkshire to seek out Mr Heversham, and it would necessitate at least one overnight stay. Ordinarily, he would have stayed at his uncle's, but under the circumstances, Claud took a room at the Angel in the nearby village of Ashbury. As well, as it turned out.

When he presented himself at his uncle's house on Wednesday morning, Mr Heversham was furious.

'What the devil do you mean by pursuing me, Devenick? Barely get my family back home, and you turn up! D'you suppose I'm likely to blab to you when your mother has expressly requested me not to do so?'

Claud jumped on this. 'So you do know about it!'

Mr Heversham, a man of portly build with greying hair and a normally even temper, showed an alarming tendency to resort to hitting his nephew-in-law. Claud stood his ground, keeping a wary eye on the fists clenching and unclenching at Heversham's sides. For a moment, he glared at Claud, his face working. And then a long sigh of exasperation issued from him and he rocked back on his heels.

'Damn you, Claud! Why couldn't you leave well alone?'

Claud was almost betrayed into sympathy. From the harsh red of anger, his uncle's face was draining of colour into an ashen hue. Were those hands, which had been ready to close with him, actually trembling? He watched Heversham cross to a table and pour out a glass of wine. He tossed it off, and turned.

'D'you wish for a glass?'

'Thank you, no, sir.'

Heversham poured himself out another and returned to where Claud was standing in his library, between two leather chairs before the fireplace. The heat of the last two days had dissipated under an overcast sky, and neither of the two big sash windows had been opened. He threw himself into one of the chairs and gestured to the other.

'Sit down, for God's sake!'

Claud obeyed, but he did not relax back as his uncle was doing. He needed to remain alert, ready for any attempt to throw him off.

His uncle's eye was on the ruby liquid in his glass, which he was turning absently in his fingers. 'The only thing I can tell you,' he began at last, 'is that what you have raked up is liable to affect each one of us.' He looked up and Claud met the challenge in his eyes. 'Make no mistake, boy. My interest has nothing to do with Lady Blakemere's. It is immaterial to me if you plunge the Cheddons and the Rothleys into scandal. I am merely trying to protect my family.'

'Which is as good as telling me that my aunt Felicia is involved!' uttered Claud in triumph.

'I did not say that.'

'No, but the implication is clear. Wouldn't redound upon your family otherwise.'

'By connection, it must always redound upon my family,' said his uncle sourly. 'Harry is Felicia's son, don't forget. Which means he cannot escape association with anything that touches the Ridsdales, the Blakemeres or the Rothleys. I might disown them. Harry can't. Hence my interest.'

Claud had no reply to make. He was lost in the sudden realisation that if Kitty was indeed Felicia's daughter, then young Harry must be her brother. Yet the boy's own father would keep him from knowing it! Would he use his son as a shield for his own secrets? His uncle was speaking again.

'I have also a wife and another son who are equally blameless and have no association with your family. I will not have their peace cut up by your foolish antics. I trust I have made myself clear?'

Claud stood up. 'If that's all you have to say to me, sir, then I'm wasting my time here. I will bid you good day.'

His uncle Heversham had calmed down, but Claud's own temper was rising as he took his leave. Did his uncle seriously suppose he would buy into the notion that his interest was merely to protect his wife and child because of Harry's connection to the family? Flimflam! There must be more to it. By Jupiter, he was getting somewhere!

On the way home, with the hood up against the drizzle that repeatedly broke out, Claud pondered his next move. His mind roved over all that Kitty had first told him, and it was then he remembered the Merricks. Kitty had lived in a hunting lodge—or he had worked it out as that from what she had said. If he could find it, people in the vicinity must have heard of the Merricks. Perhaps of Kitty herself.

The logical answer was his father's box in Leicestershire. Would the Countess have placed the child there? There was only one way to find out. Fully determined to set off for Leicestershire within a day, he arrived back at the Manor in time to change his dress for the evening meal. Coming from the stables, he entered the house by the back door, and was immediately brought up short by the sound of a voice singing and the pianoforte playing an accompaniment.

For a moment or two, Claud had the oddest impression that he had entered the wrong house. So rarely was he at home here, that he had forgotten the very existence of the instrument, and could not think where the music was coming from. Without realising what he did, he followed the sounds, drawn by the melodic rendition of the song and the sureness of the fingers that gave the singer the tune.

It did not take him long to run the phenomenon to its source in a little-frequented parlour beyond the one in general daily use. He could not recall having so much as entered the place in the last few years. Opening the door with unconscious care, he realised the explanation had been seeping into his brain even before he spotted Kitty seated at the instrument. Who else could it have been?

He stood silent, watching her, warmth cascading into his chest. Her profile only was visible, but the animation in her features as she sang enhanced her prettiness. A foreign piece, he thought, and sweetly rendered. Only Claud's attention caught upon the tumbling dark curls and the swell of her bosom in the décolletage of the spotted muslin gown. A wave of desire swept through him, but it was oddly entangled in an unfamiliar feeling to which he could not put a name. He only knew that he wanted to catch Kitty up from the stool and envelop her in a suffocating embrace.

As if she felt his thought, Kitty's head turned. She saw him, and stopped in mid note, her fingers poised over the keys and her lips forming an O of surprise that made Claud's blood thrum with longing. To hide it, he started forward, throwing out a hand.

'Don't stop! Didn't mean to disturb you.'

A flush overspread Kitty's features and she looked quickly down at her hands. Claud saw that they were trembling, and moved swiftly to the piano, throwing aside his hat and driving coat, uncaring where they went. He reached down and captured Kitty's fingers in his.

Impelled, she looked up at him, and caught a glow in his eyes that made her mouth go dry. For an instant, Kitty thought he would lean down and kiss her, and the pitter patter that had begun in her heart at sight of him increased.

But though he hesitated for a moment, Claud did nothing. His hold loosened, and he ran his fingers over hers.

'Got a light touch, Kitty.'

She thought she detected a faintly husky note in his voice, and her glance ran over the even features, secretly, while his attention was upon her fingers. Outside the nearby window the drizzle continued, but as Kitty gazed upon the blond hair, she had an impression that the sun had come out. Then the blue eyes met hers again, and he released her. His smile produced somersaults in her stomach.

'Didn't know you could play. Or sing, if it comes to that. I ain't a judge, but seemed to me you've one of the prettiest voices I've ever heard.'

Kitty's bosom swelled with delight. 'Thank you. It is one of the things I had to learn that I enjoyed.' She saw puzzlement in his features. 'You are surprised?'

'Well, you were going as a governess, weren't you?'

'A governess is expected to teach both singing and the pianoforte, as well as dancing.' A little giggle escaped her. 'To tell you the truth, they were the only subjects in which I put any effort, much to the Duck's despair. I thought I should find them of use when—'

She broke off upon the point of mentioning her ambition to marry a lord. She had told Claud at the first—but that was before she had entered into a contract that bore little relation to her foolish dreams. The sharp stab within recalled his mission to her mind.

'How did you fare with your uncle Heversham?'

To her intense disappointment, the reminder served to jerk Claud out of his preoccupation with her unexpected accomplishments. His features tightened, and he tossed his head.

'The fellow is hand-in-glove with the Countess, that's certain! Tackled him outright on my aunt Felicia's involvement, and he would only say that it's Harry he's protecting.' He saw the frown in Kitty's eyes, and added with a trifle of impatience, 'Aunt Felicia's boy. She died when he was born. Told you, didn't I?'

The apprehension that was rapidly becoming all too familiar to Kitty was beginning to invade her bosom. 'I think so. Only there are so many cousins that I cannot keep track of them all. But, Claud, what do you mean to do now?'

'Mean to set out for my father's hunting box in the morning. Might get news of the Merricks there.'

'Do you think that is where I was living?'

'Must have been. Heversham may say what he likes, but he knows the truth. If I can find any sort of clue, might prevail upon him to let it out—even if it's only in a temper. Fellow was as mad as fire that I'd gone to Ashbury Park. Don't know what he expects! What, am I to sit and wait while the Countess thinks up ways and means to rid me of you? I can see myself!'

Kitty glowed to know that his determination was fixed, but it did little to raise her from that sense of hopelessness that had briefly lifted. For that little moment, she had been convinced that he did want her. But he had done nothing more, and she concluded that she must have been mistaken.

Claud set off for Leicestershire on Thursday, defiant of the uncertain weather. Had Kitty an inkling of his thoughts, she might have bidden him farewell with less willingness. He had come within an ace of breaking his word last night! Though he had controlled himself in her presence, the vision of his wife sitting at the pianoforte had played havoc with him. The image of her velvety eyes and the clouds of dark hair had developed a tendency to sit in the back of his mind.

Arguments in favour of his strong desire to visit her bedchamber had churned through his head. He had succeeded in subduing his baser self, but it was with relief that he left Shillingford. How long he could continue in this way, he knew not. Had he been situated in London, he might have found relief with one of his ex-mistresses. Not that any female would do! It was Kitty he wanted, and it was rapidly being made clear to him that he would have to bend his mind to a solution. He consoled himself with the reflection that, once his marriage was stable, he might reasonably persuade Kitty to allow him to resume his marital rights. Which led him to the realisation that Kitty had changed.

He had thought she would be as wild to know her future as he was himself, but not a bit of it! She was withdrawn, unlike the impetuous creature he had come to know. Claud did not like to see her like this. He had found her dauntless at first. He reflected how readily she had adjusted to the violent alteration of her life, and remembered how she had fought him and berated him when she was angry. All that had gone.

Apprehension slivered into his chest. Had she taken him in dislike? Had his insistence on consummating their marriage given her a disgust of him? He knew that she thought him selfish. Had his single-mindedness alienated her completely? The thought sent him into a state of mind that was excessively uncomfortable.

It did not help when he drew blank at his father's hunting box. He knew the couple who kept the place, of course, and neither had ever heard of anyone called Merrick. Nor had they any supposition that the name was known in the surrounding area. The keeper went so far as to make discreet enquiries on his behalf while Claud refreshed himself and the fellow's wife made up a bed for him. He kicked his heels there all through Friday, but no news was forthcoming.

Claud left the place on Saturday in a mood, despite the lightening of the skies and the showing of a weak sun, of growing despondency.

Driving back to Oxford, he was spurred by a longing to see Kitty. He wished he had cheering news for her, and began to wonder whether he ought not to let the matter alone, if it produced this much unhappiness—*was* she unhappy? If she was, were his empty searches the reason?—except that he could not hold his marriage together unless he did find out.

He arrived back at Shillingford Manor in the late afternoon, walked into the parlour, and found, to his amazement, his father in company with Kitty, and looking very much at home. The two of them were seated close together in chairs dragged before an open window, and Kitty was laughing at something Lord Blakemere was saying to her. Claud was conscious of a ridiculous sensation of jealousy.

Chapter Ten

His father having been persuaded by Kitty to stay for dinner, it was not until well into the evening that Claud had an opportunity to talk with Lord Blakemere alone. Impatience chafed him as he listened to his sire boring on about an ancient temple being unearthed in a remote Grecian island. What possible interest his wife could have in such matters was beyond Claud. One would think, from her eager questions, that nothing could have exceeded her delight at the tales of worshipping of gods and goddesses with which the place was associated. She was both animated and vivacious—a far cry from the Kitty he had been privileged to see lately! Confound it, he might be pardoned for imagining that she had a better regard for his father than her own husband!

When Kitty left them at the end of the meal, saying that she knew Lord Blakemere wished for a period alone with his son, Claud felt himself tensing up with resentment. Particularly since the Earl's smiles faded with Kitty's departure.

'You wished to speak to me, sir?'

A look of surprise flitted over his father's features. But he nodded, and cast a significant glance at the butler, who

was busily removing dishes from the table to the side-
board. Claud took the hint.

'That'll do, Hollins. Leave us the bottle, will you? We'll
serve ourselves.'

The butler set the half-empty claret between Claud at
the head and his father to one side, and withdrew. Lord
Blakemere waited until the door closed behind him. Then
Claud found himself on the receiving end of an unnerving
appraisal from the mild eyes underneath the spectacles. He
was driven into instant attack.

'What the devil are you looking at me like that for, sir?'

'I am trying to make up my mind whether I have fathered merely a headstrong fool or a blind one.'

Claud glared at him. 'But a fool either way, is that it?'

He was treated to that faintly satirical smile. 'That, my
boy, I have always known.'

'I thank you! Don't doubt it's my marriage that makes
you say it this time, though it seems to me you took pleasure enough in my wife's company!'

The Earl's gaze softened. 'She is undoubtedly refreshing.'

This remark, oddly enough, set the resentment riding
high in Claud's chest. He seized the claret bottle and refilled his glass, remembering at the last minute to offer it
to his sire first. Lord Blakemere waved it away.

'My approval of your wife appears to afford you no
satisfaction, Claud.'

Claud set the bottle down. 'How should it, sir, when I
know you only mean to be sarcastic? Merely because Kitty
chooses to show an interest in your antiquities don't mean
she's the daughter-in-law you'd wish.'

'You don't know what kind of daughter-in-law I would
wish for.'

'Maybe not, but I'll stake my life it ain't a girl who is like to bring scandal into the family.'

'But that is not Kitty's fault,' pointed out the Earl, 'nor does it detract from her charm of character. Did we not agree she was a taking child the first time I met her?'

A sensation of outrage consumed Claud, and he turned a heated gaze upon his father. 'It's coming it a bit strong, sir, to expect me to believe what you say after you deliberately broke it to the Countess that I hadn't yet taken the chit! Didn't expect you to take my part against her, but I never thought you'd stab me in the back!'

The Earl gave a little sigh and sat back. 'So that is it!'

'I should dashed well think it is!' uttered Claud furiously. 'And it's the worst thing you could have done, as it chances, for I've had to act on it and it's made Kitty withdraw so far from me you'd think I was the most unfeeling brute in the universe! *And* I took the greatest care about it. But did that help? The devil it did! She's shown you a deal more friendliness than I get, I can tell you that much.'

He then threw the wine down his throat, and slammed the glass to the table with a force that nearly broke its stem. After which, he gazed at his sire in an overwrought sort of way, confused both by the tumult of emotion in his breast and his own outburst.

'Dear me.'

The Earl removed his spectacles, blinking myopically. Taking his discarded napkin, he rubbed in a painstaking manner at the two rounds of his eyeglasses. Claud eyed this manoeuvre in silence, feeling foolish and embarrassed at the recollection of what had come out of his mouth. His father finished cleaning his spectacles, and with deliberation replaced them on his nose. Claud met his limpid gaze and awaited—not without misgiving—what he might say.

'I have worked it out, my dear boy. It is not a question of one or the other. I have a son who is both headstrong *and* blind.'

Claud sank back in his chair. 'Confound it, sir, must you be so cryptic?'

'I have changed my mind.' The Earl reached for the bottle. 'About having a little more, I mean, not about you, Claud.'

Past fathoming his sire's infuriating commentary, Claud made a dismissive gesture. 'Help yourself, sir.'

His father poured a measure of wine, and sipped at it in a leisurely way. At last his gaze returned to Claud's face.

'Your mother has got wind of your activities.'

Claud sat up, all thought of his earlier confusion wiped from his mind. 'What, my enquiries? From my uncle Heversham, I'll be bound!'

'She is not pleased.'

'Ha! What did she expect, that I would sit tight and do nothing?'

The Earl set his elbows on the table, nursing his wineglass between his cupped hands. 'I have come here to persuade you to do just that, dear boy.'

Claud snorted. 'Desist, you mean? At the Countess's bidding? I can see myself!'

'At my bidding, Claud.'

Resentment made a thin line of Claud's lips, but he said nothing. Lord Blakemere nodded understandingly.

'I see what it is. But you are mistaken, dear boy. Your mother does not know that I am here.'

Astonished, Claud blinked. 'She didn't send you?'

His father winced. 'I am aware that my children uniformly regard me as a weakling, but it has never been my practice to act the role of go-between.'

'True, sir,' said Claud, abashed. 'Beg your pardon.'

That enigmatic look he had never been able to penetrate overspread the Earl's features. 'You are absolved. Setting that aside, however, what I wish to say to you is this. It is my belief that if you will practise patience, if you will just sit tight, as you so lucidly expressed it, and do nothing, you may earn your victory. And with fewer casualties than if you persist in a war.'

Claud eyed him narrowly. 'What do you know, sir? What has she said? Do you tell me you ain't in her confidence?'

'I will not tell you anything so patently false,' stated his father. 'What I will tell you is that the correspondence between your mother and Heversham has changed in tone. Your perseverance has been noted.'

'Well, and how is that supposed to help me?' demanded Claud impatiently.

The Earl sighed. 'In words of one syllable then, since you are like to fight any attempt to set the marriage aside, it is seen that a solution is called for to let it stand and avoid the scandal.'

A jolt of triumph leaped in Claud's breast. The Countess had capitulated! Jupiter, but he was winning! He had not expected her to abandon her course so tamely. Truth to tell, he did not know how to take it. Unless she had finally understood that his will was as determined as her own? His father appeared to divine his feelings.

'Before you count your chickens, Claud, let me advise you that the battle is by no means over. You stand on precarious ground. One move in the wrong direction, and this strategy is likely to be thrown aside. It has been taken only with reluctance.'

'You mean she don't want to do it, but she's been forced to it? I take that as a winning point, sir!'

'Yes, if you will only desist from trying to dig up the

dirt,' said the Earl flatly, 'if I must needs use language that you will understand.'

Claud thought it over. 'It might be worth it—for the time being. But I won't give up my right to know the truth, on that you may depend.'

'Keep it for the future,' advised his father.

'Very well. But I'm hanged if I remain cooped up here much longer. Time and past I took Kitty about and introduced her to the neighbourhood.'

Lord Blakemere sighed. 'Try not to be more of a fool than you can help, my dear boy. You will only throw everything back if you cross your mother. Keep close for a week or two, stay your hand, and that charming little creature you have married may at length be accorded acceptance.'

At breakfast, Claud gave an account to Kitty—judiciously expurgated—of his conversation with his father. She was a little warmer than she had been of late, and he wondered if it was due to having had company other than his own. With reluctance, he relayed the necessity for her to remain longer in obscurity at the Manor.

Kitty shrugged. 'I am growing used to being alone.'

'You ain't alone,' he objected. 'I'm here most of the time.'

To his chagrin, she had no answer, and the way she withdrew her regard from his face and trained it upon her plate was not encouraging. He eyed her with burgeoning resentment, and abruptly noticed what she was wearing. A pink object that looked vaguely familiar.

'That ain't one of the gowns I bought you!'

Kitty looked up. 'No, it is my old one.'

'What, the one you had on when I picked you up? Why in the world have you taken to wearing it again?'

He saw a touch of the old fire in her eyes. 'What else could I do? I have been alternating the two muslins, but they have had so many washes that I am afraid they may fall to pieces. Unless you would prefer that I wear the spangled gown to dinner?'

Guilt swamped Claud. They had been married nearly a month. Yet he had given no thought to her present needs. He had promised her she might buy whatever she chose, and he had not even arranged to give her pin money. He broke into impetuous speech.

'I'm a nodcock, Kitty! Forgot all about it once I'd seen to your immediate needs at that Frenchwoman's place. Why didn't you say something?'

'Because I didn't think of it either,' confessed Kitty frankly. 'I have been used to manage on very little, you must know, and since we cannot go visiting nor receive anyone here, it did not occur to me that I needed anything more.'

'Well, I won't have you decked out like a dashed governess! We'll go to Oxford tomorrow and purchase some gowns there.' He was annoyed to see much the same sort of look in her face as he had been subjected to by his father. 'What's to do now?'

'How can you take me to Oxford? If anyone were to come upon us there, and your mother heard of it—'

'Hang my mother!'

'That is all very well, Claud, but you have just told me that—'

'Yes, but I don't see why you should be deprived of things you need merely because my mother has set some falsehood about the country.'

'A moment ago you had not the slightest interest in my costume!' objected Kitty indignantly. 'If that is not just like you, Claud. Had I not worn this, it would never have occurred to you to think of buying me gowns, and now that you are thwarted, you must needs fly into a tantrum over it.'

'Who's flying into a tantrum? I merely said—'

'Well, don't! It is of no use to repine, for there is nothing to be done about it.'

Claud suddenly snapped his fingers. 'Yes, there is. I shall take Kate instead! She is much of your figure, if a little smaller at the bosom. But we may at least take it that what will suit her will also look good on you.'

To his relief, Kitty raised no objection to this. On the contrary, her eyes lit and he was conscious of warmth at his chest.

'That is an excellent plan, Claud. Thank you!'

Once the idea had entered his head, Claud was on fire to carry it through. He set off the very next morning, with the declared intention of capturing Kate and taking her with him to Oxford. It served a dual purpose, for he was able to seek out Ralph and find out the results of his investigations. They were disappointing. Merrick was a name unknown among the Rothley clan. Which made Claud the more certain that his wife would be found to be his uncle's natural daughter.

His enforced inaction chafed him the more, and he was glad to be up and doing, if it was only replenishing Kitty's wardrobe. His cousin Kate being only too glad of an excuse to get out of the house, his mission prospered. Claud took care not to advertise his presence to his aunt, and Ralph had only to instruct Tess to take her sister's place with the afflicted Lady Rothley.

Claud allowed his cousin to make a choice of gowns for Kitty, only intervening to check that she had made provision in the size for his wife's fuller figure. An exercise that recalled to his mind the feel of her body under his hand, and sent a surge through his loins. Watching Kate pirouette in front of a mirror in a gown of pale lemon muslin that suited well with her dark hair, Claud discovered that the feeling subsided. There was no attraction in him for his cousin. A circumstance he found inexplicable, along with an odd notion that entered his head. It seemed to him that it was now Kate who resembled Kitty, and not the other way about.

With Kate once more attired in her pelisse of mulberry cloth over her own white muslin gown, they completed their purchases, leaving the modiste with three new gowns nestling in a bandbox, and various accoutrements chosen by his cousin reposing in another. Outside, they ran straight into a matron of their London acquaintance.

'Devenick!' The woman stopped dead in her tracks, and the feathers in her bonnet quivered comically. 'And dear Katherine too? I had not expected to see you out and about together. I quite thought the two of you were in disgrace!'

Kate looked aghast as the creature gave vent to a co-quettish laugh. Claud bristled, forgetting to doff his beaver hat, and did not hesitate to give voice to his feelings.

'Haven't a notion what you're talking about, ma'am.'

The matron started back in exaggerated surprise. 'But surely—have I been mistaken?'

Kate found her tongue. 'In what, ma'am?'

A pitying look was cast upon her. 'It is all over the county that you and Devenick had been secretly married.'

'Me and Devenick?' repeated Kate blankly, with a fine disregard for grammar. Claud cursed under his breath, but the woman had not finished.

'Indeed, my dear Katherine, and against the wishes of the family. I understand Lady Blakemere is furious.'

Claud wanted to annihilate the creature, but he refrained

for fear of giving anything away. To his relief, Kate took the affair in hand.

'My dear ma'am, I cannot think where you heard such a rumour. On the contrary, it is the family who wished us to marry. Both Devenick and myself were opposed to it.'

The matron looked disappointed. 'Ah, that would explain the disgrace. Only I made sure Devenick had been married. Why, everyone is talking of it!'

'Then everyone is wonderfully mistaken,' stated Kate firmly. 'I beg you will excuse us, ma'am. My mother is unwell, and I must hurry back to her bedside.'

While she uttered spurious greetings to be sent to Lady Rothley, the woman openly eyed the bandboxes, and looked from one to the other as if she was not in any way convinced of the truth of what Kate had said. Claud was relieved to get away, and immediately they were back in the curricle, he vented his fury. His cousin cut him short.

'Claud, there is no use raging! You should thank heaven instead that you have kept Kitty close at Shillingford.'

Claud wondered if his father had heard this talk. Had this been the spur? To protect Kitty from gossip?

'It is a pity that I have been so occupied with Mama's vapours,' said Kate. 'And with Babs away too. It must be very lonely for poor Kitty with no friends of her own.'

Claud was within an ace of demanding—and forcefully!—if his cousin did not consider him any sort of company for his wife, when he remembered that Kitty did have friends. He had no clear recollection of their names, but there were two of them. They had been at that Seminary of hers, and had both of them gone out as governesses and married their employers. Of all people, they could not threaten Kitty's position as Lady Devenick. Why should she not invite them to visit her? And by the greatest good fortune, he recalled abruptly, the visit could be arranged to coincide with Kitty's birthday on the sixteenth of July.

Kitty's delight at the promised treat knew no bounds. She was a creature transformed, throwing herself pell-mell into Claud's astonished arms in a hug that caught him off balance. He grabbed her tightly as he struggled to keep his footing.

'Steady, silly chit! You'll have us both over!'

Kitty allowed herself to be righted, breathless with laughter, and immediately launched into a whirl of preparation. The letters had first to be despatched, which necessitated an explanation of her present situation. Kitty glossed it over, promising to fill in all the details when Prue and Nell arrived. She had almost sent off the invitations when Claud bethought him of the married status of the erstwhile governesses.

'You'd best ask their spouses to come along as well, and be done with it.'

Kitty stared. 'But I don't know them, Claud. I should not know what to say to them.'

'Can't expect them to stay at home while their wives go off jaunting! Take a dim view of it myself.'

A tremor attacked Kitty's pulses. 'Would you?'

'What, if you were to take it into your head to go visiting for days on end without me? I should dashed well think I would!'

It was the first time he had intimated the slightest sign of possessiveness and Kitty glowed inside. Though it was typical of Claud that it should not have occurred to him that she might be in the least discomposed by his absence.

'And if you're to be closeted with these deuced females of yours from morning 'til night,' he added trenchantly, forgetting that the whole notion had been his in the first place, 'I can do with the company.'

'Well, if you mean to entertain the gentlemen, Claud, then I don't mind asking them too,' Kitty agreed blithely, and she added a hurried postscript to each letter before begging a frank from Claud and giving the letters to Hollins for immediate despatch.

Claud found himself willy-nilly dragged into the preparations, and under instruction to think of ways to keep the gentlemen out of the house, so that Kitty and her friends might enjoy uninterrupted intercourse for at least a day or two while their guests were at Shillingford. Kitty awaited the coming of the post-boy with impatience, until both Prue and Nell had written back—by which time July was already a few days old—each chock-full of exclamation and surprise, but eager for the reunion. Nell was also to bring her stepdaughter, who, she advised, could not be left alone at Castle Jarrow.

The chambers were ready, the menus agreed with Mrs Papple, the silver polished and the whole house aired until there was at length nothing for Kitty to do but await the coming of the appointed day of arrival with what patience she could muster.

When a carriage at last drew into the drive, Kitty sprang up from the small parlour where she had been on the watch since breakfast, and flew through the hall, calling for Claud as she went. Hollins, as alert as his mistress, was already opening the front door. Kitty raced through it, just in time to see the dear sweet features of Prudence Rookham peering out of the coach doorway.

'Prue!' shrieked Kitty. 'Oh, Prue, dearest Prue!'

'Kitty!' squealed the other, and tumbled out of the coach into her friend's welcoming arms.

Claud, who had followed his wife out of the house, stopped short, conscious of the oddest sensation of mingled warmth and envy. For several moments, he drank in the reunion, which was a startling combination of laughter, tears and a flood of endearments. It struck him that the exuberance of this greeting exceeded any he had ever known. There was a degree of affection between these two girls of hitherto humble station, to which he, with all his wealth and title, was a stranger.

He became aware of a tall lanky gentleman in a mulberry coat, standing patiently by the coach, observing the two women with an indulgent expression on his face. He had his hat in his hand, revealing overlong dark hair, and his features were distinguished by a prominent nose.

Claud hastily approached him, recalling his duties as host, and introduced himself. By the time the fellow had taken his proffered hand in a friendly grip, Kitty and her friend were coming apart and Prue presented her husband.

'How do you do, Mr Rookham?' said Kitty breathlessly. 'Thank you for bringing her to me! Oh, and this is Claud. Lord Devenick, you know, my husband.'

'So much I had gathered,' said Mr Rookham in a friendly way. 'I am delighted to make your acquaintance, Lady Devenick. I have heard a great deal about you.'

Kitty flashed a panic-stricken look at her friend. 'Prue, what have you been telling him? It must be horrid, for there is nothing good to be said of me, I know.'

'On the contrary.' A gleam came into the gentleman's eye. 'You are as pretty as I was led to believe, and your ability to foretell your own future is uncanny.'

At a loss, Kitty blinked at him, and was relieved when Prue called her husband to order.

'Julius, you are not to tease her! Pay no heed, Kitty. He

has the most dreadful quizzing habit, but I shall not allow him to trouble you, never fear.'

It was plain that Mr Rookham was amusing himself at her expense, but Kitty quickly forgot about it as she left Claud to deal with him and led her friend inside, talking nineteen to the dozen.

More than two hours had elapsed by the time the second carriage signalled the arrival of the Jarrows. Over a late luncheon, Claud, forced to engage Rookham in conversation—neither being able to edge in a word with the females!—had found him an easygoing fellow, though his senior by several years. He was interested to see what sort of a man the newcomer might prove to be.

Very different was this second meeting from the first. Claud followed as Kitty ran out with just as much enthusiasm, accompanied by her friend Prue. The female who got down, a blonde creature with a strong face and taller than the other two—and dressed much more soberly—bestowed warm embraces upon his wife and the other female, and immediately turned her attention back to the coach. Extracting a little girl who accompanied her, she spent several moments explaining the various persons about them to the child, before giving her into the charge of a plump young female, obviously a nurse, and allowing herself at last to be presented to her host.

'I am happy to meet you, my Lord Devenick.' The smile, to Claud's secret relief, lit her face, softening it. She turned to the gentleman who accompanied her. 'My husband, sir, Lord Jarrow.'

Claud found a black-garbed fellow with a severe cast of countenance, much marked with grooves and shadows, though he could not have been too much older than Claud himself. There was none of the pleasant bonhomie that characterised Rookham, and Claud gave an inward sigh as he introduced the fellow to Kitty.

To him fell the unenviable duty of entertaining Jarrow, for the ladies swept off together, taking the child and her nurse with them. Claud thanked Providence for Rookham, whose easy manners thawed Jarrow a trifle, much to Claud's relief, for the thought of having to deal alone with such a brooding fellow was daunting.

Of the females, he was able within a day or two to congratulate himself on having the best of the bargain. Prudence had little to recommend her but a pair of speaking grey eyes, though she was a gentle little thing, anyone could tell that. As for the managing Nell, whose strength of character was faintly and fatally reminiscent of the Countess, though the blonde hair was striking, Claud could not by any means allow that she had a tithe of Kitty's attraction. His wife was in every way the prize of the three. She was the prettiest, the most animated, and the most talented—as became obvious when the ladies had been called upon for evening entertainment.

Prue sang a little in a pleasing way, but refused to play, whereas Nell did the reverse until she was persuaded to add her richer notes to a harmony sung by the trio that they had been used to perform at the Seminary. There were neither voice nor fingers in either, Claud decided, to match his Kitty's skill. Moreover, one could talk to Kitty freely. And if only she would look at him in the way he caught the other two looking at their spouses, he would have nothing more to wish for. Apart from the freedom wanting to advertise his marriage. From which irritant, the visit was a welcome diversion.

To Kitty, the treat proved at length a world away from the felicity she had imagined. Her first joy was unsurpassed, and the chatter among the three of them was virtually non-stop as they caught up with what had happened to each of them in the intervening few months since their last meetings.

On the Friday, two days after her friends had arrived, Kitty's twenty-first birthday was celebrated with all due ceremony. Prue and Nell had both brought her gifts, which they presented to her as they dawdled at table after a late breakfast, the gentlemen having long left them to ride out.

The jewelled comb from Prue was immediately set sparkling in Kitty's dark hair. From Nell, there was a set of pocket-handkerchiefs, hemmed in her neat stitch, with Kitty's initial embroidered at one corner. Prue having whispered to Kitty that Nell's husband was a trifle purse-pinched, she made sure to fuss over the simple gift.

'Nell, the very thing I most need! You know how badly I sew, and—'

'I know how badly you *say* you sew!' retorted Nell.

A giggle escaped Kitty. 'Well, I hate sewing. But the thing is, Nell, that I never seem to have a handkerchief, and poor Claud is forever giving me his. So I am very grateful to you.'

Nell smiled. 'Then I am happy to have served "poor Claud".'

'What has he given you, Kitty?' asked Prue.

Kitty almost betrayed herself. Claud had given her no gift, though he had remembered to wish her all happiness. She had told herself the day was yet young, and hoped he might have held back for a surprise. But the melancholy suspicion could not but obtrude that his selfish lordship had not thought of marking the occasion. She fell back upon prevarication, busying herself with the coffee pot, which Hollins had refilled with a freshly made supply, and assuming an airy manner.

'Oh, all manner of things. The spangled gown I wanted so much, for one. I shall wear it tonight.'

She was unnerved to catch Nell and Prue exchanging glances, and set down the coffee pot before she had begun to pour out. It was the latter who said it.

'Dearest, I thought you said he had bought you that gown before ever he thought of marrying you.'

Kitty flushed. She had poured out the tale of her adventures, and had in turn been regaled with fuller details of the stories of her two friends and their romantic endings. Far more romantic than her own woeful situation.

'Has he not given you a gift, Kitty?' demanded Nell forthrightly.

'Of course he has!' uttered Kitty, taking refuge in feigned indignation. 'Everything you have seen me wear was given to me by Claud. He even braved the gossips to fetch me new gowns from Oxford, though he was obliged to take his cousin Kate in my stead.'

'But for your birthday, Kitty?' persisted Prue.

Frantic, Kitty searched her mind for an excuse. And found it. 'You are my birthday gift! Both of you. It was Claud who thought of asking you both, and it was all for my birthday. And—and because he knew I had been alone here. And—and—well, it was excessively kind of him and I could not have wished for a more perfect gift!'

Fortunately, her friends appeared to accept this, and Kitty was able to congratulate herself on having deflected them from the subject. However much she might feel Claud's selfishness, she could not bear to have her friends censure him. And he had been kind. He had kept faith with her, taking Rookham and Jarrow off to a mill in another village, and then he had mounted them so they might all three ride about the country, which had left Kitty free to enjoy the company of her two friends. Only Nell had her attention a trifle divided, for Miss Henrietta Jarrow was a demanding child, and by no means content to be left with her nurse throughout the day.

Kitty's birthday dinner was a decided success, and she was exhilarated to be singled out by Claud in front of the others.

'I beg you will all raise your glasses in a toast to my wife. To Kitty!'

The echo ran round the room, and Kitty's heart warmed. After dinner, he encouraged her to entertain the company with a song. Then Prue suggested they should get up a dance or two, adding remarks that embarrassed Kitty dreadfully.

'For you must know, Lord Devenick, that Kitty is by far the most graceful dancer of the three of us, besides playing and singing so beautifully.'

'Prue, pray hush!'

'But it is true, my love,' chimed in Nell, smiling. With a brief explanation to the gentlemen that Kitty had been teaching the younger girls to dance, she added, 'I am sure Mrs Duxford must miss you dreadfully on that account.'

Kitty was betrayed into a giggle. 'You know very well that the Duck can only be grateful to Claud for ridding her of me forever!'

She was delighted when this was received with a general laugh, but the feeling became as nothing when Claud insisted, with unaccustomed gallantry, that she should immediately show off her skill on the floor. Pressed into partnering him in a gavotte, Kitty allowed herself to be persuaded, and the gentlemen having cleared a space in the parlour that housed the pianoforte in which they were assembled, she took his proffered hand and moved into position as Nell seated herself at the instrument to play for them.

It was immediately apparent that Claud was an expert dancer, and Kitty found it a source of intense pleasure that her steps matched so readily with his. It was a far cry from dancing with the other girls or Mr Duxford, and she was obliged to concentrate all her attention not to make a slip as Claud's hand, warm at her waist, guided her in the shifts and whirls of the dance.

As Kitty sank into the final curtsy, she was lifted to the pinnacle of her day. To the accompaniment of the enthusiastic clapping of the onlookers, Claud bent his blond head and kissed the tips of her fingers, and, despite a trifle of breathlessness, uttered such words of praise as rang in her ears.

'Gad—but you're light on your feet, Kitty! Like a fairy! And prettier, for my money. Couldn't have wished for a better wife!'

But still no gift was forthcoming, and Claud did not—as she had dared to hope—visit her bedchamber that night. Kitty tried to stem the flow of tears and told herself she had everything to be thankful for, considering the uncertainty of her future.

As the days passed, it became a torture to witness the undoubted happiness of her friends in their respective marriages. That intimate caress of ownership Mr Rookham was seen often to exchange with Prue, for instance. Kitty had noticed him allow his hand to slide secretly down her back or across her thigh, or tweak one of the curls she wore clustered about her face instead of being confined in the old way under a strict cap, or entwine his fingers with hers and kiss them lightly before he was obliged to let them go. And Prue's eyes as she glanced at him to accept of these gestures! None could doubt the affection between them.

She noted that Lord Jarrow was not thus free with Nell. But the odd severity of his countenance lightened whenever his eyes rested on her face, and now and then Kitty caught them exchanging a swift smile. And each instance exuded an intensity of feeling that gave Kitty's heart a horrid twinge. Of envy? She tried hard not to show it.

Yet as they sat about the gardens one heated afternoon, Mrs Papple having caused a collection of wicker chairs to be brought out and placed under the trees, Kitty could not help comparing her situation with that of her two friends. It was almost two weeks into the visit, and July was drawing to a close, but Kitty's marriage, near two months old, remained in precisely the same state of uncertainty as that in which it had begun.

Prue and Nell were engaged upon a discussion of how Lady Jarrow could best deal with the vagaries of her little stepdaughter. Henrietta, Nell had confided, though a beautiful child, was wayward. Kitty understood it to be due to the affliction of the horrid creature that had caused all the trouble at Castle Jarrow.

'She has had a difficult time of it, poor darling,' Nell excused her, 'and she is scarcely to blame for what she cannot help.'

The little girl was playing with her nurse, who had been newly engaged. From time to time, she came running up to her stepmother, either for guidance or to relate her victories. Or she would instead approach her father, who was engaged in wandering the gardens with the other two gentlemen while Mr Rookham advised Claud on what he might do to improve his landscaping.

'Gardening is a passion with Julius,' Prue had told them. 'There is nothing he likes more than to be let loose in somebody else's virgin garden, where he may revolve schemes in his head for rockeries, ponds, trellises and I don't know what else besides.'

Claud had promptly invited his guest's opinions on his wholly unmanaged grounds, which were merely kept in order. Kitty could not feel that he was likely to take up anything suggested, but it was typical of him to seize upon any novel notion. And she thought he liked Mr Rookham, having discovered in the other gentleman a skill and interest in driving equal to his own.

For her part, Mr Rookham could not hold a candle to Claud—in any respect. Whether he drove as well or not, she was not in a position to judge. But his was a lanky frame, and that jutting nose was positively ugly! He had a teasing way with him that Kitty would have found tiresome, and his relaxed manner made him decidedly dull. Claud might be impetuous and forceful, but none could deny that he had an excellent figure. She had not previously thought him precisely good-looking, but if she must compare him to Mr Rookham, or to the darkly hollow-eyed features of Lord Jarrow, whose suffering—said Nell—had made him older than his years, then she must count Claud as positively handsome! Certainly, she had rather be married to him than to either of her friends' husbands. Only she was forced to perceive that her marriage had not a tithe of the felicity that her friends enjoyed.

She became aware that Prue and Nell had fallen silent, and brought her gaze back from contemplation of the gentlemen some distance away. There was question in Nell's face, and Prue's eyes held that compassionate look she knew so well.

'What?' demanded Kitty. 'Why are you both looking at me like that?'

Nell glanced at Prue, and lifted her brows. 'Is this a suitable time?'

'There never will be a suitable time,' said Prue, 'if we do not begin.'

Kitty looked from one to the other. 'You are hatching secrets about me! You always did gang up when you wished to bring up a particularly unpleasant subject. What is the matter?'

'Not unpleasant, dearest Kitty,' protested Prue.

'That depends which way you look at it,' put in Nell. She leaned forward in her chair and Kitty found her hand captured between her friend's two palms. 'Kitty, Kitty, foolish Kitty! Why did you do it?'

Kitty snatched her hand away. 'I knew you would say I shouldn't have!'

From her other side, Prue leaned in, reaching to stroke her hair. 'Dearest, Nell is not judging you. Only we have seen how unhappy you are, and—'

'I am not unhappy!' declared Kitty stonily, flinching away. 'I have all that I have ever wanted. Or at least I will have, once Claud's mother is routed. Don't you know that I am not merely a viscountess, but I am one day to be a countess? Once everything is settled, I am to have as much pin money as I wish, and I shall go to all the balls and soirées and parties that I have ever dreamed of—'

'Kitty, stop!'

'—and I shall have gowns twice or three times as pretty as my spangled gown, and all the silk stockings I could ever want!'

Nell had used her authoritative voice, and it caught Kitty in full flood. She came to a jarring halt, and drew in a shuddering breath. She could not bear to look at Prue's tender gaze, nor face the loving disapprobation in Nell's. Looking steadfastly down at her clenched fingers, she swallowed on the tempting sobs and thrust the words out, her tone lowered against the remote possibility that she might be overheard by the object of her affliction.

'It is my own fault. I knew it was wrong. I knew you would say so, Nell. I tried to stop it. But you don't know Claud! He is so very stubborn, there is no doing anything with him when he gets the bit between his teeth. By the time I found out his true purpose in marrying me, it was too late!'

Prue's fingers were laid over her clenched hands. 'Poor darling Kitty.'

'What was his purpose?' asked Nell, in a tone that made Kitty feel herself back at the Seminary. But she answered all the same.

'It was to spite his mother. When he found out that there was a scandal attached to me that the Countess would hate to have raked up, he became determined to use me for his revenge.' Glancing at the faces of her friends she found shock, and felt impelled to defend Claud—and with violence. 'Don't look like that! You have no notion what he suffered at her hands. All his life has been a misery because of that woman. I have met her, and if her manner to me was a sample, I can readily believe how horrid she had been to poor Claud. Truly, I don't blame him for it.'

'You don't blame him for taking you in a marriage that must condemn you to scandal and put you through the unhappiness of knowing some dreadful past history?' Thus Nell, as was to be expected. But Prue's reaction was different.

'Dear Nell, you must not judge him. If Kitty can forgive him, then you should too. And she does forgive him, do you not, Kitty?'

Kitty was moved to shaky laughter. 'I can hardly do otherwise. If you knew Claud well, you would forgive him too. He is so very impulsive—and excessively selfish!—

but he is kind. And when he is put in mind of his obligations, he is generous.' Recalling her birthday and the lack of a gift, she added quickly, 'He does not mean to be thoughtless or to think only of himself. He admits it for a fault. I believe that is what is most admirable in him—he is wholly honest. It is to his credit that he will not pretend to care for me.'

Realising what she had said, Kitty drew back. Her voice became gruff as she tried to conceal her distress.

'The Duck always prophesied that I would come to a bad end, did she not?'

'You have not done so!' uttered Prue, quite crossly. 'And you could not help what happened years ago, Kitty. That must be laid at the door of your parents—whoever they may prove to be.'

Kitty had not withheld the various possibilities that had been postulated within the family. She did not feel that Nell would absolve her, and instinctively she looked to the woman who had always been the guiding light for herself and Prue. She received a burst of Nell's rare laughter.

'Kitty, Kitty! Don't look to me for salvation. I have enough on my hands as it is!'

There had been time to learn of Nell's difficulties. She and Lord Jarrow were obliged to remain in Castle Jarrow for the present, while they hoped for a sale of a larger family home that had not been lived in for many years. Although she had been spared the company of her husband's manic brother-in-law—a creature who had very nearly done for Nell with his crazy machinations about an emerald necklace!—the castle was uncomfortable and Nell wanted to remove Henrietta from the influence of its shadows of the past. The madman had evidently left the place, and was rumoured to be troubling his own family in the north. Once the Jarrows had removed, it was expected that he would return to the castle, for Lord Jarrow had said he might live there if he chose. Meanwhile, Nell had all to do to teach her little stepdaughter basic manners, and to keep her spouse from brooding.

Notwithstanding these troubles, Kitty found an urgent need in herself to have words of comfort from Nell. 'But you do think I did wrong, don't you?'

'Is that what you wish me to say?' asked her friend, smiling. 'Or do you instead hope for my blessing?'

Kitty was grateful for Prue's intervention. 'For shame, Nell! You know she is dreadfully unhappy, and it is unkind to tease.'

'I wish you will not keep saying how unhappy I am!' uttered Kitty, frustrated.

'Well, but aren't you?' asked Nell straitly.

Kitty sighed and capitulated. 'It is only not knowing what is to happen. And to know that once I discover the truth, it can only serve to make me more miserable, for it must be the most hideous scandal when everyone is so anxious to hush it up.'

'And?'

She frowned at Nell. 'And what?'

'She means what else is making you unhappy, dearest.' Thus Prue.

'Nothing! At least—I should not call it unhappy precisely.' It was out before she could stop it. 'Only frustrating!'

'What is frustrating?' demanded Nell.

To Kitty's relief, she heard the nearer voices of the gentlemen, and found them much too close to allow for any further secret exchanges. What had possessed her to blurt that out? The last thing she wished for was to be obliged to explain the horrid predicament of her lack of marital intimacy.

But if Kitty thought herself safe from any more questions that day, she reckoned without the persistence of her two friends. Scarcely had she settled into her bed when there was a gentle tap at the door, followed immediately by the stealthy entrance into the room of Nell and Prue, both clad for the night.

'Julius and Lord Jarrow are still downstairs with Lord Devenick,' confided Prue, 'so we thought we would join you for a comfortable cose.'

They looked so much less like married ladies in the dressing-robes that Kitty remembered, and so much more like her Seminary friends, that it was no time at all before the two ensconced themselves within her massive wooden bed to engage in just the sort of conversation they had enjoyed together in the past. The curtains were closed upon the window side and the base, containing them all three in a cosy haven.

Prue sat cross-legged, elbows on her knees and her chin resting in her hands—just as she had always done. While Nell lay at her ease, facing Kitty, her long legs stretched towards the pillow, and the fall of golden hair tumbling over one shoulder. The three candles set upon the bedside cabinet threw brightness over Nell's strong features, but set Prue's face half in shadow. It was she who began it.

'I have wanted to tell you both—for I have not mentioned the matter to Julius—and I am not *quite* sure, but—'

'You are increasing!' exclaimed Nell.

'Prue, never say you are going to have a baby?' broke in Kitty at exactly the same moment.

All three burst into laughter, and then there was a deal of hugging and commentary at such exciting news. Then Nell touched upon her own situation.

'I hope I may not follow you too swiftly, Prue, for we have so many matters to settle before I dare think of having my own children.' Kitty saw a gleam of fun light at her eyes. 'Only since my darling Eden cannot leave me be for so much as a night, I am very much afraid that he will do the thing long before we are ready!'

Prue giggled, and Kitty dutifully dredged up a laugh or two that had no foundation in her feelings. Worse was to come.

'I am in just the same case,' announced Prue, with what Kitty felt to be odious self-satisfaction. 'What Julius will say when he learns that he cannot have his way quite so much now, I dare not think!'

'There is no harm in it, Prue, if only he is careful,' Nell advised.

'Well, the doctor told me that it can be excessively dangerous if there is too much enthusiasm in the early stages.'

The argument persisted for several minutes, and Kitty was conscious of a hollow opening up inside her. To her dismay, she saw Prue reach out to silence Nell with a touch upon her arm, and give a significant nod in Kitty's direction. Nell uttered words that crushed the heart in her bosom and awakened a nagging ache.

'Don't tell me those memories of yours have risen up to haunt you, Kitty?' She sat up, reaching to take Kitty's reluctant hands into her own. 'Have you been troubled by them, is that it? Has it proven a barrier between you and your husband?'

'What in the world are you talking of, Nell?' asked Prue anxiously.

Kitty sat mumchance, unable to find words to correct the false construction put upon her silence.

'Kitty had memories of having heard and seen what she should not when she was very little,' Nell was saying to Prue. 'She spoke of it once to me, that's all.'

'It is not all!' declared Kitty indignantly, her tongue

loosened by a thrust of old resentment, long buried until this moment. She wrenched her hands from Nell's hold. 'If you had not scolded me for it, Nell, I should have told you then how much it frightened me!'

'Frightened you?' echoed Prue. 'Oh, Kitty, no!'

'Frightened you how?' asked Nell.

'Because I thought the women were crying out in agony.'

The ghost of a laugh escaped her friend. 'Agony! I think not, my love. They must rather have been expressing pleasure.'

'Yes, I know that *now*.'

'But you did not know it when you married,' uttered Prue distressfully.

'Heavens!' exclaimed Nell. 'If my tongue is to blame, Kitty, I am sorry for it indeed.'

'Oh, poor Kitty, what a horrid thing! Was it very bad?'

Kitty burst into overwrought tears. By the time her friends had petted and soothed her into quiet, she had been coaxed into revealing all too much of the true state of affairs. There was balm in the unburdening of her woes, but she could by no means subscribe to the prognostications of her friends.

'You may believe that he will return to you, my love,' said Nell, predictably matter of fact, 'for men have their needs, and why should he look elsewhere when he has a wife at home?'

This was scarcely comforting, and Prue said so. 'Besides,' she added in her overly sentimental way, 'I believe he will come to care for Kitty. Who could fail to love you, dearest?'

Kitty could not repress a watery giggle. 'The Duck, for one.'

Her friends laughed, although Prue protested. Neither was slow to offer advice, however.

'Show him a friendly face,' suggested Nell.

Prue went further. 'Flirt with him.'

'That you surely know how to do,' laughed Nell.

'I promise you, he will not mistake such signals,' Prue told her earnestly.

'At the least, Kitty, do not let him suppose you are still afraid.'

'If he should approach you, return his gestures of affection.'

If she had only the opportunity! Her friends went away presently, leaving Kitty prey to a worse yearning than had previously afflicted her. And all for a faint ray of hope! Convinced that it was vain, Kitty blew out her candle, drew the curtains shut and prepared for sleep, half-sunk in gloom.

She was just dozing off, when the sound of an opening door brought her fully awake. Freezing where she lay, her heart leaping into her mouth, Kitty listened intently in the darkness. A creak indicated the movement of a floorboard, and she could distinctly make out a shuffling of steps. Her pulse quickened.

Chapter Eleven

Faintly, through a chink in the bed curtains, Kitty spied a light. Common sense told her it must be Claud, and her heartbeat quickened mercilessly. Unable to bear the suspense, Kitty reared up and flung back the curtains.

Claud started back, his candle wavering. In the dim light, Kitty saw him put a finger to his lips.

'Sssssh! Don't sh-shriek! Wait, while I p-put thish down.'

Puzzled by the slurring of his words, Kitty waited while with exaggerated care he placed the candlestick on the bedside cabinet. Her pulse was thumping wildly, and a raging hope had taken possession of her bosom.

Then Claud swished the curtains aside a little more, and tugged at the bedclothes. Kitty saw that he was in his nightshirt and a wave of heat swept through her. Dumbly, she flung back the bedclothes and looked up at him in desperate invitation.

'Oh, Kitty!' he uttered, his tone guttural. 'Kitty, Kitty, Kitty!'

In a very short time, he had struggled under the bedclothes—with a little cursing and difficulty!—and was snuggling down beside her.

'Come here! Want you sho very mush—'

Kitty found herself clasped tight against the length of him, and fire swept through her from her head to her toes. Then all thought left her as she began to drown in the intensity of his kiss.

A faint awareness in the far reaches of her consciousness gave her a strange taste to puzzle over. Then came an odd aroma when his mouth left hers and his hot breath roved her cheek and travelled into her neck. Under the urgent pulsing of her need, that flamed to meet Claud's passionate demands, a memory played at the corners of her mind.

Her own breath hissed as the lipping at her neck set her shivering with desire, but the chord tracing back through time yet nagged, seeking for enlightenment. There was a flash of an image. Of a man with red cheeks who took her on his knee and blew a close kiss into the dark curls about her face. And he had radiated that self-same aroma!

She thrust at Claud's shoulders as the recognition hit. 'You're drunk!'

He lifted up a little way and grinned down at her in that engaging look of his, the short gold locks tousled. 'Trifle foxed, thass all. Had to come, Kitty! Couldn't—couldn't shtand it any more. Muss have you! Need you, Kitty. *My* Kitty.'

Kitty's breast was swept with waves of warmth, and the fumes on his breath no longer mattered. She pulled him down to her and kissed him with all the fervency that had attended her longings in those lonely nights. And Claud responded with every evidence of enjoyment.

His hand slid down her flank and splayed across her belly, and his probing fingers shot Kitty into feverish need. She arched involuntarily, gripping his arms and welcoming the velvet invasion at her mouth, giving of her answer in a wild union tongue to tongue.

Claud's convulsive shifting gave her his weight, and Kitty automatically spread herself in invitation. A world of difference this time in that first invasive thrust! Inflamed, Kitty drew it in and cherished it, sinking her teeth into the flesh of Claud's shoulder. He grunted his satisfaction and in a few short movements pressed himself home. Kitty's breath came in gasps, and she gave voice to her need.

'Oh, Claud—pray don't stop. Don't stop!'

As if she must give him reason to yield, Kitty seized his mouth with her own, expressing with her lips all that she knew not how to say.

'Kitty, little witch! What y'doing to me?'

And then he was riding her, plunging deep. Kitty's senses soared away, and all that was real was the urgent pulsing rhythm, the fervid heat between them and the harsh sound of Claud's breathing, close against her cheek. Of a sudden, the intensity of feeling escalated, boiling out of control, and Kitty knew nothing more than the violent movement of her own pelvis and the harsh cries that issued from her throat. She heard her own name, in a frenzied call,

'*Kitty*. Gad, you passionate little minx!'

And then all thought was gone in one mindless instant of total abandon.

When awareness began to return, Kitty became conscious of the heavy weight of Claud's body upon her own, his panting breath in her ear, and her own drenched skin. She felt utterly replete, and could not mistake the intense feeling in her breast for anything but affection. Truth, like a whispering breeze, entered her consciousness. She was in love.

Kitty awoke to the seeping brightness of a promising day, and a sensation of utter contentment. Instinctively she sought for the source of it, and discovered that Claud was gone. For a moment or two, she blinked at the space beside her, hovering on the edge of disappointment. Had it all been a dream? Had she conjured him again and imagined the fervent writhings that were creeping back into her mind?

Her heart refused it. They must be memories! From where could her untutored brain have envisioned these things? It could not have been her distant fears, those childhood images of forbidden sights. Impossible that she could have translated what she had then heard and seen into the exquisite pleasures of last night.

She pulled herself up, and took in the rumpled bed-clothes and her own near nakedness. Her nightgown was gathered all about her waist, and the ache deep within her had nothing to do with dreams. It had happened! Last night Claud had come to her, had mastered her so completely that she was his—wholly and forever.

Kitty hugged the knowledge to her, and relished the discovery of her own feelings. How long had she loved him? It must have been coming upon her for some time, the deeply hidden source of her unhappiness. For her affections were not reciprocated.

Oddly, she felt no resentment now. At the least, she had proof that Claud desired her. It was scarcely flattering that it had taken overindulgence in drink to awaken his need, but Kitty forgave him for that. As she would, she knew now, forgive him anything. Almost. He was who he was, but he had married her. He had signalled his ownership in no uncertain terms. 'My Kitty', he had called her, she recalled with a thrill of delight. And he had taken his rights without mercy! Oh, that he would do so again—and soon.

Recalling the advice she had been given, Kitty was able

to laugh now as she prepared herself for the day. No need
for flirtation or friendly faces. Kitty needed no further instruction on how to signal her need. She knew it would be
in each look she gave him, in every smile. Oh, he would
hunger for her now! What had he called her? *Passionate
little minx*. Well, she would be. For Claud, she would be
passion incarnate—if that was all she could be to him.

She went down to breakfast presently with a light step,
and a bosom bursting with expectancy, only to discover
that chance, awaiting its moment to pounce, had not given
up its relentless pursuit of her.

Claud was at table, frowning over a letter in his hand.
There was no sign of their guests. He looked up. There
was no record in his features—infinitely dear to her now—
of the indelible impression he had made upon his wife last
night. He was instead looking alarmed.

'Fat's in the fire now, Kitty, and no mistake!'

Her heart skipped a beat, and she grabbed hold of the
back of a chair. 'What is it? Has your mother done something?'

'Not the Countess, no.' He waved the sheet of paper in
a manner that showed clearly his agitation. 'It's my grandmother. The Dowager Duchess of Litton, y'know. She's
got wind of the marriage, and she's summoned me to Derbyshire to give an account of myself.'

The whole of Kitty's happiness vanished in a thrust of
dismay as she recalled the hideous uncertainty under which
she laboured. She had foolishly forgotten it all, convinced
that last night's revelation had settled everything. Unable
to fathom what this latest turn betokened, she eyed Claud
in gathering apprehension.

'But—but has she been alerted by the Countess, or—'

'Can't have been, for she's warned me to say nothing
of it to anyone.'

Kitty tried to think, and could only take in that he was leaving the house. 'When must you go? I mean, we have guests at this moment, but—'

Claud shook his head. 'I've made my excuses to Rookham and Jarrow. They'll be off tomorrow, and their wives with them. I've said Hollins and Mrs Papple will see 'em all right. But we must set out today.'

'We?' gasped Kitty, horrified. 'But, Claud, she cannot wish me to go!'

'Well, she does. Expressly stated I should bring you with me. Look.'

Kitty took the sheet in nerveless fingers, and read where Claud pointed. It was true. Indeed, the instruction was heavily underscored.

'Hanged if I know what to make of it,' Claud said, trouble in his voice. 'But one thing's clear. She's as mad as fire. And when Grandmama is on the warpath, she's a deuced sight more dangerous than the Countess ever could be!'

Kitty did not know what she had expected. Indeed, her apprehension had grown steadily through the relatively short journey to Buxton, accomplished within the day, where the Dowager Duchess of Litton had resided since the death of her spouse.

'She says it's for her health,' had confided Claud, 'but if you ask me, there ain't a female in the land of her age who can boast a stronger constitution.'

If Kitty had cherished a vague hope that the intimacy they had shared would change Claud's behaviour towards her, this upset had put paid to the possibility. There was no echo in his manner of her newfound feeling towards him. Kitty, on the other hand, had felt all his unease as if it were her own, with the result that her fears had worsened.

And this, on top of the horrid necessity to bid a hasty farewell to her friends, cutting short their visit. Prue had noticed the change in her, but there had been time only to whisper of the unexpected visit from her spouse in the night, before Kitty had been whisked away. She had left her friends with promises to meet again at the earliest possible moment, and had shed tears at leaving them.

Claud had glanced round as he drove and spied her distress. 'It ain't as if you won't see 'em again, silly chit. I liked that fellow Rookham, and I dare say I can bear Jarrow's company if I must. We'll have them to visit again whenever you wish.'

Only as the miles had passed, and Kitty's attention had turned to the visit they were obliged to make, she could not but wonder if there might never be another opportunity. If the Dowager Duchess of Litton was more powerful than Lady Blakemere, the marriage might already be doomed.

Kitty had formed a hazy vision in her mind of an elderly version of the Countess of Blakemere, but very different was the reality with which she was confronted, when they presented themselves that Wednesday evening in a pretty south-facing saloon, with sun streaming in through an open French window upon pink-tinted walls.

The Dowager, attended by a faded creature introduced as her companion, was a lady of no great stature, with fine bones in delicate features and a pair of exceptionally keen grey eyes. What hair could be seen escaping from under a frivolous lace confection that passed for a cap was almost wholly white, offering no clue to its former colour. Her skin was pale, but little lined, and she might as easily have been in her fifties as the much greater age Claud had mentioned. The whole effect was singularly unnerving, and oddly familiar.

'Ha! So you've arrived, have you?' was her greeting, and her gaze remained fixed upon Kitty as she held out her hand for Claud to kiss.

'You're looking well, Grandmama.'

Relieved that the penetrating eye shifted to Claud's face, Kitty kept her distance. 'Never mind how I look! What do you mean by it, you young rascal, setting the family by the ears?'

Claud threw a glance at the companion. 'Tell you anything you wish, ma'am, but in private.'

The old lady flung her hand out in a dismissive gesture. 'Off you go, Moston!' She added, as the unfortunate female shuffled from the room, 'Not that you need mind her. Deaf as a post! Besides, I'm bound to speak of it to her. No one else likely to listen to my ramblings.'

Her gaze returned to Kitty's face, and she wondered if she was expected to speak. The door closed, and a finger beckoned. Kitty looked instinctively to Claud for guidance, her heart beginning to hammer.

'Can't she talk without your say-so?' demanded the old lady, evidently catching the look.

'Of course she can,' he retorted, crossing quickly to Kitty's side, and putting an arm about her. She sank against him, her heart filling with gratitude. 'She's had short shrift from the Countess, though, and she's scared of you!'

'Piffle! Why should she be? I ain't angry with her. It's you I'm fit to fry with a fishbone!'

'I know, ma'am, and you ain't the only one.'

'What did you expect, noodle? But I'll wager there ain't one of 'em with my reason.'

Claud's blue gaze frowned upon her. 'Which is?'

The Dowager threw up hasty hands. 'You've got hold of a girl of dubious birth who looks more like Kate Rothley than Kate does herself, and you didn't think to bring her straight to me?'

'Hang it, that's the last thing I'd do!'

'Then you're a pudding head!'

'And you'd try the patience of a saint, Grandmama! Why should I distress you with it all?'

'Use your noddle,' snapped his grandmother. 'It don't take a genius to know there's been dirty work afoot. And don't tell me you didn't realise it, or you wouldn't have married her. I know what your game is, young Claud!'

'Oh, do you?'

'Do you take me for as big a noodle as you are yourself? Why your father didn't drown you at birth, I'll never know!'

Kitty listened to the quick give and take of words in growing wonder. The likeness of manner was uncanny. She had assumed Claud had his strong will from his mother, but seeing him head to head with his grandmother, she felt obliged to revise this opinion. The frail appearance of the elderly dame was as deceptive as Claud's insouciant attitude. She would not be at all surprised to find an echo of her husband's impetuosity in this extraordinary female, who obviously behaved precisely as she chose. Indeed, defiant of fashion, she was dressed in pomona green silk, made up in a style Kitty instantly recognised to be long out of the mode, with a large muslin handkerchief crossed before and tied behind.

Claud had fallen silent after her last stricture, a heavy frown descending on his brow. But Kitty was sure he was not exercised by the unkind aspersions upon his intelligence. To her dismay, the Dowager's eyes reverted upon herself. The delicate features softened all at once, and a smile creased her mouth.

'Don't look so terrified, child, I won't eat you! Come here to me.'

It was the first time she had addressed Kitty directly. Swallowing down a surge of fright, Kitty took a reluctant pace towards her. She felt Claud at her back, and found herself shifted willy-nilly closer to the old lady. The grey eyes inspected her, drinking her in from head to foot. Close up, the pale skin was like stretched parchment, and the years were more visible. The Dowager Duchess Lady Litton reached out a dainty hand. Kitty took it. The fingers were dry to the touch, and they closed about hers with surprising strength, drawing her forward.

'Let me look at you.'

The fingers left Kitty's hand, and instead reached up and took hold of her chin, tilting her head. Kitty stood still, her gaze never leaving the eyes in the Dowager's fine-boned face. Despite what the old lady had said to Claud, she thought that a faint look of sadness came into those eyes. But there was nothing of it in the voice, which was as vibrant as ever when she released Kitty.

'Very pretty.'

'Isn't she just?'

Kitty flushed with pleasure and gave him a shy smile. He returned it with a quizzing look, which caused a flutter in her heartbeat. Her mind leaped to the night they had shared, and Kitty was conscious of a tug at her loins. She felt it a mercy when the Dowager claimed her attention.

'Sit by me, child. There's a deal I want to ask you.'

At the old lady's bidding, Kitty turned a chair and sat so that she half-faced the Dowager Duchess. Claud hovered beside her, until his grandmother acidly recommended him to fetch another chair if he meant to stand guard over the chit.

'How old are you?' demanded the redoubtable dame.

'I have just turned one and twenty, ma'am.'

'Ah, that explains why my grandson took you to Gretna.'

'Wish I knew where you had your information,' interrupted Claud.

The Dowager flicked a smug glance at him. 'I have my spies.'

'Then they must be in the family, for there ain't anyone outside it knows we went to Gretna.'

'Piffle! Nothing ain't secret when you've a parcel of servants around you. Though how Lydia managed to keep this one dark is a mystery.'

Claud leaped from his seat. 'How did you know it was the Countess who did this? Do you know who Kitty is, Grandmama?'

'If I'd known, boy, you'd not have found her. Which reminds me, where did Claud find you, child?'

As Kitty explained the error that had been made, she thought she spied a tell-tale motion at the old lady's mouth. But the slight relaxation did not prevent the Dowager from catechising her about her life at the Seminary and how she had arrived there in the first place, before turning to her early years. Kitty found herself explaining much of what she had told Claud, about her life in the hunting lodge, the lady who used to visit her, and the man who might have been Lord Rothley. The Dowager's brow grew blacker, and Kitty faltered a little.

'Don't stop. What was the name of the people who had you in charge?'

'The Merricks, ma'am. I was named for them. It was said that Mr Merrick had made a misalliance and I was the result. Then they both died and I went to the Seminary.'

The Dowager turned to Claud. 'Heard of the Merricks before, boy?'

'Only wish I had,' Claud returned. 'I looked for them in Leicestershire, but—'

'Where in Leicestershire?'

'My father's hunting lodge.'

His grandmother snorted. 'Should have gone to Hinkley. I'll lay you any money you'd have had word of them there.'

Claud stared. 'You mean my grandfather's hunting box? But it belongs to Litton. The Countess wouldn't have put her there.'

'Noodle! It belongs to Litton now. But you forget, Claud. Your grandfather was Litton then. Thought the name Merrick was familiar the moment I heard it.'

Kitty could see the burgeoning excitement in Claud's blue eyes, as strongly as she felt it herself. If only this snippet of her history did not threaten to deprive her of him!

'Grandmama, I believe you've hit it!'

A second snort nearly blew Kitty's head off. 'Didn't I say you'd have done better to come to me?'

Claud grinned. 'You did. I'd best be off there as fast as may be!'

'You'll do nothing of the kind, boy.'

'But, Grandmama—'

'It'd be a wasted journey. They'll have covered their tracks. Besides, you don't need to go to Hinkley when you've got me.'

Claud's gaze was arrested. Kitty turned from him to the Dowager again, and found in the delicate face a look reminiscent of the stubborn determination of her husband. She heard Claud's indrawn breath, and there was awe in his voice.

'D'you tell me you're on my side?'

The grey eyes flashed. 'I ain't taking sides! But I'm coming back with you to Brightwell Prior.'

'Eh?'

Kitty felt as aghast as Claud looked. 'I don't understand.'

A grim smile curved the old lady's mouth. 'Yes, it's time you woke up. Pair of madcaps! Did you think to sail through without let or hindrance? Can't expect to pull a stunt like this and not face the consequences.'

'We have faced them,' snapped Claud, rising to his feet. 'At least, I knew the Countess would cut up rough, and I was ready for that.'

'Ready for it? It's what you wanted. Don't tell me, boy, for I can read you like a book. Only you didn't suppose it'd come home to roost on *my* doorstep, or you'd have shied off like a startled pony.'

'But what has it to do with you, Grandmama?'

'I'll tell you when I've found out the truth,' said the Dowager Duchess of Litton, 'which I intend to do, or die in the attempt. Someone in this family has a deal of explaining to do.'

Kitty could wish that she had been excluded from the party that met, two days later, in the great drawing room at Brightwell Prior, but the Dowager Duchess Lady Litton would not hear of it.

'Piffle, child! Who has more right to the truth, I should like to know? Dare say you won't like to hear it, but it's high time you did.'

She had learned already that the Dowager was not a woman to be flouted. Throughout the journey, which the elderly dame had insisted upon taking in her rumbling coach that had lengthened the time considerably, Kitty had been obliged to relate not only her life's history, but the entire story of her abduction and elopement. She had desperately missed Claud's presence, and his shielding of that too close probing she had endured. Kitty guessed the Dowager knew he would have intervened, which was why she had insisted upon Kitty's company while Claud escorted them in the curricle.

They had been obliged to break the journey on Thursday night, for the old lady meant to arrive at Brightwell Prior in prime condition to confront her daughter Lydia and the rest of the family whose presence had been commanded at this meeting. It was taking place in the great drawing room, which was less grand than Kitty remembered from her brief entrance there on that fateful Monday long weeks ago. Yet it had all the stamp of cold grandeur that she had come to associate with Lady Blakemere.

The whole room was done out in the same blue brocade, the woodwork all around impartially white or silvered, with branches of silver candle holders extravagantly swirling on the blue-papered walls. There were sofas on either side of the fireplace, the one to the left occupied by Lady Rothley, looking despairing and ill. Kate, obviously anxious, sat beside her, while Ralph stood close by. Mr Heversham, summoned by special messenger, had come alone, looking frosty, and was stationed by a vast window, its blue drapes raised high in billows below the silvered pelmet. Lord Blakemere, hovering ill at ease, seemed uncertain whether or no to seat himself next to his daughter Babs, fresh returned from her visit to her prospective in-laws and agog on the other blue-upholstered sofa at his back. His wife had taken up a position in front of the empty grate, one hand resting on the ornate mantel, where her feathered coiffure was mirrored in the vast glass behind her.

She was plainly furious. 'I cannot think why you must needs interfere, my dear Mother. Heversham and I have the matter well in hand.'

'Yes, indeed,' agreed Mr Heversham, casting a harassed glance at Lady Blakemere before turning to the Dowager. 'We are almost resolved upon a course which—er—promises to scotch any pending scandal.'

'Oh, are you?' demanded Claud belligerently, from where he stood off to one side of Kitty, who flanked the Dowager facing the opposing forces. 'I'd give something to know what you've hatched between you!'

'Be quiet, Devenick!' snapped his mother. 'If you imagine your disgrace is rescinded, you are very much mistaken.'

'*His* disgrace?' piped up the Dowager, from the chair she had caused to be prominently placed. 'Claud's to blame that the chit's a bastard now, is he?'

There was a concerted gasp, followed by a short silence. Kitty's pulse skittered as she encountered a black look from Lady Blakemere. She wished she had the courage to reach out for the reassurance of Claud's hand, but she dared not. Besides, she did not wish to appear afraid. Then the wintry eyes moved across to the old lady's face.

'That was uncalled for, Mama.'

'I ain't mealy-mouthed, Lydia, you know that. A spade's a spade in my book, and I don't care who hears me.'

Mr Heversham, who had dignified the occasion with a sober coat of blue cloth over dark breeches, intervened. 'You may not care, ma'am, but the rest of the world is not as accommodating.'

'But that's your objection to the girl, ain't it? Both of you, as I understand it.'

The gentleman coughed. 'It is not as simple as that.'

'Ain't it?' The penetrating grey stare was bent upon him. 'Care to enlighten me on the complications then, Heversham?'

Claud gave vent to a short bark of sardonic laughter. 'The devil he will!'

'Devenick, I will not warn you again!'

Here Lord Blakemere was seen to move across to his wife. A brief murmur drew the Dowager's fire.

'Say it for all of us, Blakemere! I'll have no more secrets in this family.'

The Earl turned to his mother-in-law and gave a slight bow. 'I was merely suggesting to my wife, ma'am, that a confrontation with Claud at this juncture was less than desirable.'

A grunt from the Dowager acknowledged this, and she returned her attention to Heversham. 'Well, man?'

'I beg you will excuse me, ma'am,' he answered. 'It is a subject upon which I prefer to maintain silence.'

'Been too much silence on the subject, that's what I complain of!' uttered the old lady. Her gaze veered suddenly upon her other daughter. 'You, Silvia? Sitting there looking like a wet hen! Will you speak?'

Lady Rothley, her unnatural girth encased in muslins but swathed in a profusion of shawls, groaned and turned her face away. Ralph looked across. 'I beg you will let her be, Grandmama. She has been ill of late.'

'Vapours, I take it?'

'Grandmama, pray don't!' begged Kate, suddenly entering the lists. 'It has been a trying time for poor Mama, truly.'

Balked, the Dowager's glance swept the room, passing over Babs without a check, and coming to rest upon Lord Blakemere's face. He threw up a hand.

'Don't look at me, ma'am! I am sworn to secrecy and will not break my word.'

Unable to bear the suspense, Kitty dipped her head, gazing at her hands clenched in the lap of the gown of lemon muslin that Kate had chosen for her in Oxford. The Dowager had been so positive that she would prevail! Apparently, she had overestimated her power. She felt a hand on her shoulder and found Claud beside her. Her senses swam slightly as he leaned down and spoke in a voice meant only for her ears.

'Don't look like that! If I know Grandmama, she's only beginning. The old tartar has just been priming her guns.'

The Dowager's voice broke in upon him. 'Claud, no whispering, I said. What are you telling the girl?'

Claud jerked up, and cast a glance around the company. 'That you're not finished yet, Grandmama.'

A stifled giggle drew Kitty's attention to Babs. She was not the only one to notice, and the Countess shot her daughter a look that quelled her instantly. There was another stony silence while the old lady once again passed her glance around the assembled members of the family.

'Very well, Lydia, I'll leave it alone,' she said at last.

Kitty could almost hear the sighs, above the muttered exclamation that emanated from Claud. She longed to leap up and hide herself in his sheltering arms. A swift look around showed the family in varying degrees of disappointment or relief, according to their interest.

'On one condition.'

The room froze. In the steely silence, every eye turned upon the Dowager Duchess of Litton. It was as if the whole assembly held its breath. Lady Blakemere broke the tension. Ice was in her voice.

'What condition?'

Across the room, her eyes met those of her mother. Kitty

could scarce believe she was witnessing the hint of real fear in the Countess's look. But it was there.

'On the condition,' said the Dowager straitly, 'that you give me an unequivocal assurance that a girl who was known as Kitty Merrick was not in fact Miss Katherine Ridsdale, daughter of Lady Felicia Ridsdale.'

The oddest sensation overtook Kitty, as if she floated out of reach of the meaning of the words. Vaguely she took in the totality of the silence, and, inconsequently, her mind turned upon the proverbial saying. If a pin did drop, she was sure she would hear it.

Lady Blakemere's cold tones fell into the silence. 'I cannot think where you came by such a notion, my dear Mother.'

Kitty discovered that she was holding her breath. It seemed an age before the Dowager spoke again.

'You're telling me it ain't true?'

The Countess did not answer, and the old lady's gaze turned upon Heversham.

'Well? You married her. Was Felicia concealing a daughter about her?'

Heversham coughed. 'You know that Felicia died in childbed.'

'Yes, with young Harry. But that don't answer me.'

Kitty saw Heversham exchange a glance with the Countess, and into the sensation of vagueness that had overtaken her came the certainty that the Dowager was right. She knew her mother now. That mysterious lady who had visited her in secret, a lady whose identity was certain. From the mists of time came the image—fine bones in a delicate face—and fitted itself upon the features of the Dowager Duchess. She was hardly aware that she spoke.

'She was used to show me the jewelled watch at her waist, and a medallion which hung upon a spangled rib-

bon. They fascinated me because they caught the light.'
Eyes were trained upon her, but Kitty noticed them only
as a blur, for the image was clarifying. And she could hear
the musical tones. *'See, little one, see the sun dancing on
the wall.'*

She had no idea that she had said it. Heversham spoke,
a hush in his voice. 'My God, it's a like a ghost! Felicia
to the life!'

Kitty barely heard him, the image strong in her mind.
'She had grey hair—was it powdered?—and she looked
like you, ma'am.' Her gaze focused upon the grey eyes of
the Dowager. 'I could not think why I had thought you
familiar, but now I see that must have been it.'

'How convenient!'

The arctic tone penetrated Kitty's cloudy mind, and she
turned to face the woman who must be her aunt. But Claud
was before her, shielding her from his mother's attack.

'It ain't Kitty's fault that her memory is hazy! She's the
victim here.'

'Claud, pray hush,' begged Kitty, catching at his hand.
He turned swiftly, frowning down at her. 'You must see
that something had to be done. If—if Lady Felicia was
unmarried, then my birth must indeed have been scandal-
ous.'

Intervention came in the form of the Dowager's snort.
'Yes, but that ain't it, child. They could have got over that
easily enough. She'd only to marry to give you a name. If
Felicia had come to me, I'd have arranged it. Only Lydia
wouldn't let her, would you, my girl?'

Once more, the Countess took refuge in silence. Kitty
looked about, and found puzzlement in the younger element. Of the elders, Lady Rothley had her handkerchief to
her eyes, Mr Heversham looked as if he had been stuffed,

and the Earl, from the fidgeting with his spectacles, was clearly uncomfortable.

Then Claud spoke up. 'Well, it don't matter. For my money, it's a relief to know my aunt Felicia was Kitty's mother. For that makes it certain my uncle Rothley couldn't have fathered her—and we had it down that it must have been he, for she looks too like Kate and Ralph for any other explanation to be...'

His voice died, and the implication hit Kitty in the same instant that she took in the frozen significance of the faces round about. There could be no doubt. So impossible that it had not entered their minds. She and Claud had looked for one or the other—Rothley or Felicia—but not *both*. Now the whole hideous dilemma was there for all to see. No remedy. There had been no possible remedy. Her real mother's illicit liaison had been with her own brother-in-law. And Kitty was the embarrassing result.

As if it were contaminated, her hand opened, releasing Claud's fingers. Yet, with their loss, a tumult of agony clattered into Kitty's breast and there encysted, tight, tight against a future time. Like an automaton, she gazed about the room, taking in reactions.

Lady Blakemere's winter gaze was trained upon Claud in a look of brutal hatred. Heversham's jaw was so tight his lips were pouting. The Earl looked distressed. Lady Rothley sat frozen, all her pain in her face. For the rest— shock, disbelief, a gradual awakening to the horror.

'There now, Silvia,' came flatly from the Dowager. 'That's what comes of ignoring my advice and marrying a ne'er-do-well like Rothley. Headstrong, that's what you are, for all you're a ninny with it.'

Lady Rothley flinched. Then she cast one desperate glance at her mother and buried her face in her hands. Kitty felt the held-in breath within the room. More acutely, she felt beside her a weight of some emotion she dared not name. She could not yet contemplate Claud's agony, for it must lead to her despair. She turned instead to the Dowager, and knew that none dared speak as the old lady's sharp eyes left her youngest daughter and travelled around the room. They stopped at Lady Blakemere.

'You, Lydia. Another one with a head like a rock and a quiverful of pride! Beats me why Felicia turned to you instead of me. Might have known you'd spike her guns.'

This proved too much for the Countess. She strode forward, eyes blazing. 'If you must have it, Felicia did not come to me! I guessed at her condition, and the whole stupid story came tumbling out—in Silvia's presence, if you please. What would you, for God's sake? I had to act!'

'You should have brought her to me,' uttered the old lady, and Kitty heard a catch in her voice. 'Instead you took her to Hinkley and forced her to give up the child.'

The Countess turned again, her cold glance resting on Kitty. She met it, for in her present state of numb despair she could not feel its enmity.

'Had I been successful in that, we would not be in this mess. A country farmer's daughter who bore a resemblance to Rothley would have given us no trouble.'

Kitty felt a convulsive movement at her side, but it subsided. Almost she could feel Claud's disgust. Was it directed at her? Or at his mother? Not that it mattered now. Listless within, she watched the Earl step in, laying a restraining hand on his wife's arm, as he addressed himself to the Dowager.

'The case is, ma'am, that Felicia sought to marry so that she might keep the child. But Heversham—who can scarcely be blamed under the circumstances—would not be persuaded to shelter the little girl.'

'Not when I knew Rothley had fathered the brat, by

God!' came forcefully from Mr Heversham. 'I was willing to provide for the child when Rothley refused, but there it ended.'

Ralph, who had been tending his mother, looked round at this. 'My father knew?'

'Then it was he who came to see me once!' Kitty found all eyes swivelled upon her, and she shrank a little. She had spoken without thinking, armoured against the cruelty of the words she heard by the numbness that possessed her. But this had caught at one of those unexplained memories. 'It must have been he—there was something in Ralph that reminded me, but I could not think of it until this moment. He stood me on a table and—and inspected me. I remember he laughed.'

She looked, as if for confirmation, from one to another, and found the unyielding features of Lady Blakemere. It did not occur to her to withhold her questions now. It was merely information. There was no more horror to be heard here.

'Was it you, ma'am, who took me to the Seminary? You—and Mr Heversham, I think,' her glance flying to the man who had rejected her too.

He reddened and coughed. 'Nothing else to be done. At least it was suited to your station. Lydia would have had you turned over to a farmer or his like, even then.'

'And I fervently wish that I had done so!'

'Hold your tongue!' came irately from the Dowager. 'We'll have words presently, my girl.' For a dangerous moment, the Countess glared at her mother. Then she turned and swished back to the fireplace. The old lady's gaze shifted. 'And what prompted your leniency, Heversham?'

'I knew my late wife's wishes, ma'am. The least I could do was to ensure the child a decent future.'

'As a drudge of a governess. Generous!'

A moan from Lady Rothley drew attention to her. There was wildness in her aspect, and in her voice. 'Why should she have had so much? She had no right to more! She had no right to be *born*. And Devenick has married her. *Married*. Oh, it is cruel and unjust!'

'Yes, Sylvia, it is,' agreed the old lady brutally. 'Cruel and unjust to *my granddaughter*.'

Kitty's gasp was drowned in a concerted babble of exclamation as Lady Rothley collapsed against the squabs of her chair.

'Heavens above, it's true! And she is my half-sister.' Kate was up, ignoring her mother's state, and shifting across the room to seize Babs, who was also on her feet.

'And cousins too. My cousin, your cousin, and Claud's cousin!' Babs uttered a hysterical laugh. 'The most delicious tangle!'

Kate's fingers tightened on her arm. '*Scandal* is what you mean.'

Their excited whispers became inaudible. Heversham crossed quickly to engage the Countess in a low-voiced colloquy, while Ralph attended his mother. The Dowager sat silent, her sharp gaze shifting from Lady Rothley to Lady Blakemere and back again, and there was nothing to be read in her face. Kitty took it all in, caught in that feeling of deadness, as if she stood outside it all and watched the mayhem unfold.

Again, she felt Claud's tension. Taking her courage in her hands, she turned her eyes upon him and found him there, silent and still beside her chair. Her heart lurched.

He was white, and the look in the blue eyes concentrated her mind so powerfully that the attendant ache, deep within, almost escaped her notice. He looked as if he had received a violent blow. She began to feel sick, but no thought of blaming him entered her head. She understood, for her heart could read him.

His impulsive nature had betrayed him. So lost had he been in his thirst for revenge that he had never truly taken in the dreadful nature of a scandal that could cause the furore to which his marriage had given rise. Now it had hit him. How bitterly must he repent and begin to wish her otherwhere. And who should blame him? Certainly not the creature he had so unfortunately chosen to make his wife!

Kitty knew what she must do. It was not difficult. Indeed, she had known she must do it almost from the instant that the truth had revealed itself. Moreover, the moment could not have been more propitious. She rose from her chair, and discovered that her knees were shaking. But she did not reseat herself. Instead, she grasped the back of the Dowager's chair and held it tightly.

'What's to do, child? May as well sit yourself down again, for I ain't done yet. Just waiting for them all to settle.'

To her own surprise, Kitty's voice was steady. 'I must beg you to let me withdraw, ma'am.'

The keen gaze appraised her intently. Kitty hoped that her determination was not visible in her face. 'Dare say you can do with a period of quiet reflection. But don't you go far. We've yet to settle what's to be done, and I want you back in here.'

Kitty had no intention of returning to this house, let alone this room! As for what was to be done, she was taking that into her own hands. Her love—that love she had found and cherished so pitifully short a time—was too deep to do otherwise.

She made a curtsy that could be taken for agreement. Turning, she sought for Claud, and found that he had come a little out of his stupor. His gaze was upon her, and the expression in his eyes caught at her heartstrings. He was already learning to regret!

He frowned as she took a step away from his grandmother's chair. 'Where are you going?'

Her voice almost betrayed her. She thrust down on the rise of distress, and tried to smile, aware that her lips were trembling. 'I—I need to be alone for—for a little while.'

There was bleakness in his eyes. 'Shall I come with you?'

That was the last thing he could want! She had to relieve him of the necessity. He must not feel obliged to her in any way. She shook her head.

'I will be better alone, if—if you don't mind.'

'Mind! Lord above, you must do anything you wish, Kitty, without reference to me. I have done damage enough!'

The guttural note of self-blame was almost too much to bear. And it was plain he would do nothing to stop her, even did he know her intention. But she could not leave him feeling it so deeply.

'Don't reproach yourself. We did it together, Claud. But there is—there will be a way to mend it.'

With which, she slipped quickly past him and made for the door. In the hall, she looked for a servant, and found none. She headed for the stairs. The Dowager Duchess had kept her captive after their arrival here, and she had gone with her to a chamber where the old lady had rested while she awaited the coming of Heversham and Lady Silvia, whom she had summoned. Kitty made for that chamber.

From there, she might call for a servant and order a carriage to take her back to Shillingford Manor. They would do as she wished. She was still the Viscountess Devenick—for now.

Chapter Twelve

Claud had been unsurprised to discover, from the message conveyed to him by Vellow, that Kitty had returned to the Manor. It was late when his curricle turned in at the gates, and as he glanced up at her window and saw no light, he was conscious of a feeling of relief. He wanted to see her, for the news he brought was cheering, but the lash of his conscience could not but make him writhe in her presence.

Such an ill turn as he had served her, and all for his own ends! Kitty had told him long ago that he was selfish, and he had allowed it to be so—but until today, he had not known how true it was. She had begged him to reconsider even as they were on the road to Gretna. Had he listened? Had he given the notion consideration? He had not! His thirsting vengeance had been all in all to him, and he had cared nothing for the innocent creature he had made his victim.

The dull thud of conscience had afflicted him so strongly that he had taken in little of the ensuing scene. The realisation of what he had done to Kitty had thrown him into a state of semi-torpor that had fogged his mind. He had felt like a drowning man, who sees his life's crimes flash across his mind and knows there can be no forgiveness.

When Kitty had turned to leave, the despair in her face had jolted him back to awareness—and to feeling in full the guilt he must ever feel. It had been hard at first to take his part in the discussion that had followed. But his determination had been all for Kitty's relief. He dared say it was the first time in his life he'd had not the slightest attention on his own interests.

He gave up the reins to Docking, who was awaiting him in the stables, jumped down from the curricle, and made his way into the house. Mixon met him in the hall.

'Will your lordship go directly to bed, or—?'

Claud waved him away. 'I'll manage on my own. Go to bed, Mixon. I'll be downstairs for a while yet.'

To his relief, his valet made no demur, but left him with a bow. Claud made for the study and took up the brandy decanter that Hollins kept filled for him there. He drank a little, remembering with a faint lift of his spirits, how his sire had taken his part when the Countess had dared to scorn him.

'What's the scheme you've hatched with Heversham?' his grandmother had asked her. 'Claud is ready to hear it.'

He had received a sardonic look from her ladyship, the Countess of Blakemere. 'A trifle late in the day, Devenick. If you had been this dutiful earlier—'

He had cut her short. 'My duty, ma'am, is to my wife. If there's a way to mitigate the punishment to her, my personal feelings must be sacrificed.'

'Bravo, Claud!'

That was his sire, who had come up and laid a hand upon his shoulder. His father's approval had made him self-conscious, but he had acknowledged it.

'I'm learning, sir. Late, I grant you.'

Papa had smiled, wholly ignoring, to Claud's secret triumph, the black look Lady Blakemere had cast upon him. 'Not too late to count, dear boy.'

But his father's support could not allay his qualms of conscience. How the wrong he had done Kitty could be righted, Claud knew not. His grandmother had her plan, and he would offer it to his wife with gratitude, for at least it must give her hope. A fitting punishment that he would have to stand by and watch while the gossips whispered behind their fans. And do nothing. How he would school himself to endure the bandying of Kitty's name from lip to lip he did not know. For her sake, he must. Grandmama would countenance no heroics, she had insisted. If they were to fly in the teeth of convention, and win, Claud must challenge none and laugh off the insults.

But none of this could make amends to Kitty for his having married her. Would pin money, gowns and gewgaws make up for the indignities to which she had been subjected on his behalf? Disgraced, rejected by his family, immured in a country house to be kept out of sight of the neighbourhood. Friendless and alone, with a husband who gave no thought to her comfort, and instead forced her into the marriage bed of which she had an unnatural terror only to spike his mother's guns. Not content with that, he recalled with a surge of feeling, he had approached her once again—and in his cups!

At which point, he was obliged to try to suppress the memory of Kitty's reception of him, lest he suffer an instant arousal. She had been wholly magical! And he knew that had his grandmother not summoned him next day, and virtually enforced a separation, nothing would have kept him from seeking her bed again. He wanted her now, this moment. *Every* moment. But he would not add insult to injury by approaching her at a time of such distress.

She had been utterly crushed by the revelation of her birth. And it had been his insistent burrowing that had caused her to suffer that hurt. There was no end to his misdeeds, and he did not know how he could begin to beg her forgiveness.

It was a mercy to be granted at least the night before he must venture upon an inevitable penitence. Yet Claud slept but fitfully, disturbed by unquiet dreams and longings for that intimacy he had purposely denied himself.

Kitty was not at the breakfast table. Nor, when he enquired of Hollins, had she been seen that morning.

'But she did come home yesterday afternoon?'

'Yes indeed, my lord. But her ladyship retired immediately to her chamber and requested that she should be undisturbed.'

Claud fidgeted with the coffee pot, prey to an unformed fear. At length he gave in to it, requesting his butler to send Mrs Papple up to Kitty's room. He drank a little coffee while he waited, a dull fog invading his brain as the vague apprehension intensified. It proved justified.

'My lord!' cried the housekeeper, puffing into the room in something of a hurry.

Claud was on his feet. 'What is it? What's happened?'

Distress was in Mrs Papple's face and voice. 'She is not there, my lord! Her bed has not been slept in!'

For a moment, Claud simply stood there, an uncomfortable thudding starting up in his chest as the implication hovered, just out of reach of his befuddled mind. Not there? She must be there!

A memory surfaced—of Kitty's face, and words that had trembled out of her mouth. *'There will be a way to mend it.'*

And then he was on the move, his steps quickening as

the realisation wheeled into his brain, blinding all but the desire that it should not be true. She could not have meant this. She could not think it a remedy—could she? She must be there. She could not have gone. Kitty could not have left him!

He took the stairs two at a time, half-aware of the butler almost on his heels and the housekeeper trailing a little way behind. The door of her room was open, and Claud hurtled through into the empty chamber and came to a shuddering halt.

Empty. The covers on the bed folded down, ready for her. But Kitty had not gone to bed. Had she been in here? Yes, she had, for Hollins had seen her.

He flung over to the press and pulled open the doors, tugging at trays within. They looked to be full. He found gowns and all manner of accessories as his fingers thrust about within them.

'The portmanteau has gone!' came the housekeeper's voice.

Claud froze and looked round. 'What? But she has taken no clothes!'

Mrs Papple was at the other end of the room. 'The portmanteau was kept in this corner behind the door, my lord. She never touched it, not since she came here.'

Claud's glance returned to the press, and he stared at the items within. If she had left him, she had gone with very little. But she had taken the portmanteau, so she must have packed something! A memory surfaced, poignant and sharp. Kitty's eyes, bright and pleading, her voice breathless with hope. 'Can it be this one, Claud? Pray say I may have it!'

That confounded spangled gown! Without thought, he plunged his hands among the gowns, tossing them this way and that in frantic haste as he searched through tray after tray. Only half-aware of the tuttings of his housekeeper as she caught at the garments that slipped from the press, Claud hunted with growing desperation, as if in the spangled gown lay his only hope of refuting the hideous truth.

At last he fell back, defeated, loosing his hold on a muslin that had been clutched in his fingers. There was no spangled gown here. He noticed neither Mrs Papple, who flew to tidy the mess he had made, nor his butler, who silently guided him away from the press and pushed him down into the window seat.

'I'll fetch you a drop of brandy, my lord.'

Claud hardly heard him. His gaze travelled about Kitty's bedchamber, and the emptiness of the room found an echo in his heart. Kitty had gone. His mind refused to grapple with the problem of how or where. One thought only went round and round in his head. The despairing notion that, though he was of less worth to Kitty than a hideous spangled gown, her loss left him irretrievably bereft.

By the time Hollins returned, bearing a glass armed with a double measure of brandy, Claud's brain was beginning to function a little. He took the glass that his butler pressed into his hand and tossed off the liquid inside it in two short gulps. His head cleared, and he was able to bend his mind to the puzzle of Kitty's whereabouts. Presently he became aware of the troubled features of his two retainers, and nodded with decision.

'Can't have got far yesterday. Had to have walked. How far? The village? That's no use. Would have had to stay overnight at the Crown.'

'Or Bessington,' suggested Hollins. 'It's only another mile or two, my lord, if her ladyship was walking.'

Claud blinked at him. 'You mean she might have picked up the stage this morning.' He thought for a moment. 'Saturday, isn't it? Yes, she could have got the stage.'

The housekeeper entered a difficulty. 'Only would it be the cross stage for Henley and Maidenhead, or—?'

'Or Reading, if it were going south,' said Hollins.

Claud cursed. If he knew which one she must have boarded, he could overtake her in the curricle before ever she reached her destination. Except that it was already well past ten, and these stagecoaches invariably rolled through at what was to Claud the crack of dawn, having left Oxford before six. By now, she could already be at Maidenhead, or well beyond Reading, having changed at either location for all he knew.

No, there was little point in chasing the coach. Better to think where Kitty might be headed. The heaviness in Claud's chest lightened. There could be no question. There was only one choice for him to make. With which of her two friends might Kitty prefer to seek refuge?

Mrs Duxford was one of those tall angular women, all elbows and shoulders, with a countenance in which the jaw was prominent, giving her a look of command useful in her chosen career. She wore spectacles, which added to the severity of a long face. Yet, as Kitty had recently discovered, a warmer heart beat under the strict exterior than her erstwhile charge had ever suspected.

Kitty had prepared herself for fury and recriminations, for in all this time she had omitted to write to her preceptress with an account of her situation. To her amazement, she had been received with an excess of sympathetic understanding.

She had arrived too late last night to do more than cast herself upon the Duck's mercy and beg for her help. Mrs Duxford had been upon the point of retiring, but she had taken Kitty in with little more than an exclamation or two of surprise, and sent the maid who had let her in to fetch

up a glass of hot milk. Kitty had been bundled into the
spare bedchamber in the Duck's own house—the place in
her old room being taken up by now—and bidden to cease
her lamentations and go to sleep.

'We will talk it all through in the morning, my dear.'

But throughout the interminable journey, during which
she had shifted from one stagecoach to another in order to
make her way to Paddington, Kitty had been unable to give
way to the overwhelming grief of leaving Claud. Several
days had been taken up, including a whole day's delay on
Sunday in a stuffy inn room in the July heat. Obliged to
make her own arrangements, and pay her way—thank
goodness she'd had a cache of coin and bills left over from
that first big shopping spree!—she had been too occupied
to dwell upon a future without Claud, and a deadness of
feeling had kept her from indulging her despair. Once in
the Seminary, and safe from noisome inns and dusty roads,
Kitty had given way at last, weeping into her pillows.

Waking on Thursday to weather as dismal as her heart,
she had partaken in a desultory fashion of the breakfast
brought to her on a tray by the round-eyed maid, and scam-
pered into her plain muslin gown in time to attend Mrs
Duxford in her study when that lady sent for her just after
ten o'clock.

'I had thought you would have scolded me dreadfully,'
Kitty said a good while later, sniffing dolefully into a wet
handkerchief.

The Duck permitted herself a rueful laugh. 'My poor
dear Katherine, so I might have done had not Helen written
to apprise me of what had transpired.'

Kitty looked up. Mrs Duxford was standing in front of
the big oak desk, from where she had been at pains to pat
her erstwhile pupil with a comforting hand as Kitty, sunk

in the chair that she had many times inhabited to receive a scold in the past, had sobbed out her history.

'Nell wrote to you?'

'Indeed she did, immediately upon her return from visiting you in Oxfordshire. I received the letter but a day or two ago. Helen took it into her head that you had forgotten to inform me of the circumstances, as was indeed the case.'

Kitty hung her head again. 'I did not forget precisely, ma'am. I meant to write again, for I knew I had not said enough in my first letter.'

'Little enough, it must be said! I confess to having been exceedingly angry with you at the time, Katherine. Particularly since the letter was franked, and I could not read the signature. That you had become entangled with a lord was patent, but for what purpose I was unable to guess.' She smiled a little. 'I may add that my suspicions, if perhaps unworthy, were perilously close to the truth.'

A huge sigh escaped Kitty. 'I knew you would think the worst, and I cannot blame you. Only you see, I—I did not know how to tell you. It was all such a tangle, and—and with this dreadful secret hanging over me, I could not think what to say.'

The Duck leaned over to pat her again. 'Poor child! I blame myself, Katherine, indeed I do.'

'Oh, no, ma'am,' protested Kitty. 'How could it be your fault?'

'I should have enquired more particularly into your history, my dear. You see, the lady and gentleman who brought you disclaimed any knowledge of you beyond what had been imparted to them.'

Kitty swallowed. 'They were lying, Mrs Duxford. They knew very well indeed who I was. Indeed, they had both been at pains to dispose of me. Lady Blakemere had been determined upon it, I believe, from the moment she learned that I was to be born.'

The Duck shook her head, tutting disapprovingly. 'Disgraceful! Not that I can censure her ladyship for doing what she might to mitigate such a terrible scandal. But to visit the sins of the parents upon an innocent child is what I can neither approve nor understand.'

'Well, it is done now,' said Kitty stonily, 'and there is nothing to be gained by recriminations. She has got her wish, for I will not trouble her again.' She looked up as she spoke, and surprised a curious expression upon the features of her old preceptress. 'Why do you look at me like that, ma'am?'

The Duck shook her head. 'I fear you will not like to hear what is in my mind, my dear Katherine. I am afraid I cannot allow you to remain here.'

Shock threw Kitty into protest. 'But you must! I am depending upon you to find me a post, Mrs Duxford!'

'Which I most certainly shall not do,' said the lady with determination.

Aghast, Kitty stared at her. 'But I cannot manage it alone! And if I cannot stay here, I cannot think what I am to do. Where shall I go? I have nowhere else, Mrs Duxford!'

She was dismayed to see the reproving look she knew so well overspread the lady's features. 'You have a home, child. And a husband, to whom you are vowed.'

Kitty got up, twisting the damp handkerchief between her fingers. 'I cannot go back! You cannot ask me to go back!'

'My dear Katherine, it has nothing to do with me. Your own sense of duty must surely tell you that there is only one course to pursue.'

Despair gripped Kitty. Unknowingly, she began to pace,

to and fro across the carpet before the desk. 'I can't, ma'am. I *can't*.'

'I do not say you must go at once,' urged her preceptress. 'By all means, take a day or two to think it over. But I believe you have no choice in the matter, my child. Is the thought of going back so dreadful?'

Kitty turned to face her, an agony of hurt in her breast. 'You did not see his face! He had not suspected—had not dreamed—'

She broke off, the remembrance of Claud's white features, which had dogged her mind on the journey here, too painful to be endured. She could not subject him to the embarrassment of her presence in his life. Without him, life stretched ahead of her as a meaningless void. But she would bear that, because the alternative was utterly unendurable.

'Katherine—Kitty—'

She discovered that the Duck had risen again, and was standing before her, looking down from her superior height in frowning question. But her eyes were kind behind the spectacles. Kitty swallowed on a painful breath.

'Yes, Mrs Duxford?'

'Do you care for your husband?'

The image of Claud swung into Kitty's mind. Blue eyes, with the short blond locks above, and that stubborn chin in features so much a part of her life that their absence yawned like a gaping wound. Tears sprang to her eyes.

'I love him desperately!'

'Then you do him great wrong to leave him,' said Mrs Duxford sternly.

Kitty turned away, shifting across the room again. 'You don't understand, ma'am. It is because I love him that I came away. I care for him too much to hurt him by remaining in his life.'

The Duck said nothing, and as Kitty turned again, she found her smiling. 'You have changed a good deal, Kitty.'

'And that amuses you?' She was aware that she sounded bitter, but she could not help it.

'I find it touching, child. Nevertheless, your judgement is mistaken. All you need is a little courage, and—'

She was interrupted by a tap on the door, followed by the entrance of Mr Duxford, a gentleman as distinguished by roundness as his spouse was by height. There was a harassed look upon his chubby features.

'My dear, do excuse me, but a gentleman has called for little Kitty here.'

Kitty's heart skipped a beat, and she gazed upon Mr Duxford with desperate eyes.

'Aha!' exclaimed the Duck. 'Lord Devenick, is it?'

'Quite right, my dear. I have put him in our parlour.'

Kitty's knees were shaking as she pushed open Mrs Duxford's parlour door. She hesitated on the threshold, but a hand thrust her from behind, and a whispered command reached her.

'In you go, child!'

Kitty almost fell into the familiar white-walled little room, with its collection of straight chairs arranged neatly around the walls, and its one small sofa in a central position opposite the fireplace. The door shut quietly behind her, and she stopped short, her eyes flying to Claud's neat figure where he stood by the window, clad in the favoured green that became him so well. He must have heard her, for he had turned. The sound of the rain pattered into Kitty's head, in tune with the hammering of her heart. He looked pale and drawn, and she could not read the expression in his eyes.

For a moment or two, Claud could utter no word. It had

been all of five days, and a nightmare in between. Though he had driven like a man possessed, he had not reached Rookham Hall until Sunday afternoon. Leaving there on Monday, he had pushed his cattle to the limit, chafing as he rested them for one night in London where he stayed at his own lodging, and pushing them on again from noon upon the following day as he headed for Hainault Forest. He had been obliged to remain there two nights to rest them again. Reaching Paddington too late to disturb the household, he had battened on his friend Jack at Westbourn Green, his patience almost at an end.

The fear that Kitty might not be at the Seminary had kept him wakeful, together with the struggle with his conscience. His relief had been considerable at hearing, from the fellow who had brought him to this room to wait, that his wife was here. But the moments before she had entered the room had been an agony.

The sight of her, the velvet eyes big with distress, the black hair tumbled in disordered curls, unsettled him utterly. She had been crying, he was sure of it. He wanted to go to her, seize her into an embrace so tight that she could never escape him! Only he had no right. How was he ever to persuade her to come back to him?

Kitty shifted a few steps into the parlour. She knew that her voice would betray the skittering at her heart, but she must say something! A question surfaced.

'How—how did you know where to find me?'

'Your friend Nell.' It had jerked out. Claud drew a breath, trying for calm. 'I went first to Rookham's house. I thought you would have chosen Prue. Only she was sure you must have gone to Nell at Castle Jarrow. So I drove there. But Nell said—'

He broke off, hardly knowing whether he could repeat it without breaking out into a despairing groan. 'My lord

Devenick,' had said Lady Jarrow, 'I believe you should look for her at Paddington.' He had protested, thinking the Seminary was the last place Kitty would go. But her friend had been adamant. Before he well knew what he was saying, out it came, and he could do nothing about the huskiness in his voice.

'Lady Jarrow said that your Duck was the nearest thing to a mother you had ever known.' He saw her eyes fill, and longed to go to her. But he did not dare.

'She has been very kind,' Kitty uttered. 'I had not expected it.'

Claud's distress got the better of him. 'More so than I have been! Kitty, can you forgive me?'

The desire to weep receded. 'Forgive you? But what have you done?'

He was moving, a step or two closer. 'Everything I should not have. Marrying you, for one thing.'

A knife cut into Kitty's heart. 'You regret it! I knew you would!' She wrung her hands. 'Oh, Claud, why did you come here? I came away so that you would be free of it all. Do you think I can bear to be the cause of—?'

'Free of it?' he broke in. 'I don't want to be free of it! Kitty, I know I shouldn't have done it, but I can't regret it! I've tried like the devil, but I can't.'

Kitty became aware of a tattoo drumming in her chest. The implication filtered into her head, but she dared not give it credence. She eyed him doubtfully. There was an expression in the blue eyes that she had never seen there before. She felt a tremor in her throat, and it was with difficulty that she got out the words.

'You cannot—want me. Not—not now that you know about—about Felicia and—and Lord Rothley.'

Claud's face twisted, and he moved so swiftly that Kitty

had no chance to escape him. He seized her in a painful grip, the blue eyes vibrant with emotion.

'I don't *care*, d'you hear me? It's nothing to me, except for how it affects you, Kitty. I don't care who your mother was—or your father. I don't give a fig for the scandal-mongers! If I go along with Grandmama's plan, it is only for your sake.'

Distracted by this last, Kitty caught at it in the whirling confusion that his words were creating in her head. 'Lady Litton has a plan?'

'Yes, but never mind that now,' said Claud impatiently, pulling her closer. 'Kitty, I'm in love with you! Didn't see it, fool that I am, until you left me.'

The tumult in Kitty's head began to echo in her breast. She hardly knew she spoke. 'In *love*? You are in love with *me*?'

The expression in the blue eyes was so tender that Kitty hardly recognised him. 'Who else? You're the one who's been warming my life like a little firecracker! There ain't anyone else, I can tell you that. Never has been. Never knew I could be in love. And of all the ways to do it, I had to go and wreck your life first! I tell you, Kitty, I meant to beg you on my knees to forgive me for what I'd done to you, but I can't. Because if I hadn't done it, I wouldn't have had you in my life, and that don't bear thinking of!'

Kitty could only gaze at him. Claud loved her? It was too impossible, too topsy-turvy to be taken in. For several moments, she forgot the horror that had sent her flying from him to spare him pain, forgot the dread future she had been trying to evade.

'I don't know what to think,' she uttered blindly. 'I don't understand any of it. I don't know if I dare to believe you.'

The blue eyes blazed. 'Oh, don't you? Then let's see if this will serve to make you!'

He jerked Kitty into his embrace, holding her so tightly that she could scarcely breathe. For a few instants, he gazed down into the shocked brown orbs, and then he took her lips in a kiss so fierce that the blood thundered in her head and she felt in danger of losing her senses.

It was only for a short time he held her thus. Relaxing his hold in a moment, he released her mouth, but only that he might enfold her in an enveloping hug.

'Oh, Kitty,' he murmured against her hair, 'that morning when I found you gone, I thought the world had ended! I love you so very much.' A lump rose to Kitty's throat and she could not speak. He pulled away again, and the blue orbs were searching her face. 'I know I don't deserve it, Kitty, but I want you back. I know you care more for that spangled gown than you do for me, and I can't blame you, but—'

'What did you say?' gasped Kitty, shocked out of her distress.

Claud let out a self-conscious laugh. 'I searched for it like a madman! When I couldn't find it, I was agonized, for I knew then you'd left me.'

'Because I took my spangled gown?' Kitty broke into weak laughter. 'Claud, are you mad? I could not bear to leave it because it was the very first thing you gave me! And I didn't *leave* you.'

'Well, I don't know what you call it when you walk out of the place without so much as telling me why! Did you think I wouldn't come after you?'

'It didn't cross my mind! But I knew from the moment I heard the dreadful truth that I had no choice but to come away. I *could* not let you suffer. I couldn't have borne it when you began to feel that you wished to be rid of me.

I wanted to set you free, Claud, so that you need not be married to a creature with so hateful a past as I have.'

Claud gentled her against him. 'My darling silly chit! I didn't care about any of that. And the moment I realised my feelings for you, the only thing I cared about was getting you back.' He put her from him and held her shoulders hard. 'It's but another instance of my selfishness, I dare say, but I can't help it, Kitty. I love you too much to lose you!'

'And I love you too much to hurt you, Claud!' uttered Kitty, bursting into sobs. 'I don't want to be an—an embarrassment to you. I can't b-bear you to be ashamed of me.'

But Claud shook her. 'Stop talking like a nodcock and say that again!'

'Say w-what?' sniffed Kitty.

'That you love me, adorable chit,' said Claud, grinning at her. 'If that's true, I don't care about anything else in the world!'

'Of course it's true!' said Kitty indignantly. 'I would not say it if it wasn't.'

'Yes, but you don't say it,' he complained.

Kitty dissolved into giggles. 'How can I, when you will behave in this typically brutish fashion?'

At which, Claud pulled her to him and kissed her again. Hard and fierce at first. And then, one hand tangling into her hair, he held her more gently, caressing her mouth with his own so that her bones melted and she sagged in his arms. His voice, when he spoke again, was husky with passion.

'Is that less brutish?'

'Distinctly,' murmured Kitty against his lips.

'Then what have you to say to me?'

Kitty entwined her arms about his neck. 'I love you.'

And she said it again and again, in many tender voices, her mouth travelling across his features, kissing his cheeks, his chin, and his eyes for each time she said it.

When she again reached his mouth, Claud seized her lips with his own in a kiss so intense that Kitty lost all ability to think for several inflaming moments. At last he let her go. 'I had best stop, or I'll end by taking you right here on the floor!'

Kitty giggled, and allowed him to draw her to sit upon the cosy chintz-covered sofa. 'The Duck would have a fit!'

'Should think she must have already had enough of them to last a lifetime, if you've told her all that I've done to you.'

'Don't say that, Claud,' she chided. 'It was not all your fault. And if you hadn't taken me for Kate and abducted me, we would not be together now.'

Claud gave her a squeeze. 'I know that, and I feel the same. But I'm too ashamed of the way I behaved to bear thinking on it. Just because it's turned out well don't make all right. I shan't easily forget why I married you.'

'You must not blame yourself, for I can't bear it,' said Kitty, clutching his hand.

'No use saying that, for I do blame myself.' He slipped his arm about her and cuddled her close. 'Only consolation is that I can now promise you you're far more to me than the revenge I took you for.' He started up again abruptly. 'Dashed if it hadn't slipped my mind! Got something for you, Kitty.'

Released, Kitty watched him delve a hand into an inner pocket and bring out a slim case. He opened it, and she caught a sparkle within. Her breath caught as Claud lifted the bracelet from its bed of satin. It was delicate, little drops of crystal inlaid into silver clips. She could not speak as Claud fastened it about her wrist.

'There. Got it in Bond Street, on my way through London. Hoped I might use it to persuade you to take me back.'

Kitty raised her eyes from contemplation of the gift. 'Oh, Claud! Did you think I needed such a bribe?'

He grimaced. 'Didn't know what to think. Knew you liked spangled gewgaws, so I thought diamonds would be acceptable to you.'

'Diamonds!' Kitty fingered the drops, a hush in her breast.

Claud caught her fingers and kissed them. She looked at him and the tears that sparkled on her lashes were more vibrant than the jewels. He drew her close again.

'Don't cry! Can't bear to see you cry! If you don't like 'em—'

'Like them?' Kitty pulled away. 'They are beautiful, Claud! Only—only they remind me of how foolish I was, to marry you for the sake of your wealth. I love you, Claud, and you have no need to give me gifts.'

'But I *want* to give it to you, silly chit! And it's because I love you.'

At that, Kitty flung her arms about his neck. 'Then I shall treasure it always!'

Claud kissed her, but his tone was rueful. 'Should've given you it for your birthday, only I'm such a nodcock that—'

'Don't say that!' begged Kitty, seizing his hand. 'It doesn't matter any more.'

'It does to me,' he argued. 'And if you want more proof of how much you mean to me, I was prepared to compound for my mother's scheme to save you from scandal.'

Kitty at once demanded to know what had been planned, and Claud, firmly settling her back into the sofa within the circle of his arm, outlined the elaborate tale that had been concocted for her deliverance.

'The Countess and my uncle Heversham had settled it that you were to be given a plausible history as offspring to some remote cousin of the Rothleys.'

'Because the resemblance is too marked not to be noticed,' guessed Kitty.

'Just so. Ralph said it wouldn't stop anyone from thinking you were Rothley's by-blow—'

'Which is no less than the truth.'

'And Babs pointed out that everyone in the family would have to be primed. Easy enough for anyone to make a slip. Too many complicated relationships involved.'

Kitty nodded. 'Yes, for I must be cousin to all of you, besides being more closely related to Kate.'

'Not only Kate. You're half-sister to all four of my aunt Silvia's children. And Babs thought of Harry too. Is he to be told the truth?'

'Harry?'

'My aunt Felicia's son with Heversham. She died when he was born.'

Kitty held his hand tightly. 'You mean that I have a half-brother on my mother's side? Oh, Claud, I don't feel as though I can take it all in!'

He drew her to him and kissed her. 'You'll do, Kitty. Chit of your courage? M'father noticed that about you, and I've come to see it.'

'Courage?' uttered Kitty in disbelief. '*Me?* You are teasing me!'

'No, I ain't. If it didn't take a deal of courage to face my family the way you did, then I don't know what to call it.'

'I was terrified, Claud, you know I was.'

'Yes, but you did it all the same.' He eyed her with

trouble in his blue eyes. 'Only I ain't forcing you into anything this time. The Countess waved aside our objections. Thought the fewer people to know the truth, the better. Said she could vouch for still tongues on her side.'

Kitty shivered. 'I am sure she could.'

'Yes, and m'father thought I'd be well advised to accept it for a solution. He said you were to be given a respectable past with a forgotten branch of the Rothley family, and that it would be given out that the likeness comes down the family tree and is seen from time to time.'

Kitty regarded him anxiously. 'Did you wish to accept it?'

Claud's arm tightened about her. 'I'd have done anything that would spare you pain. Only Grandmama wouldn't have it.'

A memory struck Kitty and her breath caught. 'You said she had a scheme!'

'She does, and it ain't an easy one,' said Claud grimly. 'I ain't such a brute that I'd make you do it. It's your decision, Kitty, and so I told her. You'll choose whether to go with what she wants, or do as the Countess proposed.'

Kitty's heart swelled. He must truly love her! A few weeks ago, it would not have occurred to him to give her a choice.

'Very well, but I don't yet know what it is the Dowager wants.'

'Grandmama wants you to be known for who you are. To take your place as her granddaughter. She said—and by Jupiter, she's right!—that you've been wronged, and she won't have you fobbed off with a false tale that will dog you for the rest of your life.'

Her pulse was beating in a slow tattoo, and Kitty almost held her breath. 'She wants me to face Society?'

Claud nodded. 'She's bent on coming to Town with us for the Little Season and introducing you as her granddaughter. We're to ignore anything anyone says and refuse to answer any questions. But I won't permit it, if you don't want the truth known, Kitty. I told her, it's your choice.'

A thrill went through Kitty, comprised both of apprehension and excitement. She looked worriedly at him. 'What would you wish me to do?'

Claud shook his head. 'I won't choose for you. You'd be living a lie, if you went with what the Countess has in mind. On the other hand, it ain't likely to be a picnic with Grandmama. She'd brazen it out, throwing you in Society's teeth. Thinks it'll be a nine days' wonder and there's an end. And none will dare to cut you, she says, when you're presented by her. *''The Dowager Duchess of Litton is still somebody,''* she said.'

Kitty gave a shaky laugh. 'I have a rival in mimicry, I see. That is almost exactly like her, Claud.'

He grinned briefly. 'Ain't so bad, eh? But, Kitty, though I dare say her position does count for a great deal, there'll be plenty of gossip, no question.'

Kitty eyed him doubtfully. 'But I am your wife, Claud. Will it not be uncomfortable for you to have people talking of me behind your back?'

He held her tighter. 'I don't care. Told you so before. All I care for is you. And since you love me, I don't give tuppence for what anyone may say.'

She drew a breath. 'Then—then I had rather trust in your grandmother than in Lady Blakemere.'

'So would I, any day!' averred Claud. Spurred by a sudden thought, he released her and sat up abruptly, catching at her hands. 'I tell you what, Kitty. We will beg your friends to come to Town with us, for I'll lay odds you'll feel a sight more comfortable with them to back you up.'

Kitty's smile was radiant. 'I should love to have Prue and Nell with us—if Nell is able to come.'

'Don't see why not. Jarrow said they couldn't move out of that confounded castle yet, and if you'd seen the place, you'd be begging your Nell to come out of it. Near midnight when I arrived, and the place was like a nightmare!'

'Then by all means let us ask them all to stay with us in London.' But Kitty released one hand, its wrist adorned with the diamond bracelet, and reached up to caress the golden locks. Her voice became husky. 'But if you wish for the truth, my comfort is wholly dependent upon my dearest husband.'

Touched to the heart, Claud drew her to him, and a tender murmur reached her. 'And mine upon my little chit of a wife.' Then he drew away a little, and Kitty saw the blue eyes alight. 'Speaking of which, my lady Devenick, I know I was foxed that night and had no right to venture into your bedchamber, but do I take it that you won't be protecting yourself with a chamber pot if I resume my husbandly duties in your bed?'

A sliver of heat fled down Kitty's veins and she swallowed. 'If you had not been so foxed, Claud, you would know how I betrayed myself that night. I had been dying for you to resume them long since!'

Claud grinned. 'I wasn't that badly foxed, my devilishly passionate wife.' He closed with her again, and his lips ran a butterfly caress across her cheek and down to tease at her mouth. 'And I'm sorry to tell you, Kitty, there ain't anything on this earth that will keep me out of your bed— even if that does make me a selfish brute.'

'You are not a brute!' uttered Kitty vehemently, and she pressed her mouth to his in a kiss that invited his urgent participation. 'You are the kindest man in the world,' she told him when she was able, 'and if you are selfish on

occasion, I am glad of it. I am such a hopeless case myself
that I could not bear to be married to a paragon!'

She was left in no doubt of Claud's appreciation of this
sentiment. But presently, he reluctantly drew away, and
stood up, pulling her to her feet.

'Let's get out of this hellish Seminary and into my curricle. I'm about to abduct you again, young Kitty—if a
fellow can be said to abduct his own wife—and though it
ain't Gretna Green this time, you may count upon the aftermath there should have been in the first place.'

Kitty eyed him doubtfully. 'Aftermath?'

He grinned. 'Ain't you ever heard of a honeymoon?'

Enchanted, Kitty said her farewells, collected up her belongings and readily abandoned the Seminary that had
sheltered her from the knowledge of her identity. With
great willingness this time, she re-entered the dashing vehicle that had once drawn her to disaster, and now promised instead to bring her to the future that would rebuild
her shattered dreams.

Sighing in deep content, Kitty settled into the curricle
beside the husband she had accidentally chosen, who just
happened to be a lord. Which was a matter of supreme
indifference to one who loved him so very dearly.

* * * * *

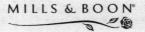

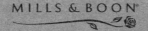

MILLS & BOON

Historical Romance™

...rich, vivid and passionate

We're on the lookout for born storytellers...

Think you have what it takes to write a novel?

Then this is your chance!

Do you have a passion for history?

Can you bring a period vividly to life, and create characters who absorb the reader from page one?

If so we want to hear from you!

Your accurate historical detail should allow the reader to taste and smell the life and times, without feeling overwhelmed by facts. The heroine should be sympathetic, the hero charismatic, and the sensuality should be supported with emotional intensity and a fully rounded plot. The Historical Romance series covers a broad range of periods from ancient civilisations up to the Second World War.

Visit www.millsandboon.co.uk for editorial guidelines.

Submit the first three chapters and synopsis to:
Harlequin Mills & Boon Editorial Department,
Eton House, 18-24 Paradise Road,
Richmond, Surrey, TW9 1SR,
United Kingdom.

0203/WRITERS/HIST

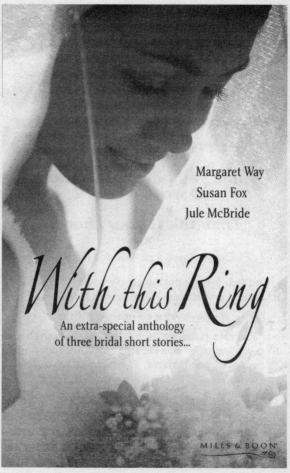

Margaret Way

Susan Fox

Jule McBride

With this Ring

An extra-special anthology
of three bridal short stories...

MILLS & BOON

Available from 18th April 2003

*Available at most branches of WH Smith,
Tesco, Martins, Borders, Eason, Sainsbury's
and all good paperback bookshops.*

0503/024/MB69

2 FREE

books and a surprise gift!

We would like to take this opportunity to thank you for reading this Mills & Boon® book by offering you the chance to take TWO more specially selected titles from the Historical Romance™ series absolutely FREE! We're also making this offer to introduce you to the benefits of the Reader Service™—

- ★ FREE home delivery
- ★ FREE gifts and competitions
- ★ FREE monthly Newsletter
- ★ Exclusive Reader Service discount
- ★ Books available before they're in the shops

Accepting these FREE books and gift places you under no obligation to buy, you may cancel at any time, even after receiving your free shipment. Simply complete your details below and return the entire page to the address below. *You don't even need a stamp!*

YES! Please send me 2 free Historical Romance books and a surprise gift. I understand that unless you hear from me, I will receive 4 superb new titles every month for just £3.49 each, postage and packing free. I am under no obligation to purchase any books and may cancel my subscription at any time. The free books and gift will be mine to keep in any case.

H3ZEA

Ms/Mrs/Miss/Mr ....Initials......................................
                                          BLOCK CAPITALS PLEASE

Surname ....

Address ....

....

....Postcode..............................

Send this whole page to:
UK: FREEPOST CN81, Croydon, CR9 3WZ
EIRE: PO Box 4546, Kilcock, County Kildare (stamp required)